She glanced back at the man

He continued to lean against the doorjamb, as if he had all the time in the world. But there was a tension around his eyes that belied his stance. He wanted her gone.

He was tall—taller than most men she knew. His muscular physique attested to the constant physical activity of ranching. He had an elemental maleness that was not something she liked. It challenged her and made her conscious of being a woman. She had had it up to her eyebrows with men of any type. Her father had been authoritarian, army through and through. Her ex-husband had been refined, sophisticated, elitist—and a crook. She plain wasn't interested in forging a new relationship. In the future, she wanted to be totally independent.

If she sold this ranch for even half of what Zack said it was worth, she could be independent for life.

Caitlin turned toward the house. "See you in the morning" was all she said.

Zack said nothing. Head held high, she walked confidently away until she rounded the corner of the house and was out of his sight. Shoulders sagging slightly, she wondered what she would do if Zack was right and the sale took years.

Dear Reader,

Welcome back to Wyoming. It's one of my favorite settings for a story. I love the wide open spaces, the wind sweeping across the plains and the stunning views of the Rockies from many vantage points.

It's a perfect setting for two people burned by life. Caitlin is the sole support of her deaf brother. Her husband walked out, taking all their money and a healthy amount of other people's money. Her father died, leaving his money elsewhere. She has spent the past year trying to keep her head above water. Now an astonishing inheritance—a ranch in Wyoming.

She arrives to find only one cowboy still left. And he's talking about leaving now that she's there. How can the ranch function with a woman who barely knows which end of a horse is which, and has never herded cattle in her life?

Zack Carson is ready to move on. He doesn't want to get involved—not with the new owner or her teenage brother. He's had enough problems in his life without taking on a needy family. Let someone else take care of the ranch.

Can two people burned by life find a way to each other?

There's plenty of Wyoming in the book, from rivers and open spaces to quiet evenings or wild rainstorms. If you ever get a chance, don't miss a visit to our least populated state. My favorite spots in the state are Laramie and the south pass area, not too far from the Triple M ranch that Caitlin inherited.

Cowboy books are my favorites. If you enjoy Zack and Caitlin's story, drop me a line and let me know. Happy reading!

Barbara McMahon

CAITLIN'S COWBOY
Barbara McMahon

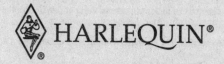
HARLEQUIN®

TORONTO • NEW YORK • LONDON
AMSTERDAM • PARIS • SYDNEY • HAMBURG
STOCKHOLM • ATHENS • TOKYO • MILAN • MADRID
PRAGUE • WARSAW • BUDAPEST • AUCKLAND

ISBN-13: 978-0-373-71472-8
ISBN-10:   0-373-71472-6

CAITLIN'S COWBOY

ABOUT THE AUTHOR

Barbara McMahon lives in rural California, but loves to visit even more rural Wyoming when she can. She's been writing romance novels for more than twenty-five years and loves her "job." Nominated for almost every award in the field, and winner of more than a dozen, she's happiest when writing stories to entertain and provide a few hours of escape for busy people around the globe. She's been published in fifty countries in thirty-five different languages and is always pleased to find that people everywhere love romances! She invites readers to stop by her Web site at www.BarbaraMcMahon.com.

Books by Barbara McMahon

HARLEQUIN SUPERROMANCE

1179–THE RANCHER'S BRIDE
1235–THE FIRST DAY
1318–THE GIRL WHO CAME BACK*
1335–LIES THAT BIND*
1353–TRUTH BE TOLD*
1406–THE LAST COWBOY HERO

*The House on Poppin Hill

Don't miss any of our special offers. Write to us at the following address for information on our newest releases.

Harlequin Reader Service
U.S.: 3010 Walden Ave., P.O. Box 1325, Buffalo, NY 14269
Canadian: P.O. Box 609, Fort Erie, Ont. L2A 5X3

To the Monday Night Bible Study Group:
You ladies rock! Thanks for all
the inspiration and encouragement.

CHAPTER ONE

CAITLIN JACKSON TURNED onto the gravel drive, noting the distance they'd traveled since leaving Wolf Crossing—almost eighty miles. If that was the closest place to shop, she was in a world of hurt. Maybe there were closer shopping centers that weren't on her map. She'd stocked up on essentials before leaving the town and hoped she didn't have to drive back in very often.

As she wound her way along the narrow drive, she felt relief at having finally reached the ranch. With their destination almost in sight, she began to relax and eagerly look around. Would she remember anything? The driveway curved along an embankment, then straightened out as the land sloped down slightly. Green grass grew as far as she could see, rippling in the breeze. In the distant horizon the purple silhouette of the Rockies rose against the blue sky, a couple of peaks tipped in snow.

The setting was beautiful. For a moment she wanted to stop the car and savor the view. It was entirely different from the San Francisco Bay Area, where space was at a premium and houses and buildings stood side by side crowded in on each other. Here there was nothing between her car and the Rockies but open range.

She glanced at her brother. Brandon leaned forward, his eyes scanning every inch of land. He'd never been here before.

Almost there, she signed.

He grinned and nodded.

The lawyer in Wolf Crossing had been handling her great-uncle Clyde's estate until she and Brandon arrived. He'd given her detailed directions to the ranch. Caitlin had been nine the only time she'd visited, and much more interested in horses and cows than the route her mother had taken. She remembered thinking she was the luckiest girl in the world that summer.

Looking back, she realized their visit had been right before her mother had become pregnant with Brandon, a little over sixteen years ago.

The graveled drive seemed to go on forever. Several minutes passed before she saw the roofs of ranch buildings. She'd pushed to complete the trip from San Francisco in the shortest time possible after she picked her brother up at the end of the school term and was tired, stiff and sick of driving. Only another few moments and they'd reach their final destination.

Her ranch. It still seemed surreal. Who would expect an army brat to inherit a ranch in Wyoming? Caitlin had never had an inkling she was her great-uncle's heir.

According to the attorney, Clyde had fifty-five hundred acres, more or less—now all belonging to her. Her family had been in Wyoming since the homestead days. Originally a large family who'd made a place for themselves on the open range, the Martins seemed to have fewer children with each generation, her mother, Tricia, being the only niece of Clyde Martin. She in turn had had two children—Caitlin and Brandon. They were the last of the family. She couldn't keep the place, of course.

Once Caitlin sold the property, she'd be able to better provide for herself and Brandon.

It seemed sad to relinquish property that had been in their family for more than one hundred years. Yet what choice did she have? She knew nothing about ranching and Brandon was only sixteen. They'd traveled the world with their father and now had settled in the San Francisco Bay Area. Wyoming was not home.

Tomorrow a real-estate agent was meeting them at the ranch at ten. Now she knew why their appointment wasn't earlier—it would take him that long to get here from Wolf Crossing.

Wire fences stretched along both sides of the drive. The one parallel on the right looked in need of repair. There were broken strands; some of the posts were leaning. She glanced around. To the left, in the distance, she spotted several head of cattle. Was that a man on a horse? She squinted to see better, but couldn't tell. According to the lawyer, there was one cowboy still on the ranch—Zack Carson. He had agreed to stay until the new owner arrived.

Caitlin hoped he'd stay a little longer—until they could sell the place.

In another minute they reached the old house and Caitlin pulled to a stop. The ranch house looked as if it had been built a century ago—two stories tall, weathered wood, sash windows. Beyond stood an old barn made of logs. It wasn't nearly as large as she'd remembered. Corrals surrounded the barn, six horizontal wooden rails affixed to upright poles. The fence looked sturdy at least. Two horses ambled over, watching them.

Brandon was out of the car, heading for the corral, before Caitlin could open her door.

"Be careful," she called, then shook her head. He couldn't hear her. And he wasn't looking in her direction so signing was out. She hoped the horses wouldn't bite.

Picking her way across the uneven ground, she wished she'd worn more suitable shoes. The high heels and tailored skirt and blouse had served her well for her meeting with the attorney, but were totally inappropriate for a ranch.

Brandon stroked first one horse, then another, his face beaming. Caitlin smiled at his delight. Since their father's death a year ago, financial concerns had been a constant in their lives. This gift from the blue was going to solve their problems, she hoped. In the meantime, it was good to see her brother behaving like a teenager again. She hated to have him worry about the future. He deserved a carefree childhood. Life was going to prove enough of a challenge to him when he went out on his own.

Want to see the house? she signed.

He shrugged. *Sure. Then can we ride?*

There was so much to do, riding came low on her list. But Brandon had been talking about the horses ever since they'd left California.

As she turned toward the house again, Caitlin's heart sank. The place needed major renovations. The clapboard siding had lost whatever paint had once adorned it; the weathered boards were warped in some spots. Was the inside as bad? What would it take to paint the entire place? It was huge, with a wraparound porch and gables jutting from the roof. Built when families needed lots of bedrooms. It looked as if her uncle Clyde had not been able to keep it up over the years.

Brandon caught up with her, studying the house.

It's bigger than I expected, he signed.

Older, too, she returned. *It needs a lot of work to make it a showplace. I hope someone will want to buy the ranch without the house being perfect.*

When she opened the door, Caitlin was assailed by a musty smell. The place must have been closed up since her great-uncle had died in March. Stepping inside, she looked around. She recognized the sofa. It was a little shabbier than before, but still looked comfortable and masculine with its dark brown nubby material. The living room was spacious, with windows on two walls. The front ones overlooked the porch and then the rolling hills to the west, with the rugged line of mountains in the far distance. The side window gave a view of the corral.

Dust coated everything. But the place was going to

be home until they sold it, or until September when Brandon would return to the California School for the Deaf. She hoped the ranch sold before then.

Brandon had gone upstairs. Caitlin heard his footsteps on the wooden floors. For a moment she tried to feel some connection to the place. The Triple M ranch had been in her mother's family for generations. Shouldn't she have some sense of belonging? But there was nothing.

She turned to check out the rest of the house. There was no point in trying to rake up sentiment for the homestead. She wasn't a rancher.

Despite her practical outlook, she tried to imagine what it would be like to live in a place steeped in family history. To trace the steps of grandparents and great grandparents. Not that she'd known any of them except her great-uncle Clyde. And that had only been for one summer. Her mother had died a few years later and her father hadn't kept in touch.

The dining room held a large rectangular table with ten chairs. For a moment Caitlin remembered some of the stories Uncle Clyde had told her and could picture a bunch of noisy children—and the chaos at mealtime. Where had they gone to school? Had any stayed to work the property? How sad that a large family had dwindled to only two members.

Caitlin continued to the kitchen. It was large and well equipped with no dust evident. While the appliances were old, they looked serviceable. She gazed out the window. No neighbors near enough to see. She felt alone at the end of the world.

Shrugging away the thought, she completed her tour and found a pantry—stocked with canned goods and packaged goods and containing a large freezer against the far wall. Peeking inside, she saw it was equally full. Living so far from town, her uncle had probably shopped for months at a time to keep trips to a minimum.

She heard Brandon clattering down the stairs and went back through the dining room.

Five bedrooms, one bath on the second floor. Two more bedrooms and a big junk room in the attic, he signed. *I want the bedroom at the front.*

All furnished? she asked.

He nodded. *What's here?*

Check it out, I'm going upstairs. Then we need to bring in the groceries and our things.

There was food for dinner, a place to sleep. Tomorrow the Realtor was coming. What more could she want? Caitlin headed up the stairs, anxious to see the rest of the house. Surely someone would want the ranch even if the house was old. Couldn't a developer tear down this place and build dozens of new homes?

But why would people want to move out here? she asked herself as she peered into the different bedrooms. There was no industry, no recreational spots, no town nearby. Who would want an eighty-mile commute? And she didn't think Wolf Crossing had so much going for it either.

This part of the country was so different from the San Francisco Bay Area where she'd lived for the past six years. And unlike any of the army bases she'd grown up on.

But at least here, no one knew about her past. She wouldn't be subject to whispers and covert glances. Wouldn't be hurt over and over by people she had once thought of as friends.

For as long as it took to sell the ranch, she was content to have a place to stay.

ZACK RODE ALONG the perimeter fence. He'd seen the car turn in to the driveway and knew it had to be the new owner. Harry Benson had said she'd be arriving today. He'd known his time on the ranch was growing short.

Damn Clyde for dying. They'd had the perfect setup. It had been two years and counting since he'd arrived at the Triple M. The longest he'd stayed in one spot since he'd gotten out of the service. But nothing lasted forever. Time for him to be moving on. It wouldn't take long to pack. He'd update the owner and be ready to head out in the morning.

Keeping one eye on the fence, he took stock of the cattle. Looking good. The grass was thick. There had been a large number of calves this year. Summer feeding would make them prime for sale in the fall.

Zack turned at the double fence, the one that separated the hay field from the grazing land. The crop was ready to harvest. More men were needed, but that wasn't his worry anymore. The level ground would make the cutting easy despite Clyde's antiquated mower. The man should have bought a new one years ago, but his old one worked—most of the time. No sense wasting money, Clyde had often said.

Zack missed the old man.

Each summer Clyde had hired four ranch hands. He'd always respected the men who worked with him. He had shared meals with his crew, spent time after dinner working on tack with them or whittling away on the steps of the bunkhouse. Winters he reduced the staff to two cowboys. Zack considered himself lucky to have been one of them the last couple of years.

Now he was the only one left. And soon even he'd be gone.

He'd learned so much from Clyde. Enough to get a good job at another ranch. He'd come a long way for a boy who grew up in the Bedford-Stuyvesant neighborhood of Brooklyn. Who would expect a kid raised dodging bullets from rival gangs to end up punching cows?

Jeez, he missed that old man.

Completing his circuit, Zack headed back toward the homestead. Once Clyde had become seriously ill, Zack had known the life he'd enjoyed for the past couple of years was doomed. Now he'd have to find another spread to work, starting over with all the grunt chores and establishing his place in the hierarchy of cowboys. At least this time he had experience going in. Clyde had taken him on almost as a greenhorn. A Wyoming ranch was a far cry from his childhood neighborhood, or even the battle hills of Afghanistan. But out here he was definitely safer all the way around.

The car was parked in front of the house. He didn't see any sign of the woman. He knew from Harry that the new owner was Clyde's grandniece—granddaughter of

Clyde's favorite sister. According to the attorney handling Clyde's estate, the new owner was planning to sell.

Not that it was any of his business, but Zack couldn't help but notice during the months he'd worked with Clyde that no letters or calls had come from the woman. Seemed to him anyone set to inherit a spread like the Triple M should have at least kept in touch.

Clyde had rarely spoken about his heir around Zack. Even at the end when the pneumonia had been so bad he could scarcely breathe, he'd only asked Zack to keep an eye on the ranch for him. Had the old rancher known this heir would sell the place for as much as she could get? Hell of a legacy for the ninety-some years Clyde had worked on the land. Still, the old man had this niece, said she'd visited once. And who else would he have left it to? She was the last of Clyde's family.

Zack unsaddled the horse and slung the heavy saddle across a stand. Slipping off the bridle, he fastened a halter and began brushing down the gelding's damp back. He'd turn him loose in the corral when finished, toss in a flake of hay and head for his room. He was tired, but not more than any other day.

He looked up from his task. Standing in the doorway to the barn, backlit by the sun, was a teenager dressed in jeans and wearing a ball cap. Zack looked at him for a moment, unable to make out his features clearly. He hadn't expected a kid. He turned back to the horse.

"You one of the new owners?" he asked.

The kid didn't answer. Zack shook his head at the rudeness. Was this the owner's son? If so, she needed to teach him some manners.

He continued brushing while mentally running through the things he had to do to get on the road in the morning.

The boy walked into the barn and came over to Zack. Tentatively he reached out to touch the horse's flank.

"Come away from the back," Zack told him. "If he decides to kick, you're right in his path." The teen was almost as tall as Zack, but lanky. His cap hid most of his hair, but Zack saw some of the dark strands. His brown eyes watched Zack's every move.

"Don't say I didn't warn you," Zack said.

"Warn him about what?" a female voice asked from the doorway.

The young woman who came into the barn had to be the new owner. Zack turned to watch as she hurried over and touched the boy, moving her hands.

"To stand clear of the back of the horse," Zack said. The woman looked to be in her mid twenties. No way was she the mother. Siblings?

Brown hair skimmed her shoulders, silky and soft in the subdued light in the barn. Her blue eyes were the color of the sky. The skirt and blouse and makeup she wore were totally out of place here. Clyde must be rolling in his grave. High heels in a barn?

"Will he kick?" she asked.

"Never can tell. Roddy isn't in the habit, but if something spooks him or startles him, he could lash out in reflex."

"Brandon is deaf. He didn't hear you. I told him to move away."

Sign language. Zack had heard of it, but he had never seen it. So Clyde's heirs were a city girl and a deaf kid. Clyde had never mentioned the boy.

"I'm Caitlin Jackson. This is my brother, Brandon. Clyde Martin was our great uncle. I've inherited the ranch."

"Zack Carson." Zack was growing uncomfortable. It happened every time he got near young women or children—flashback to women with their heads blown partway off or dead children with no chance at a future. The pleading in their eyes, the helplessness he'd felt time and again at being unable to stop the machine of war. The horrors never left. He worked hard to keep the images at bay, but he could feel himself tensing. He needed to get away. Ground himself in the reality of Wyoming and not memories of the bloody hills of Afghanistan.

"The attorney in Wolf Crossing said there was a cowboy running things. I appreciate your staying on after my uncle died," she said primly.

Zack nodded. Finished with the horse, he unhooked the lead line and led him to the corral, slapping his rump. He turned, almost bumping into Caitlin. He took a breath, confused by the light fragrance that competed with the smell of horse, cattle, sweat and hay. It'd been a long time since he'd been this close to a woman. He gritted his teeth and stepped around her.

He went to the section of the barn where the hay was stacked. Grabbing a couple of flakes, he turned around. This time it was the boy he almost ran down.

"Look, either you two help, or stand aside," he growled. "There are hungry horses to feed."

The boy reached out for one of the flakes of hay. Zack relinquished it and walked through the barn to the corral, the teenager dogging his footsteps. Zack tossed the hay over the rail, then watched as the boy did the same. The horses ambled over and began eating.

"Sorry. We'll get out of your way," the woman said

Fingers and hands flashed. The boy shook his head and moved his own hands in rapid motion. Zack didn't have a clue what they were saying, but it was definitely an argument.

Walking around them, he returned to the bench where he'd dumped his reins and began to clean the leather. Then he would head over to the bunkhouse to pack. The deal when he signed on had been no women and no kids.

"Mr. Carson?" Caitlin called after him.

He turned. "What?"

"Can you teach Brandon about the horses? Maybe tomorrow he can ride."

"Does he know how?"

"Not yet. But he learns fast."

"Look, the deal was I stayed until the new owner showed up. I'll be pulling out in the morning. If he wants to ride, he better find someone else to show him how. What about you?"

"You're leaving so soon?"

Was that panic he heard in her voice?

"I stayed on to keep the stock fed and watered. You're here now. You take over."

"I don't know anything about taking care of horses or cows," she said. "It will take a little time to learn."

"Cattle." She reminded Zack of himself when he'd first come back from Afghanistan, was determined to make a living as a cowboy. He'd wanted something as different from his past as he could get. He hadn't had a clue about ranching when he'd started. But he'd picked it up fast. "The term is *cattle*. Your uncle runs about four hundred head. There are only three horses, because he sold off a few last fall. There's enough feed to last several weeks. Hay's ready to be cut."

The uncertain look in her eyes let him know she hadn't a clue. His gut tightened. Sweat broke out. He didn't need this. He'd signed on for wide open spaces and no one dependent on him. He was used up. He absolutely couldn't deal with other people's problems anymore. Call him selfish, but he had to look out for himself if he was to make it.

Forget the saddle for now, he wanted solitude. Heading for the bunkhouse, he fought his curiosity. He would not turn around and see what they were doing. It was their ranch now, let them deal with it.

Temptation proved too much. As he swung the door open to the bunkhouse, he glanced over his shoulder. Caitlin stood in the barn doorway staring after him. The boy hung on the rail, watching the horses.

Not his problem. He'd had his fill of trying to save the world. Let someone else be the hero in this scenario.

CAITLIN WATCHED Zack Carson go into the low building. He closed the door and she was alone with Brandon and three horses she hadn't a clue how to take care of. She swallowed hard. Taking a deep breath, she tried to organize her thoughts. What was she going to do? If the only person who knew how to run the ranch left, she was in big trouble. She didn't even know how much hay to feed the horses. How soon could she find another cowboy?

She made her way over to the corral. Brandon was mesmerized by the horses. They ignored the humans, munching contentedly. The water trough was full, with a device on the side that looked like a paddle. Was it some kind of automatic device that kept water in the tank? She remembered riding with her uncle and hanging around the horses and playing with the dog. How long had she and her mother stayed on the ranch? She couldn't remember. It had seemed like forever. That stage of her childhood had been carefree and happy.

When she got Brandon's attention, she signed, *It's late and I'm tired, let's unload the car and fix dinner. The horses will still be here in the morning.*

Everything she owned was in the used car she'd bought a few months back. Twenty-six years old and she had very little to call her own.

Of course she'd had to sell everything to pay some of her ex-husband Timothy's debt. And even then she'd come up short. But the judge had waived the balance given the circumstances.

Six months ago, she'd started life as a single woman again without any debt.

But without any assets either.

They had to make a quick sale.

BY THE TIME THEIR THINGS had been unloaded and carried up to the bedrooms, Caitlin was exhausted. She quickly changed into clothes more appropriate for a ranch. Tomorrow she'd begin cleaning the house so it'd be habitable for the few weeks they planned to stay. She was pleased Brandon liked what he saw so far. Part of the reason she'd decided to come to Wyoming was to give him a summer on a ranch. She thought the experience would be good for him, and they would have time to spend together. But she'd had no idea how far they were from town.

Maybe she had better reevaluate her summer plans. If Zack Carson left, she'd have to scramble to hire another cowboy. How long did it take someone to get up to speed on a ranch? Surely an experienced cowboy would be able to step in and take over until the property sold.

Once they had money from the sale, Caitlin would need to decide what to do with her life. Brandon had two more years of high school. Would he want to go to college? He'd never talked about a particular career.

It would take more than two years of college to finish her own degree. She had been working toward a major in French literature, but there weren't many jobs in that field other than teaching. She had had so much fun when she'd first started college. Then she'd met Timothy and the world had become a magical place.

She'd quit college to marry him, despite her father's arguments. If only she could have seen the future, she'd have done so many things differently. How many other people had said that over the years? She couldn't change the past, only make her best shot for the future.

When the phone rang, the sound startled her. No one knew where they were. She hadn't told anyone of her plans, not even their stepmother. Marjorie had been horrible after Caitlin's father had died. She'd been cordial to her husband's children while he'd lived. Once he was gone, her true colors showed. She wanted nothing further to do with her dead husband's children. Bob Jackson had left his estate to his wife and a small stipend for Brandon until he turned eighteen. She didn't have an obligation to make sure his children were provided for and surely would never try to track them down here.

"Hello?" Caitlin answered.

"Ms. Jackson?" an unfamiliar voice asked.

"Yes." She'd taken back her maiden name when the divorce became final. No sense in advertising that she'd made a monumental mistake in marrying Timothy Soames. Enough people knew in Palo Alto, but she was in Wyoming now. Maybe that part of her past could stay hidden. She had done nothing wrong— except marry Timothy.

"Jeffrey Bradshaw, from Wolf Crossing Realty? Just confirming our appointment in the morning."

"Yes, at ten," she replied.

"Are we going to be able to see over the property?" he asked.

"See over it?"

"Ride the boundaries, take photographs of the lay of the land. I need to know about rivers or other water rights. Any mineral rights? Things like that."

"I don't know the answers to those questions," she said. Did she need to contact the lawyer again?

"I'll have one of my assistants look up the legal description," he said. "And Zack can show me around."

She should have expected something like this. When she'd sold the house in Palo Alto, the real-estate agent had examined every inch. But somehow a house and a ranch didn't compute as the same thing in her mind. Wasn't it enough to know how many acres the ranch had?

"Fine. See you in the morning." The agent hung up.

Caitlin looked for Brandon. He had his head in the freezer. She went over and pulled out some meat—steaks. Figured.

She pointed to the microwave and handed him the frozen strips. Signing quickly, she told him she had to check on something with Zack and would be right back.

Knocking on the bunkhouse door a moment later, she waited. It seemed like a long time before Zack opened it.

"You don't need to knock on this door. It opens into the communal living room. My bedroom is one of the ones in the back."

"I'll remember that next time. I need to ask you a favor. I don't know yet what my uncle paid you, but I'd be happy to pay you the same if you could stay a little longer. I'm putting the ranch up for sale. A real-estate agent is coming tomorrow morning and wants to see around the place. I haven't ridden a horse in forever. Plus, I haven't a clue about where the boundaries are or what special features the ranch might have. Do you know where the water supply is?"

He nodded slowly. "There's more than one. A portion of the river runs through part of the property and there are some wells that produce a steady supply."

"Could you show the man around?" If he refused, she'd have to hope Jeff Bradshaw would be satisfied with riding out to the nearest hill and taking pictures from there.

Zack narrowed his eyes, his gaze never leaving hers. Caitlin felt awkward. She wished she'd handled the entire matter from California. But she'd jumped at the chance to stay at the ranch for a few weeks until it sold. Brandon had the summer off. Marjorie had made it clear they were no longer welcome at the home their father had provided for her. Spending time at the ranch had seemed like a good idea. Now she wasn't so sure. Nothing was turning out the way she'd expected.

Caitlin was still hurt and angry at her father for leaving almost everything to Marjorie. Surely he could have left something to his only daughter. Granted, he'd thought she was well taken care of by Tim. The will had been written when Timothy was flying high. At least her father could have left her a picture or a watch. And he should have provided more for Brandon.

She knew why he hadn't. And that hurt, too. She just hoped Brandon never learned the reason.

But right now she had more immediate things to think about. Was Zack going to help her out or not?

"I'll show him around," he said at last.

She felt the relief like a tangible weight being lifted.

"Thank you, I appreciate that. He'll be here around ten."

"I can leave in the afternoon as well as the morning."

"Please reconsider. It'll only be for a little while—until the ranch sells. I really need help. If you leave, how would I go about hiring someone else?"

"Run an ad, I guess."

"Are there are lot of unemployed cowboys?"

"Not that I know of around here. Most get hired early for the summer months."

"Oh. Still, there may be one or two looking for work. Will you stay until I find someone? And if you'll stay for a few weeks until the ranch sells, you can leave with a hefty bonus in your pocket." She'd gladly pay a substantial sum to keep him here.

He shook his head slowly. "I wouldn't count on this place selling fast."

"Why not?" She looked around. "It's not in the best shape, but I'd sell as is. Cut a deal because of it. Someone could make a real killing on it."

"Do you know how much this place is worth?"

"No. I expect once the real-estate agent sees it, he'll give me an estimate."

"I can give you an estimate right now. Probably more than five million dollars. Do you think buyers with that much money are a dime a dozen? It could take months or years to sell a spread this size."

She stared at him, dumbfounded. "Five million dollars?" she repeated. She had no idea the ranch would be worth that much. Or even half that much. She'd been hoping for a few hundred thousand, enough to enable her to return to college and provide an education fund for Brandon. The amount staggered her.

Could Zack be right? She glanced around at the log barn, the weathered house. The gravel driveway.

"If it's worth so much, why does it look like it's about to fall down around our ears?" she asked, reality taking hold. How would a cowboy know what a ranch was worth?

"Land rich, cash poor. The plight of many ranchers." He leaned against the door frame, crossing his arms over his chest. "Your uncle ran a good spread. The cattle are healthy and prolific. The hay supplies feed with some left over to sell. Cattle sales in the spring and fall provided enough income for him to live the way he wanted. But it's an iffy way to make a living, subject to beef price fluctuations and weather."

"I thought maybe I could sell to a developer," she said.

"Do you see tract homes going up all around here? Who would live in them? There's not a lot of industry around Wolf Crossing, much less out this far. And the winters can be pretty bad—we get snowbound occasionally for a couple of weeks at a time. Not ideal commuter weather."

She glared at him. "Someone will want this place. Besides, if it's worth all that, maybe I can get a loan until it sells." Not that she needed to run her ideas by him. Especially if he was set on leaving.

"And pay it back how? If you don't have the income to service it, you wouldn't qualify. And if selling is your way of repaying, the bank won't lend you money unless it knows you have a buyer lined up."

"Any more good news?" she asked. It was wrong to get angry with him. It wasn't Zack's fault that she was at the end of her rope.

He shrugged. "Sell some cattle if you need some ready cash. And be prepared to ride out the sale of the ranch. It's fine property. Someone or some conglomerate will want it eventually."

She turned and gazed out over the rolling hills. "Mr. Bradshaw will be here around ten."

"I'll be ready and have a horse saddled for him. You coming with us?"

She debated. It had been an eon since she'd ridden. But surely they wouldn't be out for too long. The purpose was to look over the land, not have some endurance competition. Chances were Mr. Bradshaw wasn't any more used to being on a horse than she was.

"I'd like to." It would give her a chance to see the entire ranch. And she could hear firsthand what the real-estate agent had to say.

"We don't have enough horses to include the boy," he said.

"His name is Brandon. He needs to learn to ride around the homestead before taking off cross country. He'll be fine here on his own. He's sixteen."

She glanced back at the man. He continued to lean against the doorjamb, as if he had all the time in the world. But there was a tension around his eyes that belied his stance. He wanted her gone.

He was tall—taller than most men she knew. His

muscular physique attested to the constant physical activity of ranching. He had an elemental maleness that was not something she liked. It challenged her and made her conscious of being a woman. She had had it up to her eyebrows with men of any type. Her father had been authoritarian, army through and through. Timothy had been refined, sophisticated, elitist—and a crook. She plain wasn't interested in forging a new relationship. In the future, she wanted to be totally independent.

If she sold this ranch for even half what Zack said it was worth, she could be independent for life.

Caitlin turned toward the house. "See you in the morning," was all she said.

Zack said nothing. Head held high, she walked confidently away until she rounded the corner of the house and was out of his sight. Shoulders sagging slightly, she wondered what she would do if Zack was right and the sale took years.

CHAPTER TWO

WORRY KEPT CAITLIN from falling asleep as soon as she went to bed. Brandon had regaled her with stories most of the evening, fascinated at everything he'd seen that day. He asked if Zack would teach him to ride and rope cattle. Asked if there were any neighbors nearby, or was the town the closest place to visit. His enthusiasm was wearing—not invigorating. She knew she'd been as carefree when she was sixteen, but now worry about the future threw a pall over everything. She wanted to get some sleep and have the real estate agent show up and tell her he had a buyer in his back pocket.

It was great to be with her brother again, though. Brandon attended the deaf school as a resident student, staying with her only on holidays and during the summer break. Their mother would be so proud of her son. She'd grieved that he'd been born deaf, but he was so adorable she forgot his difference and focused on his delightful personality. Not that Brandon was perfect by any means. He could sulk and be as annoying as any teenager, Caitlin thought. But their mother would have been happy at how well he did in school and how successfully he'd adjusted to a hearing world. Caitlin wished again that Tricia had survived that drunk driver. The unfairness of his walking away unscathed still rankled though the accident had happened ten years ago.

She turned onto her side, her thoughts moving to Zack. Could she come up with a way to persuade him to stay? If not, how long would it take to find someone to replace him? And what was she going to do in the meantime? Would Zack give her a crash course in the feed and care of horses and cattle before he left? She was beginning to think coming here had been a huge mistake. It sounded as if Zack might have stayed had she not shown up.

But she couldn't leave. Not with Brandon loving the place so much.

Maybe Zack was wrong. Maybe there was a neighboring rancher who had been longing to buy this property and would jump at the chance.

Five million dollars. Unbelievable. Could Uncle Clyde's spread really be worth that much?

With thoughts of spring vacations in Paris and winter ski trips to Gstaad, she finally drifted off to sleep.

BRANDON HAD A dozen questions at breakfast, all to do with Great-uncle Clyde and the ranch property. Caitlin was sorry she didn't know more about the family history. She knew Clyde was the older brother of their grandmother—their mother's mother. As the oldest boy, Clyde had been the one to inherit the property when his father died.

You've been here before, right? Brandon asked.

I told you—when I was nine. Uncle Clyde had lots of horses and several cowboys and a cattle dog then. I remember riding a horse and feeling scared and excited and so proud. Then eating with him and Mama. Remember, Dad didn't like kids at the table until they were older, so I felt all grown up that summer. She smiled at the memory. Uncle Clyde had frightened her at first. He'd been a large man like Zack. But he'd been kind to a little girl who had been so enchanted with his ranch. Much as Brandon was today.

How long can we stay? Brandon asked.

Until the property sells. Or school starts, whichever comes first. She hoped she could stick with that. She decided not to raise his hopes about the amount of money Zack thought the property would bring. She'd believe it when she had the cash in hand, not before.

Tell me more about when you were here, he signed.

It was hard to sign a conversation and eat at the same time. She told him about her riding efforts, the little calf that had to be bottle-fed, and of course playing with the dog. Brandon laughed at some of her comments.

Can we get a dog? he asked.

We won't be here that long.

We could take it with us when we leave. I've always wanted a dog. I can't keep it at school, but it would be company for you. I graduate in another two years. Then I could look after it.

Not if you're going to college, she returned. *I don't think they allow dogs in dorms.*

He shrugged. *Don't know what I want to do when I leave school. Not sure about college.*

College, she signed with emphasis.

He stared down at his plate and didn't respond. Caitlin tapped his arm to get his attention.

He looked at her, frowning.

College, she repeated.

Maybe.

He glanced away, essentially ending the conversation. Caitlin studied him for a long moment. They had never really discussed college, but she'd always thought of him attending Gallaudet University in Washington, D.C., the school for the deaf. Maybe they needed to make some plans. Or at least get him thinking in that direction. What else would he do? It was hard to think of her little brother growing up. But he was right. In two years he'd be graduating from high school and he had to decide whether to continue his education or get a job.

She had never thought beyond college for him. What kind of work did Brandon want to do?

She heard a car on the gravel and glanced at the kitchen clock. It was almost ten. Jumping up, she carried her plate to the sink and quickly ran water into it.

The real-estate agent is here, she signed and headed for the front of the house.

Today she wore jeans and a long-sleeved shirt. Cross-trainers were the best she could do for shoes. If she planned to ride a lot, she'd have to get boots. Just thinking about making the trek to Wolf Crossing for a single pair of boots was mind boggling. If she'd thought ahead, she could have asked Jeffrey Bradshaw to bring out a pair in her size.

The dusty pickup truck that pulled to a stop near the barn didn't look like the vehicle a prosperous real-estate agent would drive. Or was she letting Timothy's prejudices influence her? She needed to get past those.

"Ms. Jackson?" The tall, lanky man who stepped down from the truck seemed to be in his mid fifties. He wore a cowboy hat, faded jeans and boots.

"Yes. Mr. Bradshaw?"

"Call me Jeff. Sorry about Clyde's passing. He was a good man."

"Thank you. Please, call me Caitlin. Did you want to see around the house first or any of these buildings? I've asked my uncle's cowboy to show us the place. I haven't seen it all myself."

"Zack? Seems like he's been here longer than he has. Worked well, according to Clyde, which is high praise. Your uncle was a stickler, that's for sure."

Before Jeff finished his sentence, Zack came from the barn, leading three saddled horses.

"Hey, Zack, just talking about you," Jeff said, walking over to greet the man.

Zack handed him the reins to one of the horses and shook hands. He glanced at Caitlin.

She smiled politely, feeling awkward again at the fact they had been talking about him, though the comments had been positive.

"Can't believe this place is going up for sale," Jeff said, turning back to Caitlin.

"Why? Is there something wrong with it?" she asked.

"Not a thing. It's been in your family for more than a hundred years—since the area was first settled back in the 1870s. Seems odd its being sold off."

"I'm not a rancher," Caitlin reminded him.

"Could get a manager in," Jeff said. Then he smiled and shook his head. "What am I doing, trying to talk myself out of a sale? Let's get riding." He mounted his horse easily.

With another look at the dusty truck, Caitlin turned back to Zack and eyed the two horses standing docilely.

"I've given you Bonny Boy. He's the gentlest we've got. But he shies if things blow by him. Shouldn't have any problem today, but if the wind kicks up, beware. Even a little leaf will cause him to sidestep out from under you."

She patted the brown gelding's neck and then prepared to mount. He was tall and the stirrup was higher than she could reach. Before she could even ask about a mounting block, Zack's hands encircled her waist and lifted her up and into the saddle. She clutched the horn and glared at him.

"I could have managed." She felt breathless. How strong was the man? She was no lightweight.

"Doubt it. Anyway, we need to get going. There's lots to see. You need a hat."

"I'll be okay. I put on sunscreen earlier."

He didn't respond, but went back into the barn. A moment later he returned, carrying an old felt cowboy hat. He handed it to her. Caitlin considered refusing, but she still didn't have an answer about whether or not he'd stay. She couldn't imagine managing the ranch without someone who knew what to do. Taking the hat gingerly, she grimaced as she set it on her head. It was large and came to rest on her ears.

Zack swung up easily into his own saddle. Jeffrey Bradshaw was already walking beyond the barn.

Caitlin settled herself, gathered the reins and looked at the real-estate agent. "Is he really good?" she asked softly, leaning closer to Zack.

"One of the best around as I hear," Zack said, urging his mount forward. "You think differently?"

"No, but his truck is sort of old and run down. Doesn't seem very prosperous."

Zack looked at her for a moment, then glanced behind him at the truck. "You think he should drive a Mercedes out here? Fording creeks sometimes, spinning up dirt and rocks?"

Put that way, no, she didn't think an expensive car would be a good choice. Once again she felt Zack's disdain. Once again she realized the summer was not starting the way she'd hoped.

By THE TIME THEY'D RIDDEN to the far boundary of the ranch, Caitlin was saddle sore. Her legs ached and her butt was numb. Yet she was having a fabulous time. She loved the freedom of riding across empty acres of range with only cattle and wild grass. Zack was a good guide, pointing out watering holes, the area where a river meandered through a corner of the ranch, the fields of hay ready for harvest and the fencing that needed constant monitoring.

She listened attentively, contributing little. There was so much she didn't know, but the men did. Sometimes it sounded as if they spoke in code with their discussion of cattle and how many head the land could support. They talked about the possibility of sporting activities for a resort, but there were no large stands of trees for game, and only a small portion of a river for fishing.

Brandon would love to come fishing. She'd have to ask Zack later if Clyde had any poles.

On the ride back, Caitlin couldn't wait to get off the horse and sit in a soft chair all afternoon. But she kept her back straight, ignored the pain and kept up. She'd learned how to provide a false front to the world this past year. She wasn't a quitter and she wasn't letting anyone get the better of her again.

"Good number of calves this year," Jeff said as they moved through a portion of the herd.

"Clyde used Borroff's bull, should provide a lot of beef, too."

"Thought he had a bull of his own," Jeff said.

"Does. One mean son of a gun we keep in his own field over by Tally's place, double fenced. But Clyde wanted some fresh blood in the herd. And I think this is the largest percentage of calves he's had for a long time. Damn, I wish he was here to see them." As he rode, Zack's gaze constantly swept the land.

Both men spoke well of her great-uncle. Caitlin wished she'd made more of an effort to correspond with Clyde. Once her mother had died, her father had shown no interest in keeping in touch with his wife's only living relative.

But Caitlin had lived away from her father's home for years. She should have made contact herself. She could have invited Clyde to San Francisco, or visited him. Why hadn't she?

It was something she would always regret.

ZACK LISTENED as Jeff talked about some of the bulls he'd heard about in his travels. As one of the major real-estate agents for the county, Jeff knew everyone and could find out anything about a ranch with a few minutes research. Zack wondered how he felt about finding a buyer for the Triple M.

They were approaching the rocky area of the ranch. Though he'd worked for Clyde for two years, Zack still grew tense when he approached one of the rocky outcrops. They were perfect hiding places for snipers. The rest of the land was open, unable to offer concealment.

He shook his head, consciously forcing himself to relax. He wasn't in Afghanistan. He didn't have to witness the death and destruction that had once been a daily part of his life. No more women raped and mutilated. No more children blown up by a car bomb or shot by marauding insurgents. No more soldiers groaning in pain or bleeding to death on the dusty desert a million miles away. He couldn't lose his best friend in Wyoming. That had happened outside Kandahar. The danger of being shot on the Triple M was nil.

And he didn't make friends anymore.

Zack focused on the herd as they rode through. Clyde would have been happy with this year's numbers. He would have culled the older heifers, kept the most promising of the young ones, and sold off the rest of the calves after a summer of fattening.

Clyde hadn't been any better at making friends than Zack, but the two men had hit it off. Despite the age difference and their unrelated backgrounds they had formed a working relationship that had benefited them both.

Clyde had talked a lot about the past at the end, those last two weeks when he knew his time was coming to a close. He'd hoped the girl would take on the ranch, but didn't really think she would. His niece and nephew were city people. A person needed to be raised on the land to really know it. Still, the ties of family went deep in this Wyoming soil.

If the ranch belonged to him, Zack would fight tooth and nail to keep it.

He wondered what Caitlin Jackson planned to do with the money when the place sold. Buy a fancy condo in some major city probably. Indulge herself with expensive clothes and jewelry and fancy cars. She'd never have to work. Never have to find ways to pinch pennies to buy food the way his mother had.

"Zack!"

He looked over at the real-estate agent.

"Hey, man, you already planning the next roundup or something? I asked about the well over there near that clump of rocks."

Zack looked at the high windmill turning steadily in the light breeze. "It produces several gallons a minute, keeps the troughs full. Hasn't run dry once since I've been here. We rotate the sections where the cattle graze. There's either a seep or a well in each one. Water's never been a problem."

"What has been a problem?" Jeff asked. He reined in his horse and leaned over to rest his arm against the saddle horn.

"Getting enough men hired to handle everything. No one wants to live so far from town." He glanced at Caitlin. She frowned at his comment, but she might as well learn now that it wasn't going to be easy to get men to work the ranch. "Distance also plays a part in shipping the beef. The cattle have to be driven to the homestead and trucked out from there. Clyde erects—erected—a holding pen to contain them until loaded. There's only one area big enough to let the cattle trucks turn around. Winter can be a bitch, too."

"That's true all over Wyoming. Don't see anything to stop a sale. This is good land," Jeff said.

"I have no idea what property values are around here," Caitlin said. "Zack gave me an estimate yesterday, but I'd like your valuation of the ranch."

"I have to see the house and buildings, but I'd say the land alone is worth about $1,200 an acre—so that'd be about six million or more. Won't be a fast sale, however. Not a lot of call for start-up ranches in this area."

Caitlin frowned. "Start-up? It's a working ranch.

Someone could move right in and be all set. We could leave with hardly any notice."

"Sure it's a working ranch and makes a profit most years, I expect. By start-up, I meant someone coming in to start up in ranching. It would take a lot to buy the place. Someone needs to come in with expansion ideas, not start-ups."

"Any neighboring ranches interested in more land?" she asked.

"Well now, I asked around after you first called to list the property," Jeff said. "No one can take on the expense right now."

Zack knew Jeff had probably been hoping one of the neighboring ranches wanted to double in size. A quick sale meant faster commission for him. That kind of money, however, was hard to come by these days.

They headed back to the homestead. Zack had already finished the crucial chores, but there were more to be done. The ranch usually had three to four men working. For the first time, no one had hired any hands this spring. He was barely keeping up with the basic day-to-day running of the place. Now that Ms. Jackson and her brother were here, he could dump the entire problem in her lap. It was her ranch now.

Yet for some reason, he was loath to do that. Maybe he felt an obligation to Clyde for giving him a chance when he'd been so green. It wouldn't hurt to stay another day or two to give her an overview of what needed doing. He had no place to go; he'd be hunting work himself when he left. Maybe he'd give it a chance.

WHEN THEY REACHED THE BARN, Jeff easily dismounted and tossed the reins over the top rail of the corral fence. Zack slid off his horse and looked around for Caitlin. She had ridden to the corral and sat looking at the fence as if planning to use it as a ladder to get off Bonny Boy. He'd like to see that. But she'd probably fall flat on her face.

He studied the glossy sheen of her hair now that she'd discarded the hat, and wished the Triple M was a men-only ranch as it had been with Clyde.

Reluctantly, he tied his horse and went to assist his new boss.

"Need help?" he asked.

"Please," she said, looking uncomfortable.

He lifted her down and set her on her feet. She hardly weighed anything. She was tall enough, but thin. He could feel her ribs through her shirt.

She took a step and almost fell. He caught her and held her upright. The fragrance of her perfume filled him. He took a deep breath. The warmth of her body wasn't unpleasant. Instantly Zack stepped back, releasing her slowly.

"It'll take a minute to get your bearing if you're not used to riding," he said gruffly. She was warm and feminine and it had been a long time since he'd been with a woman. But he wasn't going down that road. No involvement—with anyone. He'd set his path a few years back and nothing had changed.

Jeff ambled over. "Shaky legs?"

"Yes." Caitlin grimaced. "I'll be fine in about ten years, I'm sure."

He chuckled and swept one hand around. "I'll check

over the outbuildings, then we can look over the house," he said, ambling away.

Zack wasn't needed. Soon she'd have her land legs again. He'd see to the horses and then start a list of everything to cover before he left.

"I'll take care of the horses," he said, unlooping her reins from the rail.

Brandon ran out of the house and headed for them. Caitlin looked up at Zack. "Could you please give him some pointers? No matter how long the sale takes, we'll be here a couple of months. It may be the only chance he has of being on a ranch and I'd love for him to learn as much as he can."

"I'm not a babysitter," Zack said.

She gave a small sound of annoyance. "No one is asking you to babysit him. He just needs to learn. I can't teach him. I don't remember that much from when I was here before. Consider it on-the-job training so you can have someone else helping out."

She'd hit probably the only reason he'd agree. He'd been as green as grass when he'd started out. Who was he to deny passing on what he'd learned to a relative of Clyde's?

"I don't know sign language." The last thing he wanted was some kid around. Yet he had a feeling he was going to end up being a kind of temporary teacher until the boy got up to speed.

"He can read lips a bit. And follow any directions if you show him instead of tell him. Please?"

Brandon reached his sister and grinned, signing.

Zack watched the hands and fingers move. Did the boy's entire family and circle of friends sign?

"Tell him to follow what I do," Zack said, remembering back when he'd been a kid in the neighborhood and Tony Bartotelli had given him instructions on tearing apart a car engine and building it back. He'd hero-worshipped Tony for years. Zack looked at Brandon. There was no way he planned to be a hero to the kid. Maybe a few honest pointers on how hard it was to work a ranch would have Brandon backing away. Ms. Jackson had made it perfectly clear they weren't staying long. Maybe he could hasten their departure.

He handed the kid Bonny Boy's reins and took the reins of the other two horses, leading them into the barn. Brandon followed with the gelding.

Zack showed the teen how to put on the halter, cross-tie the horse, take off the saddle and begin grooming. The kid had the most delighted expression on his face. For a moment Zack felt the sense of accomplishment Brandon experienced. When he'd first come back from Afghanistan, Zack had decided city life wasn't for him. His first job on a ranch in Texas was really the pits, the dregs of ranch chores—but he'd relished every new skill he'd mastered. Anything was worth the freedom of the range and the peace he felt away from crowds of people.

He took care of the other two horses in the time it took Brandon to finish grooming Bonny Boy. For a moment, Zack could almost imagine he was working side by side with Clyde. Neither had been much on talking. The silence was not awkward, just companionable.

Caitlin appeared in the opening to the barn. "Touch Brandon on the shoulder and point to me," she called. When the boy turned, she signed and spoke. "I'm going inside with the real-estate agent. You can stay with Zack if you don't bother him or come with me. I'll fix lunch after we discuss the sale. I'll ask Mr. Bradshaw to join us. And Zack." She looked at him. "Can you?"

His first inclination was to refuse. But he was interested in what Jeff had to say about the ranch. He nodded. He was even more interested in what Caitlin planned to do until the ranch sold. Would she and her brother really stay for the entire summer or would the reality of a working ranch have them returning to California within a few days?

CAITLIN FELT HERSELF growing stiff as she and Jeff walked through the house. As soon as he was gone, she planned a long hot bath. In the meantime, she wished she'd been able to thoroughly clean the entire dwelling. It looked shabby and run-down.

"Good solid home," Jeff said as he knocked on walls. "They built them well back then. And the modern improvements, while not completely up to date, will make it easier to sell. But the big advantage to your property is the land—most of it useable. Your ancestors chose well."

Every time Jeff commented on the place being in the family for so long, Caitlin felt another twinge of guilt. As if she were essentially selling her birthright.

After Tim's defection, she'd sold the house they'd bought together. No loss there. It cost a fortune in upkeep, the mortgage was astronomical, and it had been a constant reminder that the happiness she'd expected had gone terribly wrong.

But this was something else. If their background had been in ranching, maybe she and Brandon could have lived here and made the Triple M their home. There was no mortgage on this property. Renewable assets roamed the range.

That was fanciful thinking and she had to be practical. An experienced rancher would buy the place and love it. And with six million dollars, she could do anything she wanted.

She just wished she had some goal in mind.

Jeff accepted Caitlin's invitation to lunch. After the house tour, they ended up in the kitchen. While she was making sandwiches from leftover steaks, the bread she'd brought from town and a salad from the cans of fruit in the pantry, Jeff sat at the kitchen table, discussing strategies.

"I'll talk some more with the ranchers in the area to see if anyone might consider expanding. If no one wanted the entire ranch, would you be willing to sell some acres to adjacent neighbors?"

"Is that a good idea, breaking it up?" she asked.

"Might get you some ready cash. Don't know if there's any interest of course. I'll list the property with a national brokerage service, on the Internet and with cattlemen's associations. Then I'll target resort venture capitalists. You never know—this could be the next place for a destination resort. Unlikely to be another Disneyland since the winters are so harsh. You don't have enough height in your hills to encourage a ski resort. Still, a resort sale is worth a try. I won't kid you, this sale is likely to take a long time."

"But you do think it will sell eventually?" she asked.

"Sure to. But it's not like houses in a residential market where sales are expected in days or weeks."

Caitlin bit her lip in discouragement. She had thought she'd swoop in, list the property and have it close escrow before Brandon returned to school in September. Could she stick it out here until it sold?

What choice did she have? At least she'd have a roof over her head and plenty of food to eat.

When Brandon and Zack joined them for lunch, Caitlin put on a brave front, unwilling to let Jeff or Zack know how desperate she was for money. It had taken all she had and then some to settle the legitimate debts Timothy had left, not counting the thefts. His case was in the hands of the police. She'd obtained a divorce and wanted nothing more to do with the man she'd once loved.

Her foray into working for herself had proved a bust, though she was wiser now. She drew in a deep breath, meeting Zack's eyes. Looking away, she forced the anger aside. She wouldn't dwell on the past. Nothing could be changed. She'd learned a hard lesson. Now it was time to move on.

Brandon signed his excitement at working with the horses. He asked if Zack could teach him how to be a cowboy.

Caitlin looked at Zack, not sure which way she wanted him to answer. He had a scowl on his face. So far he hadn't exactly welcomed them with open arms. She hadn't forgotten he'd said he'd be leaving soon. She should make certain Brandon knew.

"He sure can make those hands fly," Jeff said, watching.

"It's American Sign Language. My mother had us learn when he was just a baby and we found out he was profoundly deaf. He attends a school for the deaf but does fine in the hearing world. He can read lips a bit, too." While she was talking, she also signed so Brandon could be part of the conversation.

Ask Zack if he'll learn enough sign so he can teach me about being a cowboy, Brandon persisted. *Or use you as interpreter. I can watch him and pick up a lot.*

"What was that?" Jeff asked.

"He wants to know if Zack will teach him how to be a cowboy," Caitlin said, watching the man in question from the corner of her eye.

"I won't be here long enough," Zack said without looking up.

CHAPTER THREE

"YOU'RE LEAVING?" JEFF ASKED, surprised.

Zack nodded. "I signed on with Clyde. After his death, I agreed to stay until the new owner showed up. Time to move on."

"Where you heading?"

"Don't know yet. Wherever the truck winds up, I guess."

"If you don't have another job lined up, please consider staying here until we sell the ranch," Caitlin said, signing for each speaker so Brandon was included.

He can't leave. We need him! Brandon looked shocked.

I know that, but I can't make him stay if he doesn't want to, she replied silently.

Jeff rubbed his chin. "Don't know of many ranch hands hunting work right now. Could be dicey finding a good worker on short notice."

"So post an ad and I'll stay until she does find someone," Zack said, taking another bite of his sandwich.

Caitlin didn't know why he was so anxious to move

on. "Seems to me this is a good setup. With me knowing so little about ranching, you really get to run things. I'll make you manager and throw in a bonus for staying, and for teaching Brandon and me what you can." Once she had the money from the sale, she could afford to be generous. Would it make any difference to the man if he stayed a bit longer?

Zack thought it over for so long she was afraid he would say no. But finally he nodded.

"You post a job opening in town. I'll stay until someone comes along that's suitable, or you sell, whichever comes first," he said. "I figure I owe it to Clyde."

"Thank you." She wanted to throw her arms around him in gratitude. For a long moment she'd faced the fear that he'd leave, and she and Brandon would make a complete mess of trying to keep animals fed, watered and cared for.

Can we get a dog? Brandon signed.

"One thing at a time," Caitlin said, signing back at him.

"What's that?" Jeff asked.

"He wants a dog."

"A good cattle dog would be an asset," Zack said. "Clyde had one that died last fall. I think the old man was too tired to train a new one. But that dog sure was a help."

"Charlie Johnstone has a couple he's letting go. He might sell one to Ms. Jackson," Jeff said.

Zack looked skeptical. "I saw one of his dogs in action at the branding last spring. Why would he sell any?"

"He's cutting back on his herd, going into buffalo, can you believe it? Anyway, wouldn't hurt to ask."

Caitlin looked at Zack. "Could you?"

ZACK MET HER GAZE then glanced away. She was asking him as if he were the one to make the decision. He didn't want to be manager of the ranch. Too much responsibility. Too much like putting down roots, becoming involved.

But it wouldn't hurt to call Charlie Johnstone and talk about the dogs. No denying that old dog of Clyde's had been a big help on the range. Some of those dogs were scary they were so savvy about cattle.

"Yeah, I can give him a call after lunch," he said. Was he doing this for Clyde, or to help Caitlin Jackson? He wasn't sure which. He glanced at the boy.

Brandon could hardly sit still. He ate his lunch, smiling all the while at Zack.

The kid was fast becoming a pain. Zack didn't want hero worship. He knew firsthand how fast circumstances could change. In the blink of an eye, lives were altered forever. One kick in the wrong place by a horse and the kid would be injured or killed. An unexpected rattler could wreak havoc, or an angry bull.

And he didn't even want to think of that pretty woman out on the range fending for herself.

He wasn't a damned babysitter. He had work to do.

After he'd finished his meal, he said goodbye to Bradshaw and headed back outside. Within seconds, Brandon was on his heels.

"I have work to do," Zack said gruffly.

The boy watched his mouth, then nodded. "I wan' to help."

Zack stopped and looked at him. "You can talk?" His voice sounded rusty from lack of use, and he spoke in monotone. Yet Zack understood every word.

"Yes. Part of teaching so hearing people can understand me. Not everybody learns sign."

"Does your sister know?"

"Yes. But she can sign. That easier."

"How much can you understand me?"

Brandon frowned, watching Zack's lips. "Slow, please."

Zack repeated the question slower.

Brandon smiled and flicked his index finger up and down near his forehead. Pointing to his chest he said, "I understand."

Zack mimicked his hand movements. "I understand." Son of a gun, he had learned his first bit of sign language.

Not that he wanted any part of it. He turned and strode to the barn. Dammit, he was not putting himself on the line again. He knew he was burned out.

He'd get the kid started on cleaning tack and then go call Charlie. And Jeff Bradshaw better get that job opening posted today!

ONCE JEFF LEFT, CAITLIN quickly cleaned the kitchen, getting food from the freezer for dinner. The supplies were plentiful. The only things she didn't have a lot of were eggs and milk. Anything that could be canned, packaged or frozen was available. With a trip to town taking most of a day, she could see why.

Deciding to take a quick hot bath, she headed upstairs to the only bathroom. Her legs were so stiff she used the railing on the stairs to pull herself up. She loved the large claw-foot freestanding tub in the big bathroom. An oval rod hung from the ceiling with shower curtains. But today she wanted to soak in hot water and get her muscles loosened.

She gathered clean underwear and her silk robe. Stepping into the hot water a few moments later, she gave a sigh of pure bliss. It felt heavenly. Stress eased away as she leaned her head back and closed her eyes. She could feel the warmth soaking in, feel some of the strain of the last few weeks melting away.

Events had been put into motion. There was nothing further she could do. The sale of the ranch rested in Jeff's hands. She'd have to ask the attorney about money to carry the place until it sold. He'd mentioned an account at the local bank, but had said there wasn't much in it. He was working to get her as a signatory on the account. How much money was there? she wondered. Enough to pay Zack? How had her uncle managed? There must have been some regular income she didn't know about. Hadn't Zack said she could sell some cattle? Maybe she should sell the entire herd if they weren't going to stay on the ranch. Would the next owner up the buying price to cover the value of cattle? Not likely if he wasn't a rancher.

She wished she'd asked Jeff about that.

Caitlin felt much better by the time the water began

to cool. She dried off and slipped on her silky dressing gown—one of the few items she'd kept when trying to salvage the mess Timothy had left. It made her feel glamorous. She brushed her wet hair, fluffing it up a bit with her fingers, and went to change into fresh clothes when she heard a knock on the front door.

Had Brandon locked himself out?

As she ran down the stairs, she was pleased to feel her muscles respond with hardly a whimper of protest.

Opening the door, she stopped in surprise. It was Zack.

He looked at her. Caitlin was immediately conscious of her damp hair, her flushed skin, and the fact she wore hardly anything beneath the slinky material.

"Is Brandon hurt?" she asked. Why else would Zack have come back? He'd gone out of his way to make it clear he didn't want anything to do with her.

"He's fine. I called Charlie Johnstone about the cattle dog. He's willing to sell you one or two of the dogs he's letting go. No other buyers yet but he has had another call about them. If you want first choice, you'll have to head over there in the morning."

"Oh." The message could have waited.

"I didn't know you'd be lounging around in a bathtub all afternoon," he said. "I thought I could go over some things about the ranch with you."

"Hardly lounging. I took a hot bath to loosen up my muscles. I'm not used to riding. I'll be changed in a minute. Come in."

"I'll wait out here," he said, turning and going to sit on one of the old wooden rocking chairs on the wide porch.

ZACK HEARD THE DOOR CLOSE. Dammit, he did not need to see his new boss rosy from a warm bath and wearing some feminine thing that made her look alluring and sexy. He'd been away from women too long. Nothing like abstinence to make a man horny as all get out for the first woman he saw.

He drew in a deep breath. Caitlin was strictly off-limits. Even if he wanted to become involved with someone, she was not what he was looking for.

For a moment the thought stunned him. When he'd come back from overseas, the pain of losing Billy, of futilely trying to save lives had been too fresh. He'd sought a different life from what he'd known. And he'd sworn not to let himself become involved with anyone. It hurt too much when things went wrong.

He'd found a certain peace working with Clyde. The old man had never pushed, never tried to change him. Maybe that was the ticket, finding acceptance where he could. He hadn't been able to save people when death had summoned. But working cattle and dealing with horses made it possible to find peace in his portion of the earth.

It was selfish, but he liked the way things had been the last two years. Clyde's death had been sad, but the man had been in his nineties. He'd lived a good life, one Zack wouldn't mind looking back on. Clyde had been a good neighbor, had the trust and respect of all who knew him. He hadn't changed the world, but he hadn't contributed to its problems, either.

Zack frowned. He was becoming philosophical. Billy would have laughed. They'd been two boys from a poor section in Bedford-Stuyvesant, bound and determined to make the army their jumping-off point for great things. Instead, Billy died, and Zack was more messed up inside than when he'd joined.

Caitlin came out onto the porch. Her hair was still damp and she wore no makeup. Not that she needed it, in his opinion. He stood. The sooner they finished their business, the better.

"Tell me about the cattle dog. Is one really necessary?" she asked as she walked over to stand near him.

"Maybe not if you're planning to hire more help. But I can't move the entire herd myself when it's time to rotate fields. I don't think you and your brother are going to be much help. Especially if you only plan to stay until September."

She leaned against the railing, looking out over the rolling land. "Even if we stayed forever, we wouldn't be much help. I know nothing about cattle. Our lives are in California."

"You could hire a manager, have him run the place. Probably what you'll have to do until the ranch sells." Zack stayed back by the chairs, watching her gaze out to the horizon. Did she miss the city? Find the empty land desolate?

"That's why I want you to manage it. I'd like to know that the man running things had known Clyde and would do his best because of that."

Zack didn't say anything. He didn't want to be a manager. But he wouldn't mind her leaving soon. The solitude of the ranch these last few months had suited him to a T.

"It's really pretty here, isn't it?" she said. "I almost

forget how crowded the Bay Area is until I look out over all this empty land. Traffic isn't much either around here." She smiled wryly and turned to face him. "Not that lack of traffic makes Wolf Crossing any closer. Long way to go for groceries."

"It's the largest town in the county, but Fallworth is closer, about twenty miles. Just a wide spot in the road, small store, video rentals, few hardware items. It's on the way to Johnstone's ranch, we'll pass it tomorrow. Need anything?"

"I sure do. I'll make a list. So how much would a good cattle dog cost?"

Was that the real issue—lack of money? Zack found it hard to believe with the clothes she wore. Yet the car was an old heap of junk, and she kept alluding to the cost of things.

"I have no idea. Want me to call before we go?" If she couldn't afford a dog, how would she hire a new hand?

"It's bound to be cheaper than hiring another cowboy, wouldn't you think?" she asked, almost reading his mind.

"Yes."

"Brandon's always wanted a dog. We didn't have one when we lived with my father, he couldn't stand dogs. Brandon's been in a boarding school for the last decade, so no pets there."

"These aren't pets. They're working dogs. They'll be friendly and loyal, but their focus is their work. Queensland Heelers are bred for cattle. Don't expect a cuddly puppy to share his bed."

She nodded. "Maybe that will make it easier to

leave it here on the ranch when we return to California. What time tomorrow should we be ready to go?"

"Before ten—after chores, and time enough to get home in time for chores."

She motioned to the rockers and went to sit in one. "So, give me a crash course in all I need to know about ranching for the time I'm here."

Zack sat and thought a moment before he began. She didn't have to know much. They would only maintain things until a buyer was found. No repairs beyond the basic necessities. No painting the house or installing new lights in the barn. But if Jeff was right and it took months or years to sell, they'd have more work to do.

Maybe she should sell the herd, take the money and live on that until the land sold. That would eliminate the most pressing work.

Zack began to tell her what he'd learned over the last few years.

CAITLIN LISTENED, TRYING not to panic. The place was way too big for one cowboy to run, and she and Brandon were next to useless. She tried to remain confident, but nothing in her past had prepared her for a challenge like this.

And her most recent experiences had shattered whatever confidence she used to have. She was feeling overwhelmed. There was no one to turn to. Worse, Brandon depended upon her.

Her brother wouldn't be so complacent if he knew the full extent of her screw-up with her marriage and her attempt to go into business for herself. She glanced at the man beside her. Zack wouldn't either. She drew a deep breath, concentrating on what he was saying. She had to succeed at this, to hold on until the place sold. It was her only hope for the future.

Brandon came around the house and saw them. He looked tired. Caitlin hoped he wasn't pushing himself too hard in his desire to learn all he could about working on a ranch. Yet he also seemed happier than she'd seen him in a while.

Finished, he signed, looking at Zack as if for approval.

"Whatever he was doing, he's finished," she said. "Tomorrow we'll go see about a cattle dog to help move the cattle," she said as she signed to Brandon. "Zack knows someone who has a couple of dogs to sell. But they are working dogs, not pets. If they're suitable, we'll get one."

"Brandon can be in charge of it," Zack said. "The dogs work better following directions from one person. And he could feed and play with it when they aren't working. They're high energy dogs."

Caitlin told Brandon and his grin grew broader. Nodding, he said he was going in to wash up before dinner.

Caitlin glanced at her watch, it was almost five. Even though she felt they'd just finished lunch, it was time to get started cooking dinner.

"Do you want to eat with us?" she asked. "You could tell me more over dinner."

Zack rose and shook his head. "I've got chores to

do before I can eat. Tomorrow you and Brandon can step in and help. I'll fix my own dinner. We'll leave in the morning around ten."

She watched him amble toward the barn, struck by the difference between this man and Timothy. Zack was even better looking than her ex-husband, and he certainly was more masculine, with broad shoulders and muscular arms. But he seemed totally unaware of it. He was completely focused on the work to be done rather than on himself.

She thought back to her time with Tim. She'd been so crazy about him when they'd started dating. He'd already done well in the dot-com arena and had pots of money to show her a good time. After the rather austere life-style her father had espoused, it had been a heady experience. When they married, the sky had been the limit. Fancy home, expensive cars, trips to Hawaii and the Caribbean. And constant parties. She could throw a dinner party for thirty at a moment's notice.

She looked at the ranch land. Nothing in her past had prepared her for this.

She thought of selling the place and having a lot of money again. What would it be like to never have to worry about money?

But the sale was not a reality yet. And tomorrow she was expanding her holdings by acquiring a cattle dog. Maybe Fallworth would have a store that sold boots. If she was going to do any riding this summer, she needed proper attire. A hat that fit was also on her list.

Sighing at all she had to figure out, Caitlin rose and headed in to start dinner. At least she could cook.

Brandon claimed the small office after they ate, e-mailing his friends in California. Clyde had a dated computer with dial-up capabilities. Brandon's ease in using the computer gave her hope he might pursue a career in that field. But he'd need to go to college. And if the ranch sold, he could go to any school he wanted.

WHEN CAITLIN AWOKE the next morning, she could hardly move. Her legs screamed in protest at the slightest attempt. Even her shoulders ached. Slowly she eased herself out of bed, limping to the bathroom. Standing beneath a hot shower didn't help as much as she wished. Still, she could walk with only an occasional twinge. She dressed slowly and headed downstairs.

Entering the kitchen, she saw the note Brandon had propped up—*Gone to help Zack. I got food.*

She shook her head. She bet the teenager had scarfed down last night's leftovers. Checking the refrigerator, she saw she was right. What else was there? He wasn't one to fix an omelet or even fry a couple of eggs. She should get some cereal for him. Zack had said there was a small grocery store in Fallworth, and she was planning to stock up on things she hadn't thought about in Wolf Crossing.

The phone rang. Caitlin answered, slowly stretching her leg muscles, hoping to have them loosen up before she saw Zack again. She did not want to be limping around him!

"Ms. Jackson, Harry Benson here. I'm calling about the bank account. The bank will mail new checks with your name to you this week. With the card you signed in my office, the account is now in your name. In the meantime, I can arrange for some money to go into your current checking account if you like. I'll continue to pay Zack until you get the new checks, and I'll see to some of the other current bills. If you can come to town next week, we can transfer the utilities into your name, like the electricity and phone."

"That would be fine. What day?" She was relieved to have the attorney handle these things for her, but how much would it cost? Was she running up a huge bill?

"Thursday works for me, early afternoon."

"How much will you transfer?" she asked, jotting a note on the calendar hanging by the phone.

"I told you the account doesn't have a huge sum. Clyde didn't have any medical insurance so the hospital took up a lot of his cash. You'll have to think about selling some cattle or something before things get critical. I can transfer about five thousand now, but you'll need more before long."

She blinked. "You'll transfer five thousand dollars?" She thought he'd said there wasn't much in the account. Not much was the four hundred dollars in her own account. Five thousand sounded like a fortune.

"Only around fifteen thousand remaining after the transfer. Not a lot when running a working cattle ranch. But you've got time to get some cash before you run short. Clyde often sold off some cattle in the spring, but the big sale is in the fall."

If fifteen thousand wasn't a lot in his mind, she wondered what was. Yet she had no clue about the expenses of a ranch. Zack's salary probably ate up a lot. Did they have to buy food for the horses, or did the hay she saw cover that?

"That will be fine. I'll discuss it with Zack. He'd be able to tell me what we need to do, wouldn't he?"

"He would. I'll see you next Thursday. I'll wire the funds now."

"Thank you," she said, feeling safe for the first time in months. She could stretch that money a long way.

She grabbed some canned peaches and ate them for breakfast, then got ready to leave. As she headed out to her car, she didn't see Zack or Brandon. Turning toward the barn, she met Zack as he walked out.

He looked at her, glanced at his watch. "Time to go?"

"It's ten."

"I'll get my wallet and keys."

"We can go in my car," she said.

"I don't think so. Where would you put that dog and all your supplies?"

"Dog in back seat, supplies in the trunk."

"You need more than that car of yours will hold, and you don't know where that dog's been. Told you they aren't pets. They don't go into the house. We'll fix him up a place in the barn. Good for guarding the ranch at night as well as working cattle. We'll take the pickup."

"Fine."

She walked out and over to the truck. It was a big one, dented and dusty. Opening the passenger door, she peered in. The cab was larger than she'd expected, and higher. Stepping up put a strain on achy muscles. She kept quiet though, not wanting to give her hired hand any cause for more disparaging remarks.

Brandon joined her in the cab and slammed the door shut. He quickly told her about his work that morning, how he'd learned how to tack up the horses, groom them and pick their hooves. Zack said he was a quick learner and that maybe he could be a rancher when he got out of school and—

Caitlin interrupted him. *You have to go to college first. And we won't own a ranch by then. This one is up for sale, remember?*

It's been in the family for generations, maybe we shouldn't sell.

We are not ranchers.

Our family has been. We can learn. Anyway, the real-estate agent said it could take years to sell. We could learn all we can, and if we like it, stay.

Caitlin was dumbfounded. Her brother thought they could stay and raise cattle? They'd been here two days. She didn't know one bit more about the job than she had when she'd arrived. She had no intentions of staying in this out-of-the-way place. She wanted a big city like San Francisco or Dallas or Miami. She wasn't going to live eighty miles from the nearest town, which didn't even have a movie theater much less the ballet or symphony.

Yet she could see his enthusiasm.

Give him time, she thought. Once he had to do chores in the rain, or was bone tired and still had to do chores before dinner, he'd be excited about something else. She wouldn't argue with him, that would only strengthen his defense.

Zack joined them a moment later. The cab, which had seemed so spacious, now seemed crowded. With Brandon on one side and Zack on the other, Caitlin felt hemmed in.

"How long is it to the store?" she asked as he backed around and headed out.

"Less than half an hour this time of year. Longer in the winter. Roads don't get plowed a lot."

Snow. Caitlin remembered snow in a couple of places her father had been stationed. But she'd been a child then. There wasn't a lot of snow in the Bay Area.

She didn't need to worry about that now, though. She and Brandon would be long gone before the winter came to Wyoming.

Settling back to enjoy the ride, she tried to ignore the man beside her, which wasn't easy. He took up a lot of space. She studied his hands for a moment, capable and large. She noted a couple of scars. How had he gotten them?

She could smell the scent of hay and horses and man. Swallowing, she glanced at her brother. He was all arms and legs. Slender, he'd shot up over the last couple of years and now was several inches taller than her own five feet six inches. But he didn't reach Zack's height, and it would be a few years before Brandon filled out.

She wondered what he'd look like as a man if he worked on a ranch. Muscular and fit, she was sure, if Zack was anything to go by. But she had thought of

Brandon working with computers or something, not such a dangerous, physical job as ranching.

For a moment she let her imagination run with the idea of staying on the ranch and learning how to manage it. She could see herself wearing jeans and boots and a Stetson, striding around the property. She'd meet her neighbors and be the belle of local dances, having cowboys hanging on her every word. No one would know she'd foolishly married a man who'd stolen from investors. No one would know how her second client, Tiffany, had stiffed her for the money she owed Caitlin for that lavish big party. Unable to pay her bills on time, Caitlin had lost her chance to continue in events planning.

As a successful rancher, she would be respected.

The truck hit a pothole and Caitlin was thrown against Zack, Brandon slamming against her right side.

"Umph," she said, straightening. That was the end of her daydreaming.

"I thought we'd go to Charlie's first, get the dog, then stop for supplies on the way back. That way if you get cold things, they won't spoil while we look at the dogs," Zack said. "Plus we can pick up anything we need for the dog that Johnstone doesn't throw in."

"Fine." She should have thought of that. In fact she needed to begin thinking like the owner of a ranch, and not someone on vacation. The surroundings might be foreign, but the realities weren't going to change. She was the sole person responsible for her brother and herself. And the ranch was their one hope. Daydreaming didn't get things done. She needed to make concrete plans and follow them.

CHAPTER FOUR

FALLWORTH WASN'T MUCH MORE than three or four buildings along the highway. There was a small feed barn, a
grocery store connected to the gas station, and a bar.
Cowboys probably kept it in business. How many other
ranchers found this the closest place to shop? There were
several pickup trucks parked along the road, only one car.

I need a hat and boots, Brandon signed as they
passed the feed store.

Me, too, she returned. As well as another pair of
jeans. Should she get leather gloves as well? Jeffrey
had worn them. Zack's hands were hard and calloused.
The skin was tanned, and nicks and scars dotted the
backs of them. A man's hands. Timothy had had his
nails done. She almost shuddered when she remembered how much she'd loved the man—or the man
she'd thought he was. And how blinded she'd been to
his actual character by the lavish things he'd provided.

In retrospect, he now seemed ostentatious, shallow
and not worthy of another second's thought. Yet she
couldn't let go. She'd been married to him for almost
six years. How could she not have suspected something was wrong during those years? Had she been so

shallow herself that the parties, the fancy clothes and trips to exotic locales had blinded her to honesty and the truth?

"What's he saying?" Zack asked.

"He wants boots and a cowboy hat. I need them, too."

He glanced at her, his straw hat curled and shaped to shadow his face without interfering with seeing. Sometimes he wore it low on his forehead, other times pushed back.

"They'll probably have a small selection here," he warned. "You could wait to get into Wolf Crossing. The feed store there has a lot of clothes, boots and hats."

"Too long, we want them today."

He didn't say anything and Caitlin wondered if she'd sounded impatient, as if she was dismissing his suggestion?

"Unless the quality isn't good here. We'll need you to help us make selections," she said in appeasement.

He clenched his jaw. "You're on your own."

No matter what she did, she missed the mark with the man. Why should she care? If she found another cowboy to hire, she could let Zack go on his merry way. Not that *merry* was exactly the word to describe Zack Carson.

A short time later they arrived at the Johnstone ranch. Dogs came running to the truck, barking and prancing around. Zack got out without a worry. He said something to the dogs and they wagged their stubby tails like crazy.

Brandon jumped out almost as fast and went around the truck to the dogs. They immediately turned their attention to him. He leaned over and began to rub their necks, laughing when they jumped on him.

Caitlin wasn't as brave. She didn't know these dogs or they her. Zack had said they weren't friendly house dogs. What if they bit Brandon? After a minute she slid across the passenger side and got out. Her muscles protested. Thankfully a man was coming from the house. If that was Charlie Johnstone, he could control his dogs.

"Hey, Charlie," Zack said, coming round the truck.

"Thought that was you." Charlie and Zack shook hands.

Then Zack introduced Caitlin and Brandon. The teenager reached right out to shake Charlie's hand and smiled. He then turned his attention back to the dogs.

Caitlin also shook hands, feeling the toughness of the old rancher's palms.

"I knew your mother a long time ago," he said. "She came to visit Clyde one summer."

"I came with her. The only time I've been on the ranch."

"And now it's yours. Nice spread. Seems odd to have Clyde gone. He was ranching before I was born. My dad always spoke highly of him. So you want a dog to help Zack here?"

Charlie Johnstone looked to be in his late fifties. He carried a bit more weight than Caitlin would expect of a busy rancher. His place looked in tip-top shape, though. She wished her own place looked better. Would the run-down condition hinder sales?

"Maybe," she said. The dogs swarmed around the truck and spotted her. They came over, tails wagging.

"Get away," Charlie said, and they backed away a

little distance, sitting, almost vibrating with excitement, their entire attention focused on the man.

"That blue merle is for sale and the spotted one next to him. The merle is the better dog, canny like you wouldn't believe. I can let you have one or both."

"Can we see them work?" Zack asked.

"Sure." Charlie turned and headed around the house. "I've got some cattle in one of the fields nearby. Saves getting the horses out. Come along."

A five-minute walk led them to a fenced section where several steers were grazing. Charlie gave a command and all the dogs lay down. He pointed to the blue merle and whistled. The dog ran into the field, circling the cattle, watching them, glancing back at Charlie once in a while.

Another series of whistles and the dog began moving the steers toward them. Caitlin watched, fascinated. The cattle were huge in comparison to the little dog. But the Heeler knew his business and darted here and there, keeping the steers bunched and moving steadily toward the fence.

She glanced at Brandon. He was entranced. A quick look at Zack and she was surprised to find him watching her.

"Amazing," she said in a low voice.

He nodded. "Charlie, will the dog work to hand signals?"

"Some. He'd need some conditioning to get used to that. You can't whistle?"

"I was thinking Brandon might like to work with him," Zack said.

"Don't even suggest that," Caitlin said. "He can't ride yet. How do you think he'd manage out on the range where anything could happen? We're only here a short time."

"You're not staying?" Charlie asked in surprise.

"No. I've listed the ranch for sale."

Charlie looked as if he was going to say something, then closed his mouth. Glancing at Zack, he raised an eyebrow.

"She's hunting another ranch hand. Once she finds one, I'm moving on."

"Sorry to hear that," Charlie said. "She won't be wanting a dog if she's only staying a little while. What will happen to him next?"

Caitlin didn't like the two men talking as she wasn't there. "Actually the real-estate agent said it could take a long time to sell. We only have two and a half months before Brandon has to get back to school in September, but we'll be here until then. Whoever runs the place will need help until it sells. How much for the dog?"

Charlie rubbed his chin, then shrugged. "Six hundred."

Caitlin paused. It seemed like a lot of money for a dog. Yet the attorney had transferred funds to her account. A dog was cheaper than hiring another cowboy. "I can write you a check."

"Be fine with me. You taking him today?" Charlie asked easily.

"Yes. What's his name?"

"Hank. I have some papers for him. And I can show Zack the hand signals so he can get the dog to work."

Caitlin signed the information for her brother. His eyes lit up. He insisted on staying with Zack and Charlie to learn the hand signals as well. Caitlin argued to no avail. The men climbed through the barbed-wire fence and headed for the cattle and the dog. She watched anxiously, hoping the large steers didn't charge Brandon. But the bovines drifted away as the men approached. They were talking and watching the dog. Knowing Zack and Charlie were comfortable gave her some reassurance Brandon would be okay. She returned to the truck to get her checkbook from her purse.

She wrote out the check, then continued to sit in the cab of the truck. She leaned her head back, feeling as if things were spinning out of control. She would soon own a Queensland Heeler dog in addition to several hundred head of cattle and thousands of acres of Wyoming. A far cry from a woman who had loved to party and had briefly wished for a career as an event planner.

Now she'd need to become proficient in riding. Learn about raising cattle. Show Zack that she could run a ranch.

What was she thinking? She wasn't here to impress Zack Carson. Running a ranch was hard work. She wanted Brandon to have a fabulous summer, but she couldn't let him think they'd be staying—no matter how much he thought he wanted that right now. The novelty would wear off soon.

She wasn't sure how long she sat in the truck, but when she saw the men heading back, dogs dashing around them, she knew her quiet time w ˙s over. Reality always had a way of intruding.

BY THE TIME THEY REACHED the Triple M later that afternoon, Caitlin was stiffening up again. She and Brandon had bought boots, hats and jeans at the store. She'd also stocked up on as many items as she thought they'd need for the next few days. If she was going into Wolf Crossing next Thursday, she would do more shopping there.

Hank rode in the back of the truck without a problem. Caitlin hated to admit it but the purchases would never have fit in the trunk of her car. If she were staying, she'd have to get a pickup truck to haul things around.

"Did my uncle have a truck?" she asked. From what she'd seen, every man in Wyoming owned a truck.

"Yes. It's parked in the shed behind the barn. I've been using mine for supplies and things, but that one is yours."

Thursday she'd drive it into Wolf Crossing.

After dinner, Brandon headed back outside to practice commands with Hank while Caitlin went into the small room that served as Clyde's office. It was as dusty as the rest of the house before she'd cleaned. Only the computer that Brandon had been using was clean. She quickly ran a cloth over the desk and bookshelves then sat down. Turning on the computer, she looked at the programs listed. Her uncle had been an orderly man. There were only two programs—an accounting program and a database. She clicked on one and was confronted with financial records going back several years. She skimmed through them quickly, not understanding all the ins and outs, but recognizing he'd made a solid income from the ranch, though in spurts.

He'd sold hay to help his cash flow. A few months later he'd sold some cattle. That had brought in a larger amount. And Clyde had invested money in fairly conservative funds, which paid quarterly. There were expenditures to a medical facility through March—then nothing after he'd died. She was too tired to study this right now, but maybe in the morning she'd get a better handle on things. Maybe she could liquidate some of the remaining investment. Brandon would be in before long, wanting to e-mail his friends. She could imagine the stories he had to share with them.

Feeling a little lonely, she wished she had someone special to e-mail. Her friend Beth was away on a cruise with her husband. There was no one else that Caitlin wanted to talk to.

She heard the dog barking so she went to the window and raised it. Leaning out, she saw Brandon throwing a stick. Hank raced after it, barking the entire way, then picked it up and raced back to drop it at her brother's feet. The two of them looked as if they were having a great time. She smiled. This was a summer Brandon would always remember.

Besides the barking dog, she could hear the breeze rustling through the old trees near the house and in the distance the lowing of cattle. She rested against the window frame to absorb the evening. There were clouds gathering over the peaks. The sunset would be spectacular. It was peaceful and beautiful. No wonder her uncle had loved it. And her mother. She'd spoken fondly of their summer visit. And of Wyoming.

Caitlin should have come to visit again after she was grown. Vague guilt rose when she thought of how mindless her life had been. She was twenty-six and had nothing to show for her years. What did she want to do in the future?

ZACK SAT IN THE SHADE of the bunkhouse steps and watched the woman gazing at the horizon. She annoyed him no end and it wasn't even her fault. He couldn't expect her to know how to help around the place. When she asked to be shown how to do something, he resented the time to teach her. Yet if not him, who would show her?

He didn't like the way she had him feeling emotions long dormant—ones he didn't want to feel. As if he'd been asleep for a long time and was now awakening.

Which was stupid. He had his life just as he wanted it. He had no family except his grandmother. And she was back in Brooklyn. He called her every Sunday. He could pick up and move whenever the mood struck. And if things didn't go the way he liked, he could always pack up again.

Yet he sat in the shadows of the bunkhouse stoop watching Caitlin. What was she thinking—how she'd spend all those millions when the ranch sold?

She hadn't been feigning surprise when she'd learned how much the land would bring. It had flat out astonished her. But it would not take long before she got used to the idea. Once she had all that cash in the bank, she'd be gone so fast he'd probably only glimpse the dust.

Or was the magic of the place getting to her? He'd felt it soon after he'd arrived. The timelessness, the feeling that the land had been here at the beginning of time and would be long after he was dust in the ground. The breeze carried secrets from long ago, and the peace invaded a person like a slow caress. He took a deep breath, breathing in the scents that defined this part of the world. He could smell the green grass, with a hint of the hay that was ready to cut. The stink of cattle and the mud flats by the river. The small pond in the center of the trees near the house.

He had needed this healing place when he'd shown up. Maybe Caitlin Jackson needed some healing herself. Her eyes looked sad and fearful. As if the weight of the world rested on her shoulders. What could a woman like that have to mourn? A broken marriage? He needed to pull back, do his job and not get involved. He did not want friends—and especially did not want involvement with a woman needing rescue. She was on her own.

The kid was working out better than he'd initially thought. The boy learned fast. If he stayed long enough, he could conceivably become a competent cowboy. He had an endless thirst for information and a willingness to try anything. Sometimes Brandon taught him the sign for an object or action. The boy was cut off from the world through no fault of his own.

Zack had cut himself off from the world. But he could join back in if he ever wanted.

He rose and headed for the barn. There were endless tasks to be done. Working kept thoughts at bay. He'd spent his entire life not knowing the Jacksons. Two days acquaintance didn't fundamentally change anything.

BY THE TIME ZACK TURNED OFF his bedside lamp, the wind was blowing hard. He hoped it wasn't going to storm. He hated storms. Running through the list of chores he needed to see to in the morning, he soon drifted to sleep.

Thunder rumbled. The wind blew. Rain began to fall, softly at first, then with a drumming beat on the roof. The temperature dropped drastically. Zack tossed and turned.

A sudden crack had him sitting upright with a yell that shattered the night.

For a long moment he sat in the darkness, breathing hard. The images wouldn't go away. Another crack of thunder, or was it gunfire? Lightning lit up the night, or was it explosions in the distance?

He could smell the gunpowder, hear the screams, see the unrelenting landscape that offered little hiding space and no protection from the rockets that rained down.

"Medic!" The cry echoed over and over.

He gritted his teeth and dashed across the room and out into the pouring rain.

The cold air hit him instantly and snapped him out

of the flashback. For a long moment he stared out, seeing nothing, becoming soaked in seconds. He shivered. This summer rain was nothing like the arid climate of Afghanistan. Lightning illuminated the horses standing beneath the lean-to along the wall of the barn. He felt the cold nose of the new dog brush his naked thigh.

"Hey, Hank. It's okay, fellow." Zack reached out to pet the wet dog. The scent was nothing like the blood and dust of a war zone. It grounded him in the present.

"Sorry to disturb your first night in your new home," Zack said, stepping back on the stoop out of the downpour. He shivered with cold, but wasn't ready to go back inside.

Thankfully these nightmares didn't happen often. A jagged lightning bolt lit up the sky. Seconds later a large crack of thunder reverberated. Zack was prepared for it. He took a breath, holding on to Hank. Sinking down on the wooden stoop, he ignored the cold and talked to the dog. He was in Wyoming. He was alive and no longer responsible for trying to patch up the wounded. He no longer had to identify the dead.

The storm gradually moved east, the rain settling into a gentle downfall, soaking the ground.

It would mean a delay in cutting the hay. The crop needed to be dry. But only a couple of days of hot sunshine and it would be ready.

After a long time, he was too cold to remain sitting buck naked outside. With a final rub on the dog's neck, he rose and headed inside. A hot shower, something to drink, and he'd see if he could get any more sleep without the nightmares of the past catching up.

CAITLIN LAY IN HER BED, listening to the rain on the roof. Her window was open a crack and she could feel the coolness of the wind as it blew across the room. Water might be getting in, but she was too cozy beneath her covers to get up to see. Once again thunder rolled. She smiled, remembering other storms through the years.

The Bay Area rarely had thunderstorms, but when her father had been stationed in Texas, they'd been almost daily occurrences during the summer. She'd always loved the freshness of the rain, the fury of the thunder and the power the storm represented.

How was Hank doing? she wondered. Brandon would sleep through the entire storm, but she worried about the dog—new to the ranch, alone in the barn. Should she go check on him?

Reluctantly she rose and went to the window. Despite the heat of the afternoon, the air now stirring was cold. Her bare feet felt the rain on the floor. She pushed the window closed and went to the bathroom for a towel. She blotted the floor until it was dry, her muscles still protesting. Dressing quickly, she tried on her new boots. Seemed a shame to get them wet and muddy, but they'd do better for her than her cross trainers, which would be soaked in no time. Boots weren't for show.

Pulling on a light jacket, she went downstairs and out to the front porch. It was pitch-black outside. She could hardly make out the silhouette of the barn against the dark sky. The rain had slowed and was now more of a sprinkle. But it was so dark she wasn't sure she could make it to the barn without running into something.

A light caught her attention. She walked to the edge of the porch and looked at the bunkhouse. Lights were on. Was something wrong or had the storm wakened Zack, too? Had he thought about Hank? Probably not. Hadn't he said the dog wasn't a family pet? She didn't feel the cattle needed to come in out of the rain, but she did worry about the dog.

She stepped off the porch and carefully headed for the bunkhouse, using the light from the windows as a beacon. A moment later she knocked on the door. Then opened it. Zack had said not to knock.

"Zack?" she called.

He stepped out into the hall, wearing only jeans, with a towel slung around his neck.

"What are you doing here?" he asked, walking into the communal room.

"I got up to see to Hank. I thought the storm might scare him or something."

"He's fine."

"Are you sure?"

"I was out on the porch for a while. He came and sat with me."

"Oh." Caitlin didn't know what to say next. She glanced around the room. Comfortable sofas and chairs were scattered around. A large-screen television sat in one corner. A card table in another.

"I'm not used to storms like this," she explained. "I wondered if the dog would run or something and not come back since this is his first night here." She hoped she didn't sound too foolish.

"First night, but I think he knows this is home."

He just stood there watching her. Caitlin grew nervous. She'd found out what she wanted. Might as well return to the house.

"I was going to make something hot to drink. Want to join me?" he asked.

She blinked in surprise. It was the first friendly gesture Zack had made.

"Sure. Do you have hot chocolate?"

He nodded. "I'll finish getting dressed and be in the kitchen in a minute. It's through that door if you want to wait there."

Caitlin went to the large kitchen. When Zack joined her a few moments later, he'd donned a shirt and socks, but no boots. His hair was still damp.

"Did Clyde eat here?" she asked.

"Most of the time."

"The appliances are newer than the ones in the house kitchen," she said.

He nodded and quickly took down the cocoa, got some milk from the industrial-size refrigerator and a pan from the cupboard near the stove. "In summer we had three others working, so we all ate here."

Caitlin sat on one of the chairs circling the table, which was large enough for a dozen people.

She watched Zack get cups while keeping an eye on the heating milk. Just as he was pouring the hot beverage into the mugs, a loud crack of thunder sounded and the lights went out.

"Damn!" he said. The pan clattered on the stove.

"What?"

"The last bit missed the cup and hit my hand," he said.

"Run cold water on it."

"The well won't pump without electricity. I don't want to deplete the holding tank for this. I'll get ice."

She heard the sound of a drawer, then a flashlight clicked on. Caitlin was grateful for the glow as Zack got ice for his hand, then set the two mugs on the table. He took a chair near her and positioned the flashlight in the center of the table so that it shone up to the ceiling. It didn't give much light, but enough that she could see him.

She took a sip of hot chocolate. It almost burned her tongue. But it tasted heavenly.

"Does the power go out often?" she asked.

"Often enough. There's a generator. When we need electricity, I'll fire it up. We shouldn't need it tonight and the power may be back on come morning."

They sat in silence. Caitlin could not think of a single thing to say. She waited a moment, then took another sip of her drink. Still hot, but manageable. The sooner she finished, the sooner she could return home.

"Now that you've talked to Jeff Bradshaw, how long do you think you'll stay?" Zack asked.

She met his gaze. He looked dark and dangerous in the faint illumination.

"For the summer at least."

"You don't have a job you need to get back to?"

She shook her head. She knew she could get work. She'd been a great waitress.

It was not the life she had envisioned when she'd been younger, however. But without a degree, it was hard to get a decent job.

"Brandon has to return to school in September, so we'll be gone by then." If the ranch hadn't sold by the time they left, she'd have to find another cheap apartment, start a new job, try to get on her feet.

How hard would that be with the tantalizing thought of six million dollars' worth of land sitting in Wyoming? She still couldn't wrap her mind around the idea of never having to worry about money again. How amazing that would be.

"We don't want to be a burden while we're here," she said. "Show us what we need to learn so we can help out."

"Brandon's coming along with horse care."

"I want to learn, too."

"I'm not a teacher," he grumbled.

"Hey, until we hire someone else, you're all we've got."

He didn't say anything.

Caitlin took another swallow. She could feel the warmth spread. Finishing quickly, she put the cup down and rose just as Zack stood.

So close together, they bumped into each other. Before she could step back, he leaned over and kissed her. His arms wrapped around her and pulled her closer. For a stunned second, Caitlin could do nothing.

She had not expected anything like this. The man didn't even like her.

His lips were warm on hers, moving persuasively. She wanted to savor the touch, the feelings that built. It had been more than a year since she'd been kissed, held in a man's arms.

She encircled his waist and held on as the kiss deepened. She felt warm and safe. Forgetting all the problems she faced, she let herself go.

When he ended the kiss and pulled back, she frowned, not wanting the contact to end. Then she realized what had happened.

"I'm going back to bed," she said needlessly, moving away from the table. She stopped as she realized it was black as pitch away from the flashlight.

"Take it," he said, scooping up the light and handing it to her.

Caitlin turned and quickly left, her heart still pounding. She knew better than to get caught up with some handsome cowboy. Licking her lips, however, she could still taste him and her heart rate didn't slow.

She relished the cold air when she stepped outside. Using the flashlight to illuminate the way, she hurried through the mud to the silent house. This was so not the situation she wanted to be in. How would she deal with things in the morning?

ZACK HEARD CAITLIN LEAVE. He remained standing in the darkness, calling himself every name in the book. What had possessed him to kiss her? Granted, it had been a long time since he'd felt any interest in women, but that didn't make it a smart move to kiss this one. If he was ready to start dating again, there were plenty of women in town who had flirted with him. Any one of them would be better for him.

But when she'd bumped into him, he'd given in to instinct. The fragrance she wore drove him crazy. It reminded him of some sweet flower, pretty and innocent. Too far removed from his life.

But for a moment the kiss had driven out all other thoughts. She'd been sweet and feminine. He could have lost himself in her kiss. Desire had swelled hot and fast. And where would that have taken them if she hadn't fled?

He wouldn't go there.

Zack turned and bumped into a chair. Swearing, he made his way to the counter. There were candles and matches in the drawer the flashlight had been in. He didn't like the dark. Finding a candle, he lit it and made his way back to the community room. He wouldn't get any more sleep tonight. Maybe he could read until dawn.

He wished for a moment that Caitlin had stayed.

ZACK WAS IN A BAD MOOD by the time 6:00 a.m. arrived. He'd already fixed some breakfast and had two cups of coffee. Hay had been tossed into the corral for the horses and he was ready to work. If Caitlin Jackson wanted him to teach her and Brandon about cowboying, he'd start now.

He walked over to the house, his annoyance building. There was no reason to be mad at anyone but himself, but he felt as if he could take on the world. If she made any mention of last night, he'd quit then and there.

After knocking on the back door, he waited a moment. To his surprise, Brandon opened the door, dressed and holding a piece of toast in one hand.

"Caitlin up?" Zack asked.

"Yes." She came to stand beside her brother. "We're almost finished breakfast. Are we late?" she asked, studying him warily.

"There are a thousand things needing doing. Normally in summer we get an early start." Some of his anger faded as she stared at him. At least there wasn't going to be some big scene after one kiss.

Hell, maybe she hadn't even liked it. Zack frowned. The thought did nothing to improve his mood.

"I'll remember that tomorrow. What time should we be ready, five?" There was an edge to her tone.

"Six is fine. I'll be in the barn." Without another word, he turned and left.

TEN MINUTES LATER both Caitlin and Brandon showed up.

Zack nodded toward Brandon. "Have him saddle up two horses. You and I need to check on the hay. He can clean out the stalls while we're gone. They aren't too bad since the horses have been in the corral most of the time."

"I can saddle my own horse, if you show me how," she said.

"Fine. Catch Bonny Boy and I'll show you where

the saddles are." If he'd been in a better mood, Zack might have enjoyed watching a novice catch and saddle the horse.

Maybe a few days of hard work would scare her back to California, leaving him in peace.

More than thirty minutes passed before they were ready to leave. Brandon cheerfully attacked cleaning the stalls as they rode out into the crisp, clear morning. The only traces of last night's storm were the puddles everywhere and the cool early morning air.

The mountains looked so sharp one could almost reach out to touch them.

Pulling his hat down low on his face, Zack set a fast pace to the field. He also wanted to swing by and check the main herd.

Caitlin remained silent. He glanced at her a couple of times, but she was staring straight ahead. She'd saddled the horse, though Zack had tightened the cinch a bit more. Took forever, but so what? There was plenty of work to do, but it wasn't going anywhere.

When they reached the fenced area and looked over the hay, he almost groaned. The rain had practically flattened the entire field. He didn't know if the ground would dry soon enough to harvest. The hay was just right for cutting. Left much longer, the seeds would begin to bloom and a lot of the nutrition would be lost.

Caitlin stopped beside him.

"Will we be able to cut this? It's all in the mud."

"Once the sun dries things up, I hope it bounces back. Can't cut what's lying down. It's still green enough to have some vitality. Once we cut it, we let it lie in the sun until it dries. It's more of a problem if we have a heavy rain then," he said. "Still, everything would have been easier if the storm hadn't been so strong."

"How do we cut it?" she asked.

"Clyde had a mower. It's as old as the hills, but he could always coax it into working. If I can't get it going, you'll have to call one of the other ranchers to see if they have a machine you can use."

"Won't they be cutting their own hay about now?"

"Yep."

"So chances aren't great for borrowing one any time soon."

"Don't court trouble before it shows up," he warned. "The old machine has a bit more life in it, I'm betting."

"I'm not much of a betting person. And the way my luck has run the last couple of years, I wouldn't bet on anything to go my way."

"Your luck can't be all bad. You inherited this place," Zack said.

She looked at him. "Maybe it's changing, or maybe not. You knew before Jeff told me that it could take years to sell this place. So now it's just another problem to deal with. Maybe at the end of the tunnel there's a bright light, but this tunnel could be years long."

"You've got your health and a way to make a living until then," he countered.

She glared at him. "This ranch is not my idea of a perfect solution. I've had a man run out on me and take millions of dollars that didn't belong to him, leaving me holding the bag. A client stiffed me for more money, and my father died without leaving a penny for me and hardly any for my brother. I don't have any work skills and don't much like you or this ranch. So where is the blasted silver lining?"

Zack stared at her. She was as angry as he had been earlier. The comments intrigued him. What was she talking about?

"Start with the man who ran out," Zack said. "Who was he?"

She pulled her horse around and walked along the fence. "None of that is any business of yours," she said as she slowly rode away, studying the hay.

He stared after her for a long moment. "Truer words were never spoken, but that doesn't satisfy my curiosity," he mumbled, turning his own horse and riding after her. Maybe there was more to this woman than he'd initially thought.

"So that's all we have to do, mow it down?" she asked, glaring at the field.

"What?"

"You said we have a mower."

"After the hay is cut, then we rake it into windrows, let it dry on the ground until it's just right, then bale it up and store it."

"How do we know when it's just right?"

"Rub a few stalks in your hands, know what you're looking for, and you can tell."

She was as green as he'd been a couple years back. The only difference? She wasn't staying.

CHAPTER FIVE

CAITLIN KICKED HER HORSE into going faster when she heard Zack approaching. She felt the weight of the world on her shoulders with this ranch. But until it was sold, she had to keep things going for Brandon's sake. Zack thought she was lucky because she'd inherited Clyde's ranch. And she was, no denying that. Lots of people would love to receive a bequest like this. She just hadn't thought it would create so many problems.

Yet, as she felt the wind in her face and smelled the clean scent of grass, she felt freer than she had in a long time. She remembered riding with her mother and uncle, and sometimes just her mother. Those memories were some of the happiest of her life.

"I want to check the herd," Zack said, riding up alongside her. "If you want to come, fine, if not, I'll see you back at the barn. We'll check if the machinery fires up when I get back."

"I'll go with you." She would learn to run this ranch or die trying.

By the time they headed back toward the homestead, Caitlin's head was swimming with facts and figures. Zack had not displayed one iota of personal interest in her. He had been totally businesslike. If she hadn't been there last night, she'd never have known he'd kissed her so fervently.

But he had, and she could almost feel his hard body pressed against hers again. Without any effort she could remember how she'd responded, the wild feelings that he had sparked. She refused to look at him unless absolutely necessary lest he guess how much that kiss had impacted her.

There would be no more. She would be forever grateful the power had not come on until sometime before dawn. At least she'd got back to the house in the dark and had gone to bed—no one to see, no one to know.

She knew she wouldn't remember everything Zack had told her this morning, and if she had to ask again, well, so be it. She wondered if she could get some kind of book on ranching from the library when she went to town next Thursday.

When they reached the barn, Brandon was eager to take care of the horses. Hank danced around, but stayed away from the hooves.

"We should have taken him this morning, but I wanted Brandon to work him. Time your brother learned to ride. Guess I'll get him on a horse this afternoon," Zack said.

"Fine." Caitlin was not going to argue about it, though she planned to be nearby to make sure Brandon didn't get hurt. But if she and her brother were to pull their own weight on the ranch, they needed to ride.

"We'll start at one. You need to be here to interpret." Zack walked away.

Caitlin stared after him. "Bossy."

Brandon came over to her and she told him what Zack had said about learning to ride. Brandon could hardly wait.

Promptly at one they arrived at the barn. Zack was already saddling his horse.

"You and Brandon get your mounts and saddle up," he said.

"Me? I know how to ride," Caitlin objected.

"So you can show Brandon how. With both of us working, he'll learn that much faster. Plus you can use the practice. We'll get Bonny Boy to shy and you can practice staying on."

She rolled her eyes and went to get the horse. She was stiff from the morning ride and her muscles were still recovering from the one two days ago. She'd like nothing more than to soak in a hot tub again, but who knew what scathing remarks that would engender.

Brandon needed no help in getting up on his horse. Caitlin led hers near the fence and used the bottom rail for a step. She wished she had longer legs.

Zack hadn't said a word, but mounted with no effort and led the trio outside.

"Shouldn't we be in the corral?" she asked, seeing him heading to the open field behind the house. The old trees near the pond offered little shade.

"Why? The horses aren't going anywhere. This is home to them. Besides, it'll be cleaner if either of you fall."

She wanted to ask about his falling, but knew he probably never did. She was proud of her accomplishments over the past few days. It had been years since she'd ridden and she'd done well. Of course a lot of credit was due to the horse. Did he really shy so readily?

Zack had them practice mounting and dismounting. It was easier for Brandon with his longer legs. Caitlin persevered, however, and even when her legs were shaking with fatigue, she mastered mounting from the ground.

Then it was walking, with Zack issuing corrections like a drill sergeant. She gritted her teeth and refrained from yelling back when he barked out some order at her.

"He's helping, he's helping," was her mantra. But more than once she wanted to ride the horse back to the barn and quit.

Brandon, on the other hand, seemed to love every moment. He couldn't hear the yelled orders, so when Zack directed them at Brandon, Caitlin had to interpret. Instead of taking offense, Brandon would grin and correct what was wrong.

When Zack called it quits, Caitlin wondered if she could manage to get off the horse and crawl to the house, up the stairs and into the tub before collapsing in exhaustion.

But Zack had other ideas. The horses had to be groomed and fed. The dog had to be fed and the tack put away after a quick cleaning.

On the way to the house finally, Caitlin decided tuna sandwiches were all she could prepare for dinner. She hoped she could stand long enough to fix them. She didn't dare sit or she'd never get up until morning.

When she finally headed up to bed, earlier than

normal, but late enough in her opinion, she swung by the office to pick up something to read. One of the books on the dusty shelf looked very old. Caitlin lifted it down. It was a journal. Opening it, she read the elegant script. It belonged to Clyde's mother. Her great-great grandmother. Caitlin opened the first page and read, *January, 1914. A new year and I'm pregnant again.* Hugging the book to her chest, she hurried upstairs. She couldn't wait to begin reading.

THE NEXT DAY WAS MORE of the same. Caitlin began to regret telling Zack they wanted to learn about ranching. She hated it. It was hard work. It was hot. It smelled. It was never ending.

And she hated the fact Zack seemed to be watching her every moment, as if waiting for her to call it quits. He reminded her of her father, never satisfied, always looking for that little bit more.

But day by day, she and Brandon improved their riding and increased their knowledge of ranch life. Caitlin was so tired each night, she could scarcely stay awake much beyond dinner. The lure of the journal called, but after a page or two of deciphering old handwriting, she was too tired to keep her eyes open.

By six each morning, she and Brandon showed up at the barn, ready to work, her brother as excited as if it were a rare treat.

Thursday morning Caitlin was elated. Today she had to go to town, meet with the lawyer and buy some more supplies. A free day from the grueling schedule they'd followed all week.

Brandon had reluctantly agreed to go with her since he needed some more jeans and socks and she wanted to make sure they fit.

Caitlin had almost forgotten how far Wolf Crossing was from the ranch. It was mid morning when they arrived. Her appointment was for eleven, so she had a short time to get Brandon started on his shopping. She parked near the lawyer's office and they began to explore the town.

I'll wait for you to finish at the lawyer's before shopping, he signed. *Be easier dealing with the salespeople.*

She nodded. The stores in Fremont, California, were used to a large deaf community, but she couldn't expect the same in Wolf Crossing.

"MISS JACKSON, DO COME IN." Harry Benson rose to greet her when his secretary ushered Caitlin into his office. "So glad you could take the time to come into town."

"This is a treat," Caitlin said. "My brother came, too, but he's waiting outside. We've been working flat out at the ranch, so today is a free day for us." She smiled and sat in the client's chair. There was a folder in front of the lawyer.

"Learning everything now that the property is yours?" he asked.

"As much as we can, anyway. My brother loves it. I think I'll reserve judgment."

Harry nodded. "Big task, more suited to those born to it, I've always thought."

"We're lucky to have Zack Carson working there. He knows what he's doing."

"Good. I know Clyde thought highly of the man. Not too many can come up to speed in such a short time. He was a natural, Clyde said."

"Short time?" she asked, surprised by the comment. "Hasn't he always been a cowboy?"

"Oh no. In fact, I remember when he first hired on with Clyde. Your uncle told me he took a chance because Zack didn't have much experience, but he wanted to do something for an ex-soldier. Clyde liked the fact the man had served in the armed forces. Your uncle always said that a man from the service knew discipline."

"Zack was a soldier?" That was the first Caitlin knew of it.

"Served in the army, as I understand it."

Caitlin could feel the antipathy rise. She'd thought he was pretty bossy. A military stint would explain that. He was like her father, giving orders, expecting people to obey.

"So my uncle hired him. Was he a rancher's son before enlisting?"

"Grew up in New York as I heard it. You might check with him about it. Came in one day from Texas, where he'd been working. Told Clyde he wanted a change of scenery. I remember Clyde saying he didn't think Zack would stay long, didn't have that much experience. But he sure took to ranching. Never thought he'd outlast Clyde. Sure do miss your uncle."

"I only knew him when I was nine," Caitlin said. She'd told Harry that when they'd first met last week.

"He kept up with you through your mother's letters, until she died. That was hard. She was so young."

"Hard on all of us," she murmured, remembering how things had changed once her mother was gone.

"We could reminisce all day, but you're here to get the rest of the estate sorted out." With that, Harry launched into an explanation of the accounts he'd changed into her name and gave her a recap of the financial situation.

"I've listed the property for sale," she said once she had all the information.

"I heard that. Clyde would have been sorry to see it go out of the family. But it's yours to do with as you see fit."

She nodded, once again feeling slightly guilty that she wasn't staying to try to step into her great-uncle's footsteps.

After taking all the documents, she said goodbye and headed outside. Brandon sat on one of the wooden benches that were set at intervals along the sidewalk of the town. Friendly place, she thought, sitting beside him.

All done? he asked.

She nodded. A feeling of regret seeped in. Looking around the town, she wondered what it would be like to live in such a place one's entire life. She and her mother had moved five or six times—whenever her father had been stationed at a new base. She'd moved out on her own after starting college. Still, the San Francisco Bay Area wasn't really her home. She'd been born in Fort Dix, New Jersey, but moved when she was eighteen months. She'd never visited the place. Would she feel some kind of tie to her birth-place?

After we get my clothes, can we have hamburgers? Brandon asked, standing impatiently. *Then head back to the ranch?*

I have a list of other things we need to buy before we start back. I want to go over some of the paperwork while we have lunch, to make sure I don't have any more questions before leaving Wolf Crossing.

Caitlin didn't share Brandon's love for all things to do with ranching. She wanted to browse stores, have a meal someone else fixed, and maybe find a book or two at the library to read at night. At her current rate, she'd be finished the journal in another couple of weeks. After that she would love to delve into a good novel.

Brandon wanted to shop at the local western store, obviously considering anything non-cowboy not worth buying. Jeans, shirts, socks and another cowboy hat satisfied him.

They discussed the advantages of another pair of boots, but Caitlin didn't think it was necessary.

As she went to pay for the clothes, Caitlin signed to Brandon that they'd eat after they put everything in the trunk so they didn't have to carry it around.

"Deaf?" the woman behind the counter asked as she took the clothes.

Caitlin nodded, defenses rising.

"Paul Simmons's daughter is deaf. I see them moving

their hands all the time. Sure would like to learn that myself." The woman began to ring up the items.

"How old is the girl?" Caitlin asked.

"About fourteen or fifteen, I think. Landsake, you'd think I'd know, she's lived here all her life. Goes off to school during the year, but she's home this summer. Call them up, bet those two would love to hang out together."

Caitlin smiled politely, but didn't agree to call. Even if they wanted to hang out, who was up to driving eighty miles each direction for a few hours of visiting?

Once she and Brandon had placed the purchases in the trunk, they headed for the local hamburger place. It was crowded with people, and the smell made Caitlin's mouth water.

They found a table near the back and soon ordered.

Look at all the cowboys, Brandon signed. *Do you suppose they think I'm one?*

Caitlin almost laughed at the question, then looked more closely. With the dark hat, checked shirt, jeans and boots, Brandon did look as if he fit in. How astonishing.

I bet they do, she replied.

As they were finishing the last of the milk shakes they'd ordered with their burgers, a tall man and young girl entered the restaurant. Two people pointed out Caitlin and the newcomers headed to their table.

I'm Paul Simmons, the man signed. *This is my daughter Susan. I heard you are new in town. Welcome.* He smiled right at Brandon.

Brandon rose and reached out to shake the man's hand. He quickly signed his name and Caitlin's, then turned to Susan, asking her if she lived in town. Caitlin felt the sting of tears. His manners were impeccable. Their mother would have been so delighted with this son she loved so much.

In no time Susan and Brandon were conversing. Paul looked on, smiling broadly. Glancing around, Caitlin noticed delighted smiles on many of the other diners.

"Would you care to join us?" she asked.

He nodded and pulled out a chair for Susan. She sat, practically not noticing anything but Brandon. She was a pretty girl, almost as tall as Caitlin with dark hair and dark eyes.

Paul went around the table and sat opposite his daughter.

"Sorry to barge in like this, but it's so rare other deaf people find their way to Wolf Crossing. During the year Susan attends a school, but she's lonely in the summer."

"News travels fast," Caitlin said.

He laughed, his eyes watching his daughter. Caitlin could see the love shining through. "It does. Wolf Crossing's a small town. Neighbors look out for each other. Bettie from the store called my wife. Then one of the men here called me. Gotta get right over, they said. Here's a friend for Susan."

Caitlin relaxed. She wasn't used to neighbors watching out for each other, but she liked it. And she could tell the two teenagers were pleased to find each other.

The break for lunch extended a lot longer than

Caitlin had anticipated. Paul was interested in learning about her inheritance. He said he knew of the place and of Clyde Martin, but they had never been friends.

She told him a little about their visit, making it sound like an adventure. As she spoke, she realized it was a great adventure. She'd been looking at it as a problem, but it was a tremendous opportunity.

And her brother was loving every moment. She'd longed to spend time with him the last few summers, but other obligations had always interfered. Now it was just the two of them against the world.

As the diner gradually emptied, Caitlin glanced at her watch, surprised to find it was almost three o'clock. They'd been talking with the Simmonses for two hours.

"I've got to go," she said. "I have lots of shopping to do still and need to get back. It's not fair to leave everything to Zack."

"We've kept you. I can't say I'm sorry, however. This has been so nice. Next time you're in town, call us. My wife would love to meet you and Brandon. Maybe you can come to dinner or something."

"Love to," she said without making a firm commitment. Who knew when they'd next be in town?

He took a card from his wallet and jotted a phone number on the back before handing it to Caitlin. "Home and office numbers. And Susan's e-mail address. Maybe Brandon can instant-messenger her."

Caitlin took the card and saw that Paul was in the insurance business. "Now that he's met her, he'll probably want the computer whenever he's not on a horse. He loves riding, but there are limits." She tucked the card into her pocket.

"Susan likes to ride as well."

"Then she should come visit us one day. Zack's great with horses and could watch them." She could just imagine Zack's reaction to her volunteering him. She almost smiled at the mental image.

During the ride home Caitlin thought about what she'd learned from Harry Benson. She'd thought Zack had been a cowboy from way back when. His tour of duty in the military explained the way he ordered them about when training them to ride. She hadn't liked taking orders from her father, and she sure didn't like it with Zack.

Yet she had to admit that she was a better rider after only a week of his instructions. And Brandon was amazing. Of course, he couldn't hear Zack's scathing tone, and when she translated, she didn't tell him how bossy Zack could be. Brandon had taken to riding like a duck to water. He'd probably be on the horse all day long if there weren't other chores to do. Zack had taken him out to the range a couple of times, working Hank and getting Brandon used to longer rides. Her brother loved every moment.

Didn't Zack miss New York? She missed San Francisco, and had been gone only a couple of weeks. She glanced around at the rolling land. The road and fencing were the only signs that humans had passed this way. No tall buildings, no theater, shops, coffeehouses, restaurants—all the things she loved. Just empty land stretching as far as the eye could see. And clouds building over the Rockies again. She wasn't used to rain in the summer.

Caitlin wished she'd gotten a chance to speak to Jeff Bradshaw when she stopped in at the real-estate office. The girl at the first desk had said there was no interest in the ranch. Caitlin knew Jeff would call if someone wanted to see the place, but would he let her know if there was even an expression of interest? She'd have to check again and find out.

I'm going to the barn, Brandon signed when she stopped at the house.

Not until you help me unload, she signed right back.

Brandon could work fast when he had something he wanted to do, and in very little time, groceries had been put away and the other supplies they'd bought carried to their bedrooms. He waved and headed out to see the horses. Caitlin figured he'd sleep with them if she'd let him.

He wasn't going to return to California easily, she thought, disturbed by the idea.

By the time Caitlin reached the barn, Brandon had saddled Tumbleweed.

Where's Zack? she asked. There was no sign of him.

Brandon shrugged. He double-checked the cinch, then unsnapped the ties and swung into the saddle as easily as if he'd been doing it for years.

I'm going to ride out to see if I can find him, he signed.

Wait.

But he was already riding out of the barn. Caitlin

glared after him. He knew she wouldn't want him going out alone.

As quickly as she could, she saddled Bonny Boy and followed. The ranch was huge, but the cattle were in one area so she figured that was where Zack would be. And Brandon.

She tried to enjoy the ride, but she was concerned about her brother. He didn't have that much experience. What if something happened to him? Teenagers thought they knew everything, and Brandon was a city kid, not some ranch-savvy teen.

Reaching a knoll, she pulled the horse to a stop and looked around. She thought she saw him ahead of her, a bit to the right, near the rocks that thrust up from the earth. They looked as if a giant had stuck them into the ground for some bizarre game. Had Zack gone that way? Maybe some cattle had wandered in the area and he wanted them out before they got hurt.

She urged Bonny Boy forward. The breeze had picked up. Dark clouds were building in the west. She didn't see any lightning, but she sure didn't want to be out in this open space if a thunderstorm blew up. Caitlin continued riding. She could hardly get lost. If she came to a fence, she'd just follow it until she found a better landmark. And as long as she could see the rocks, she had an idea of where she was in relation to the house.

As she passed the rocks, a gust of wind blew a small whirlwind of dust. Bonny shied. Thanks to Zack's training, she kept her seat, though the movement startled her.

"Easy, boy," she said, patting his neck. She reached

up to pull her hat down lower and kept a wary eye out as they continued.

Finally she spotted both Zack and Brandon some distance ahead. She pulled in her horse, debating whether to join them. Brandon liked the freedom he had. He'd commented last night how different things were on the ranch.

They were for her as well, but she wasn't sure she liked the differences. The plus side was that no one knew about her past.

Yet she felt like a fish out of water. She could throw a dinner party for thirty with sixty minutes' notice, arrange a night at the opera for a party of sixteen, and knew the best deals for food for a buffet in the Bay Area. Here she hardly knew what to buy, the stores were so different from the state-of-the-art supermarkets she was used to.

She sat and looked around. When her ancestors had first arrived, there had been no stores eighty miles away. There had been only the land and the burning desire they'd had to make something of it. They'd brought stock, raised their own food, and made do with what they'd had. She was spoiled with all the modern conveniences. She never would have made a pioneer. The thought of selling the ranch for a lot of money was tantalizing. Yet once sold, it would be forever lost to the family.

Should she consider only selling a portion and keeping the rest for Brandon?

Surely once he was back at school, he'd forget about becoming a cowboy. He'd have memories and stories to tell his friends, but his destiny lay elsewhere.

Caitlin turned Bonny Boy back toward the homestead. Zack would watch out for Brandon. She needed to check in with Jeff. Maybe he'd have other ideas for making a quick sale.

As she drew near the rocky outcropping, Caitlin thought she heard a calf bawling. Bonny Boy looked toward the rocks as if he, too, heard the cry.

"Do you suppose some calf is caught?" she asked the horse. Without much thought, she turned to head toward the sound. The wind blew in gusts, and the dark clouds seemed closer than before. She would take a quick look and then head for home. She did not want to be caught in the rain.

Slowly the horse picked his way through the rough ground, ears pricked forward. Caitlin strained to see the animal, the plaintive cries sounding fainter than before. She rose up in her stirrups, scanning the area. A dozen head of cattle could be hidden behind the rocks. There was no way to spot one without riding through the entire rocky formation. When another gust of wind rattled some dead limbs from a scrub, Bonny Boy shied, snorting and half rearing, enough to throw Caitlin off balance. She tried to hold on, but was too far over on one side. Putting out her hand to stop her fall, she crashed onto the rocky ground, her head bouncing on smooth stone. Everything went black.

ZACK KEPT AN EYE on the clouds building in the west. They were in for more rain. It had been a wet spring and it looked as if thundershowers would be the norm for the next few weeks. He could handle them—if they came with enough notice. The cattle ignored the weather, contentedly grazing on the lush green grass. Hank trotted around the perimeter of the herd, attentive, watching. Suddenly he paused and looked toward Zack.

No, behind him. Zack glanced back. Brandon was riding directly toward the herd. When had they returned? Zack had left a list of chores for the Jacksons to do. Instead, Brandon was riding as if a posse was after him. If he rode through the herd, he'd scatter them all over the place, just when Hank was working to tighten the perimeter.

As if the boy read his mind, he pulled rein and slowed his horse to a walk. A few moments later he pulled up beside Zack.

"What doing?" he asked.

Zack sighed in frustration. He wished he and the kid could communicate better. He pointed to Hank, who had resumed his patrol.

"Training?" Brandon asked.

Zack nodded. He watched the dog, wondering why he didn't mind Brandon's company as much as he'd thought he would. When he'd first mustered out of the army, he'd sworn not to get close to anyone. To keep the vow, he kept to himself. He did his job, spent his off hours riding, learning some new skill or reading. Not playing cards like a lot of cowboys did, or going into town to hit the bars.

Not getting close to anyone was his protective mechanism. Friends could be killed. Family members died. Nothing lasted. The only way to escape the pain was to keep to himself.

The last thing he wanted was involvement with the Jacksons. They were as green as grass and only in Wyoming for a short visit. Yet this kid was as enthusiastic as he and Billy had been when they'd joined up. How long before something happened to Brandon to knock some of that cockeyed optimism to hell?

Zack had to give the boy some credit; he learned fast. And he remained steadfast in his enthusiasm, no matter how hard or unpleasant the task he'd been given.

Zack looked back toward the homestead. Where was Caitlin? He was surprised she hadn't ridden out with her brother. But the horizon showed nothing. He checked the western sky. Those clouds looked even closer. And the breeze was definitely stronger than before.

"Let's head back," he said. Dumb move, the kid couldn't hear him.

He waved his hand, and when Brandon looked at him, he jerked a thumb in the direction of home.

Brandon nodded, then gave a hand signal. Hank came bounding over and sat beside the teen's horse.

Zack knew they'd been practicing. He was glad to see the dog respond. Maybe he and Brandon would make a team. Tonight he'd go over some of the duties of a cattle dog and make sure Brandon could tell when each activity was needed.

They slowly rode away from the herd. Zack mentally ran over some of the tasks they could do if it rained the next day. There would be no cutting hay any time soon. If the bad weather continued for too many more days, the crop wouldn't be worth much.

Everything was more or less on hold pending the sale of the ranch, only the critical tasks being handled. He was as anxious as Caitlin for the place to be sold. Then he'd either hire on with the new owners or move on.

Habit kept him swinging wide around the rocky formation. He knew there were no snipers, but old lessons died hard.

Suddenly Hank gave a bark and stopped, facing the rocks. The hairs on the back of Zack's neck rose. He stopped and looked at the imposing boulders. No rifle barrels. No scent of cordite. No camouflaged soldiers lying in wait. Nevertheless, he could feel the tension build.

"What is it, boy?" he asked the dog.

Brandon had stopped and was looking at the dog and then the outcropping.

"Whatzit?" he asked.

Zack shook his head. He urged his horse forward, calling to Hank.

The dog trotted beside Zack for a few steps, then turned back to the rocks and barked.

"Dammit, I don't want to go over there," Zack said, calling the dog again.

But this time Hank didn't return. He took a few more steps in the direction of the rocks, barking again.

Brandon started his horse after the dog. Once Hank saw he was being followed, he took off toward the rocks at a run. Zack sighed, pulled his mount around and followed the other two. He had been in the jumble of stones before. He didn't like it, but it wouldn't hurt him. He just hoped the fool dog knew what he was doing.

As he reached the edge of the rocks, Zack thought he heard the bleating of a calf. Was one injured or stuck? The dog had good instincts.

He followed Brandon and in only a moment was startled to see Bonny Boy standing docilely by a large rock. Crumpled near him on the ground was Caitlin. Brandon had seen her first, when Hank had run to sit beside the body, nudging her with his nose.

Brandon flew off his horse and ran to his sister, Zack right behind him.

There was blood all over her face. For a moment he wondered if she'd been shot. When he turned her over would he find half her head blown away? He couldn't move for a second—scenes of other women lying on the ground overrode the present. He could hear guns in the distance. Or was it the rumble of thunder? He could see the innocent girls and old ladies, eyes wide, staring into eternity.

He swallowed hard and stepped around Brandon to Caitlin's other side. Her brother was shaking her. Zack reached out and pulled his hands away.

"We need to assess the damage first," he said, moving his hands knowingly along her legs, up to her torso, then her arms. He checked for any neck injury. Lastly he looked at her face. The blood was seeping from a scrape near her hairline. Head wounds bled freely, which was good. Minimized dirt in the wound. He brushed back her hair. There was a knot on the left side of her head the size of a small egg. Other than that and the scrape, he could find no further injury. He shrugged out of his shirt and pulled his cotton under-shirt over his head. Folding it to make a pad, he placed it against her forehead. Brandon reached out to hold it in place. Before putting his shirt back on, Zack tore off a strip to hold the pad in place. He could ride to the ranch for help and get paramedics from town, but that would take hours. The rain wouldn't wait that long.

Or he could risk injuries he hadn't discovered, pick her up and carry her back to the ranch.

If it had been a battle situation, he wouldn't have hesitated a second. But this was not a war zone. Which would be the better choice for Caitlin? How long had she been unconscious? Was she injured anywhere besides her head? And what was she doing in the rocks anyway?

The bleating sounded again. She must have heard it and gone to investigate. With the wind gusting the way it was, he could picture Bonny Boy shying and dumping her.

The moments ticked by. Zack glanced at the darkening sky. He was running out of time. A decision needed to be made.

CHAPTER SIX

ZACK MOTIONED BRANDON to stay where he was. Giving Hank a seek command, Zack followed the dog as he trotted away from the humans. In only a few moments he located the calf, caught in a small crevasse, unharmed, but unable to get out on his own.

Zack went back to the horses. He mounted his and used a rope to pull the calf free. It took off running toward the direction of the herd. He wondered momentarily where the mama cow was, but the situation with Caitlin was more critical.

He'd have to take the chance and get her home as fast as they could safely move. He couldn't leave her. Even if Brandon stayed with her, it would be dark before help arrived. And the rain would beat the dark.

With minimum fuss, he pantomimed to Brandon that he was to lead Bonny Boy home, while Zack would carry Caitlin. Lifting her, he was gratified to hear her groan softly. Maybe she was coming to. Standing on a nearby flat rock made it easier to mount his horse with a woman in his arms.

Slowly they headed for the house. Hank trotted alongside Brandon's horse, and Bonny Boy walked on the other side, not giving Brandon any trouble.

Blood had dried on Caitlin's face. Her eyes remained closed. Zack tried to keep her still, but it wasn't easy with the motion of the horse. He hoped she had no neck or back injuries; riding like this wouldn't help them at all.

He was grateful when the house came into view.

"I take horses," Brandon said, dismounting and reaching for Zack's reins. "Help her."

Zack nodded and headed to the house, hoping they hadn't locked the door. Who knew how city folks behaved?

If the situation hadn't been so serious he would have smiled. Until a few years ago he'd been as city as they came. He'd changed, so why did he persist in believing Brandon couldn't also learn ranching?

The door was unlocked. He entered and walked up the stairs. Caitlin wasn't a big woman, but a heavier weight than he was used to carrying this way. He glanced into a room, recognizing the signs of a woman's presence. Laying her on the bed, he stood up. Next step, assess the damage and fix her up. If she needed a doctor, he'd have to drive her to town. That was the nearest clinic.

Before Zack finished washing her face, Caitlin woke. She blinked at him, then glanced around the room with puzzlement.

"How do you feel?" he asked, holding the wash-cloth away from her face.

"I have the world's worst headache. What am I doing here?"

"Apparently you fell from Bonny Boy. Brandon and I found you and brought you home. I was worried you had a neck injury or something worse."

She closed her eyes just as Brandon thundered up the stairs and then burst into her room.

She looked at him and smiled wanly. "Don't tell him," she said to Zack, "but I feel awful."

Brandon signed something and she nodded slowly, moving her hands.

"Ow," she said, clutching her right wrist with her left hand. "I did more than bump my head." She looked down at the swollen wrist. "Man, that hurts!"

"Let me see." Zack tossed the wash rag into the bowl of warm water and took her wrist gently in his large hands.

"Ouch," she said, pulling back slightly.

"Sprained most likely. But it needs X-rays to be sure," he said, moving her wrist slowly to assess the damage. "I'll take you into the clinic in town."

"Great, I just got back from town."

"It's the closest clinic. You'll need to be checked by a doctor."

"There are dozens of hospitals near where I lived in San Francisco and I never needed one. Now this. I can't believe it."

"Life on the range," he said. He rose and headed for the door.

"Where are you going?" she asked.

"To feed the horses and get them settled for the night. It'll be late by the time we get back."

CAITLIN'S HEAD WAS POUNDING. She brushed against her forehead and her fingertips came away bloody. She moaned softly. Brandon sat on the edge of the bed where Zack had been and squeezed out the washcloth. He held it to her. She took it and gingerly pressed it against the burning near her hairline. It stung. Obviously a cut or scrape. She wished she had a mirror.

Holding the cloth against her skin, she assessed the damage. Her head was killing her. Her wrist throbbed in time with her pulse. She wiggled her fingers. They moved, didn't that mean no broken bones? How could she tell? Her entire arm hurt.

Want some aspirin? Brandon signed.

She smiled, and then felt tears welling. She was in a world of hurt. Aspirin wouldn't help much. Yet he looked so worried.

Fine, she returned. She closed her eyes when he left and tried to breathe through the pain. She felt awful. Riding was definitely not what it was cracked up to be. Before she let herself start feeling sorry for herself, she gritted her teeth and sat up. The pounding grew worse. But she needed to see her face.

She rose on wobbly legs and went to the bathroom. At least she didn't appear to be injured anywhere else, though there was a tenderness on one hip. The scrape was oozing blood, but it wasn't pouring down her face. There was blood on her shirt, however. She clutched the sink with her good hand and gazed at her battered appearance. That bossy cowboy was so right: she needed a doctor.

By the time Zack returned, Caitlin had washed her face, changed her shirt and, with Brandon's help, walked back down the stairs. Unable to go any farther, she had sunk on the third step and was waiting. The rain had started and she could hear it pounding on the porch roof. Out the window it looked darker than early evening. She wished the storm had held off. How much worse would it be driving in this than on a clear night?

Zack entered without knocking, surprised to see her sitting on the steps.

"Don't you dare say anything. I'm able to walk—it's my head and arm that hurt. I hate the idea of the long drive in, but I do need a doctor." She stood up on shaky legs.

He nodded. "Where's Brandon?"

"He'll be here in a minute. He needs to come as well. I don't want him home alone."

Zack nodded. "I have the truck right out front. It's raining, but it'll only be a few steps. Are you able to walk or should I carry you?"

A crack of thunder sounded. Zack glanced around, looked back at her.

She took a deep breath. "Save your heroic efforts. I got this far, I can make it to the truck."

He gave a half smile and nodded. "Good. You aren't light as a feather."

She started to say something then shut her mouth. He'd carried her up to bed, and from what Brandon had told her, Zack had carried her on horseback all the way back to the house.

Before long the three of them sat in the warmth of Zack's truck as he drove through the storm. Caitlin leaned back, trying to get semi-comfortable. Her head pounded and every jarring bounce of the truck made it even worse. She gritted her teeth, willing the aspirin to take effect.

Brandon sat still, glancing at her from time to time, but not talking. She was grateful. Her entire right arm now ached. The thought of using it to sign was almost too much.

The trip passed as a blur—the monotonous swipes of the windshield wipers, the water pounding on the roof of the truck, the black asphalt an endless ribbon stretching forever. Caitlin wished time would fast forward and she could get some relief from the pain.

When Zack pulled into the parking lot of the clinic, she almost burst into tears. She felt awful.

"I think I'm going to be sick," she said when he stopped the truck.

"Concussion, most likely," he said, quickly opening the door and scooping her up. "Hold it until you're out of the truck," he said, pulling her across the seat and into the rain.

Brandon scrambled out of the other door and ran around the truck, walking right beside Zack as they entered the double doors to the medical facility.

Their arrival startled the staff, which was quick to respond. In only seconds Caitlin was lying on a gurney, a young nurse taking vitals. An older woman began to remove the makeshift bandage to check the head wound while Zack succinctly gave his report.

Glancing at him, the younger nurse asked, "Are you a doctor?"

He shook his head.

"You sound like one," she said, returning to her task.

"You two can wait out in the lobby," the older nurse said. "We'll take it from here."

Zack nodded and touched Brandon on the shoulder, jerking his thumb in the direction of the lobby. The two walked out.

"Caitlin will be okay," Brandon said.

Zack nodded, sinking down on one of the plastic chairs that lined one wall. He leaned back and closed his eyes, letting himself relax for the first time in hours. The last thing he wanted was a situation like today's. He was trying to escape memories of people covered in blood.

Caitlin hadn't been shot, but the blood, the damage to skin and tissue still caused him to remember. Her pretty skin was now scraped and marred. She'd most likely carry a scar near her hairline for the rest of her life. She should have stayed in San Francisco and sold the ranch long-distance.

Or he should have moved on as soon as she and the kid had arrived.

Zack heard the doctor speaking. He opened his eyes. The rain was still coming down. The evening had given way to night. It would be late by the time they got home. Would the staff here want to keep her overnight? That'd mean another trip out in the morning.

And he'd be stuck with Brandon.

That wouldn't be so bad, he thought. The kid was learning fast. And loved every aspect of ranching so far.

Maybe ranchers were born, not made. Did Brandon have anything to say about the sale of the property? Zack had seen him tell Caitlin he wished they could stay forever.

Caitlin was constant in her refusal. She wanted the money.

Zack couldn't blame her. Money went a long way in making the life you wanted.

But it couldn't bring back Billy. Or his mother. Or even budge his grandmother from her flat in Brooklyn. He'd tried often enough over the past four years.

"Zack Carson?" The doctor came to the doorway and called his name.

Zack rose.

"Wait here," he told Brandon. But the teen couldn't hear and jumped up to follow Zack. The doctor looked surprised but only shrugged.

They went to the cubicle where Caitlin sat in a wheelchair, a bandage on her forehead, her arm in a sling.

"I suggested Ms. Jackson remain here overnight, but she refuses. We need to take her to X-ray. I'm thinking she might have broken a bone or two in her wrist. If so, she'll need a cast. That'll take a while. I suspect a mild concussion as well, but she won't even consider staying. Can you can keep an eye on her at home?"

Zack nodded. He knew a lot about head wounds. More than he wanted to.

"She said no one has eaten, so if you two want to go get a bite and come back in about an hour, that'll work," the doctor said.

Zack squatted down until he was at Caitlin's level. She smiled wanly. "I'll be okay. Take Brandon and go get something to eat. They offered me something, but I'm not hungry."

"Still feeling nauseous?" he asked.

She nodded, then winced.

"We'll go eat and be right back. Maybe you should stay the night."

"No. That would mean you two would have to make the trip back tomorrow to get me. I don't want that. Once they know the extent of the concussion, maybe I'll get some pain meds."

Zack reached out and squeezed her hand resting on the chair arm. "Hang in there. They'll get you fixed up. We'll be back in a little while."

"Get a tablet or something so you can write to Brandon. He needs to know what's going on and I'm hurting too much to sign."

"Will do," he said, rising.

Brandon watched as the nurse pushed Caitlin's chair out of the cubicle and down the hall.

Zack had never felt so helpless as when Brandon looked at him in expectation. He would have to find some paper somewhere and let the kid know what was going on. He put his hand on his shoulder and held it there for a moment. "Want to eat?" he asked.

Brandon frowned, not understanding. He looked down the hall.

Zack dropped his arm, stepped out of the cubicle and headed for the front counter.

"Do you have some paper I can use? Brandon is deaf and I don't know sign language."

"Sure," the receptionist said, reaching into a drawer and pulling out a small stack of paper. She handed him a pen.

Quickly he wrote an update on Caitlin and said that he and Brandon should head out to eat dinner.

"We will come back for her?" Brandon asked.

Zack nodded. Setting his hat firmly on his head, he led the way outside to the truck. It was still raining.

By the time the two returned, Zack was feeling better about things. He and Brandon had managed to have dinner together, Zack writing out his part of the conversation, Brandon speaking his. The waitress at the café recognized Brandon and greeted him with more warmth than she did Zack.

Could be her attitude resulted from his early days in town, when she'd flirted with him. Lack of response had a way of cooling a woman's interest. Not that Zack cared. He just wanted to get back to the ranch and be alone.

CAITLIN WAS READY TO LEAVE. How long did dinner take? She'd thought Zack would take Brandon to some fast-food place, eat and get right back. She looked at the clock in the reception area. It was after eleven. They'd be so late getting home. Her arm was in a cast, her head wrapped. Two stitches had drawn the skin together. She had to return in a week to have the doctor look her over. Unless she got sick from the concussion tonight.

But it was mild, they thought. She would hate to have a severe one. Was she getting used to the throbbing? She knew she was sleepy. She couldn't wait to get in her bed, cover up and try to forget she wasn't the proficient rider she needed to be to work a ranch. What had she been thinking?

When Zack and Brandon strode in a few moments

later, Caitlin couldn't help but smile. Her brother was a copycat version of Zack, hat pulled low, faded jeans and cowboy boots sounding on the linoleum floor. Both headed directly toward her.

"Ready to leave?" Zack asked.

Brandon signed. *Are you okay? Did you break your arm?*

She replied awkwardly using her left hand. It was the two-handed signs she'd have trouble with for a while. *Two bones broken in my wrist. Also badly sprained, mild concussion.*

"I'm so ready to leave," she said to Zack. "I just want to get to bed and not move for a few days." She didn't care if he thought she was slacking. She was starting to ache in places she hadn't expected. The doctor had told her she'd be stiff tomorrow and to take things easy.

"Here we go, she's all set," the younger nurse said, handing Zack an envelope. "All the instructions are here, along with the medication. We filled the prescription since the drugstore is closed now and you don't want to have to come to town again tomorrow. She needs lots of fluids, some nourishing food, as much as she wants to eat, but enough to keep her strength up if she's not hungry."

"I'm right here," Caitlin murmured.

The nurse smiled brightly. "I know, but it's best if someone else knows the drill as well." She looked as if she wouldn't mind Zack knowing lots more about herself, as well. "You can call me any time if you have any questions," she said. "My number is on the bag."

Caitlin looked away. Just because a man was gorgeous, why did women have to act so gaga over him? It had been the same way with Timothy. She'd thought it funny at the time, but later realized he'd used his looks and charm to convince people to invest. She'd married a con man and had to live with the knowledge she had been as charmed as everyone else. It was a mistake she would never make again.

"Can we go?" She sounded spoiled and peevish, but she didn't care. Thinking about Timothy always made her angry.

By the time they were ten miles outside of town, Caitlin couldn't keep her eyes open any longer. She leaned back against the seat and closed her eyes. Before long, she drifted to sleep.

ZACK KNEW THE SECOND Caitlin fell asleep. She was wedged between him and Brandon, and bonelessly swayed to rest against his shoulder. If she'd realized it, she'd have been upright in a heartbeat.

He waited a moment, then moved slightly to make it more comfortable for her.

It had been a long time since he'd been responsible for someone else. Surprisingly, he didn't mind as much as he'd thought he would. He didn't plan to make a habit of it, but for this once, it was okay. It was lucky he'd known what to do and was able to get her to proper medical care.

If she'd been on the ranch alone or just with Brandon, who knew what kind of trouble would have resulted?

He had to give some credit to the dog as well. Hank had found her. If not, she would have lain outside for a long time in the pouring rain. That didn't bear thinking about.

The rain blotted out the stars. The road was straight and empty. He made good time. When they reached the house, she woke up enough to walk up the stairs with help from Zack and Brandon. They left her alone to change into her nightgown. Zack went back and parked the truck, checked on the horses and made sure the dog was okay, then returned to the house. He had put the envelope down on one of the tables. Now he opened it and read the instructions. As he'd suspected, someone needed to waken her every few hours to make sure she was all right.

It would have to be him. He knew the signs to look for if things got worse. Brandon could sleep the night away and take over in the morning. By then, any problems would have shown up.

He fixed himself some coffee. The kitchen hadn't changed much from when Clyde had been there. The two of them had usually eaten together in the winter months, more often than not in the bunkhouse kitchen. But when the old man had grown sick, Zack had prepared the meals here at the house. He hadn't cooked in this kitchen since Clyde had gone to hospital.

Zack remembered last summer, when the seasonal cowboys had all sat around the table in the bunkhouse shooting the breeze. Clyde had always had tall tales to tell. A man could learn a lot from listening to others' experiences.

When Zack went upstairs, Brandon had already gone to bed. The door to Caitlin's room was ajar and a light shone.

He knocked then pushed the door open more. "Want anything?" he asked.

She lay in bed, looking pale against the white pillowcases. Her cast rested outside the covers. Her eyes had been closed, but she opened them to look at him.

"No. Just for the pain to go away."

"According to the instructions, once we know you're going to be okay, you get to start on stronger meds. Probably by morning. Can you sleep?"

"I hope so. I'm so tired." She closed her eyes.

Zack looked around. There was no place to sit. He put the coffee on the dresser and went to search for a chair. He found a rocking chair in Clyde's former room. It was larger than he expected, and worn with years of use. He carried it into Caitlin's room.

She opened her eyes at the sound. "What are you doing?"

"Sitting with you to make sure you don't get worse with that concussion."

"I'll be fine."

"Good, makes my job easier."

"You don't need to stay."

He settled himself in the rocker, took the coffee and sipped it. It was too hot, but Zack didn't care. Beat looking at Caitlin. He had the strangest impulse to hold her, comfort her.

He was more tired than he'd thought. It was going to be a long night.

"Really, I'll be fine," she said.

"Ever had a concussion before?" he asked.

"No. Have you?"

"Yeah, but that's not what makes me an expert."

"What does, then?" she asked.

He hesitated a moment. "I was a medic in the army. I have lots of experience with head injuries. More than I ever wanted."

"That's another thing. I thought you were a cowboy from way back. According to the lawyer, you've only worked on ranches for a few years."

"So?"

"I was surprised you know so much in a relatively short time. Maybe I can learn, too. I checked with the real-estate office when I was in town earlier. No nibbles on the ranch. And then I went by the feed store and saw the posted job opening. The local newspaper also carried an ad, and a copy was tacked up on the bulletin board as well. No interest there, either."

"There might be some summer help available with school out. Lots of ranches have kids who attend college and like to work other places to broaden their knowledge," he said. "Your uncle had a college kid last summer."

"He did?"

"He liked younger people. He was always having barbecues for the hands with lots of loud music." Zack had resisted attending. He'd go sometimes, but more often liked riding out on the range where it was quiet and he could be alone.

And remember.

"So where did you grow up if not on a ranch?"

"Thought you were going to sleep," Zack said. He had no interest in talking about himself.

"Turn off the light if you would, please," she said. "I'm tired but the nap in the truck took some of the edge off. Now I mostly feel my head throbbing."

He switched off the light. It was dark with no stars giving even faint illumination. For a moment he just rocked slowly, listening to the rain. The wild fury of the storm had passed. Now it was a gentle shower that would gradually ease and then stop.

"So where?" she asked.

"Brooklyn," he said. He wasn't one to talk much about the past, but what could a few facts hurt? He knew what it was like to be injured and unable to rest. He'd sat with wounded soldiers to help them through the night until they could be evacuated.

"You're kidding!"

He almost smiled at the disbelief in her voice.

"Went to inner-city camps as a kid. First time I saw a horse I was scared to death. First time I rode one I thought I was king of the world. Stood me in good stead when I left the army and tried my hand at cowboying."

"Ranching is a far cry from Brooklyn," she said.

"This life suits me. I would never go back to the city." He didn't return even to see his grandmother. The thought made him break out into a sweat.

She was silent for a while. He wasn't sure if she'd gone to sleep until she spoke again a few minutes later.

"You do the cowboy bit well. Don't tell Brandon

you came to it late. I want him to go to college and get
a good job somewhere—maybe in computers."

"Is that what you want to do, work with computers?"

"No."

"Once the ranch sells you won't have to worry about
work ever again," he said.

"Is that what you think? Once I have some money,
I'll just fritter away my days?"

"What else?"

Again she was silent. Zack drank his coffee, shifted a
bit on the hard rocker and gazed toward the window. The
rain was tapering off. It would stop long before morning.

"Why didn't you become a doctor when you got out
of the army?" she asked. "Seems a logical step for a
medic with a GI bill."

He started. Had he dozed off? Some watch he was
keeping if the patient stayed awake and he slept.

"Decided I didn't like it," he said shortly. She was
right on. He'd chosen the medical field thinking it
would give him a leg up into college and med school
when he got out of the service. But the realities of war
had changed his mind. The roiling helplessness swept
through him again. He'd gone to save lives and been
unable to save the most important one.

"I'm glad you had the knowledge to know what to
do today," she said softly.

"Basic first aid."

"Still, you kept your head, knew what to do and did
it. I'm grateful. I hate to think what would have
happened if it had been just Brandon and me."

"Then don't," he said gruffly.

"Tell me something about my uncle. I wish I'd known him after I grew up."

"Why didn't you come to visit?"

"I never thought about it, truthfully. My mother was the letter writer in our family. After she died, I didn't write. I'm not sure I had an address. Then it was off to college, and marriage. I wish I had. I never knew he planned to leave the ranch to me. If I had visited a time or two, he would have seen I wasn't suited to ranching."

"You and Brandon were his only family."

"Yet he only left the ranch to me. I don't know why. Do you think because Brandon is underage?"

"He never mentioned Brandon. Did he know about him?" Try as he might, Zack couldn't remember Clyde saying anything about Caitlin's brother.

"I would have thought so. He was six when Mom died. She wrote Uncle Clyde from time to time. Why wouldn't she—" She stopped abruptly.

"What?"

"Nothing. It hurts my head to talk. You talk, tell me about Clyde."

Zack settled back and started with his first month on the job, how taciturn Clyde had been. And how that had suited Zack to a T. He spoke for several minutes about the kind of man Clyde had been—old-fashioned and set in his ways, but strong, good to friends and neighbors, with a dry sense of humor that Zack had appreciated.

After a while, he didn't want to talk anymore. He

missed Clyde more than he'd expected. Now he wanted Caitlin to go to sleep and leave him in peace.

As if reading his mind, Caitlin remained silent when he stopped. A few moments later he heard her shift in bed and sigh softly. She was asleep.

The night passed slowly. He dozed, catching himself from time to time and rising to walk around. Every couple of hours he woke her and asked some easy questions to make sure she was lucid. She grumbled the last time, telling him she was fine and to leave her alone.

Which was exactly what he planned to do. Once she was well again. In fact, he'd see what he could do to hurry up finding another ranch hand so he could move on.

CAITLIN DIDN'T FEEL MUCH better the next morning when she awoke. The sun shone in through her window, bathing her in brilliant light—which did nothing to help her aching head. Turning away from the window, she saw Zack asleep in a rocking chair. She studied him, taking advantage of the opportunity to do so.

She had mixed emotions where he was concerned. She thought he was bossy, which he was. But he was so good-looking it almost made her stop thinking and start drooling, except she was immune because of Timothy. She'd seen how the nurse at the hospital had flirted with Zack last night. Caitlin was not going to get involved with another heart-stoppingly gorgeous man.

When the ranch sold, she'd be a wealthy woman.

Even splitting the money with Brandon would leave her set for life, with proper investments. If she ever did get involved with another man, it would be a partnership—equals going in the same direction. Not some bossy cowboy who obviously had issues she wasn't capable of dealing with.

For a moment her heart was touched, however. Zack looked uncomfortable in the rocker. He'd sacrificed a night's sleep to watch over her. He hadn't had to do that. He could have arranged for Brandon to check her.

Slowly Caitlin slid out of bed. She stood and frowned as her head started pounding again. She was good enough this morning to take those pain meds the doctor had prescribed. But first a shower.

She quietly gathered her things and headed for the bathroom. A few minutes later she eyed the shower, wondering how she could manage to get clean and not get the cast wet.

A sharp knock sounded on the door.

"Caitlin, are you okay?" Zack asked.

She opened the door and looked at him, suddenly conscious of the intimacy of the situation. She was wearing only her nightgown. Not that she could be considered alluring—she'd glanced in the mirror and almost groaned at the picture. Bandage covering half her head. Eyes bruised and bloodshot. Speckles of blood still scattered on her skin. Zack would have to be a lot harder up than he was to have any interest in her.

But seeing him with a night's worth of beard was tantalizing. She must be getting better. She wanted to reach out and touch his cheek, run her fingertips over that raspy beard and feel his mouth against hers again.

"I'm fine. I wanted a shower." At this rate it had better be a cold one.

He ran his hand through his hair and blinked again, as if still waking up.

"I'll get you a plastic bag to cover your hand and cast. Can you manage?"

"I think so. When will I be able to wash my hair?"

"We can check the stitches later today. If the cuts and scrapes have scabbed over, we'll manage something. Wait here."

Like where else would she go, she wondered. He returned with duct tape and a white garbage bag. He covered the cast, taping the plastic bag against her upper arm. She felt clumsy, but it would be worth it to have a shower.

"I'll wait right out here. If you need anything, yell," he said.

What she needed was privacy. She glanced at the door several times as she got ready for the shower. It was awkward maneuvering with the cast, but at last she was beneath the hot water. It felt heavenly. She wished she could soak her hair, but knew she wasn't to get those bandages wet.

At last she finished. Then she faced the daunting task of getting dressed. Pulling on jeans one handed proved almost more than she could manage—until she considered the alternative of having Zack help. That was motivation enough to get the job done.

"Ready to eat?" he asked when she opened the door.

He was leaning against the wall in the same position she'd last seen him. Had he really stayed there the entire time?

Brandon came out into the hall and looked at the two of them. He asked Caitlin if she was feeling better and she nodded. Once she had those pills and some food, she'd feel halfway to normal.

Zack cooked pancakes and sausages for breakfast, and as soon as they were finished told Brandon they had to get to work.

To Caitlin, he merely said, "You rest up. If you feel sick, call me on the cell phone." He wrote the number down on a notepad on the counter. "Your uncle held on to that old mower but had all his men carry these for communications. It doesn't get reception everywhere, but I'll try to stay in range."

By the time Zack left, Brandon had already dumped his dishes in the sink and headed out, too.

Caitlin cleaned up the breakfast dishes one handed. The pain medication helped immensely. It made her tired, however, and after she finished, she went back to bed to lie down.

She wasn't sure how long she slept, but the sound of Hank barking and an engine in the driveway woke her. Going to the window, she saw a truck she didn't recognize. Brandon came from the barn and motioned Hank to sit. The dog obeyed but kept his eyes focused on the arriving visitors.

When Paul Simmons stepped down, Caitlin stared. She didn't remember inviting them to visit. They'd made vague comments, but nothing firm. Quickly she went to the dresser to run a brush through her hair. No time to do more. The bandage stood out like a beacon. Her arm ached. She was a mess, not up for company. But she could hardly turn them away when they'd driven so far.

CHAPTER SEVEN

BY THE TIME SHE GOT downstairs and out on the porch, Brandon and Susan were busy conversing while Paul looked on. He spotted Caitlin and headed toward her.

"What happened to you?" he asked when he took in the cast and bandage.

"I fell off a horse," she said, hating to admit it.

"When? I'm sorry, I didn't know. This is a bad time to visit. Susan and Brandon have been e-mailing back and forth already and I had today free so I brought her out. We won't stay, of course."

"No, don't leave. I just won't be much company. But it's too long a drive to turn right around." Caitlin saw Zack come from the barn. The two teenagers turned and headed for him, their hands flying. "This will be great for Brandon. Come in and I'll make some coffee."

"I'll make it. My wife tells me I'm handy in the kitchen. And you look as if you're about to fall down. Peggy wanted to come but Friday is a busy day at her office, she couldn't get the time off. We still want you and Brandon to come to our place for dinner one evening. Looks like it'll be a while, though."

"I'm so much better than I look," she said, happy the pain meds worked. The nap had refreshed her. She could handle a little company as long as he didn't expect much from her. "Once I'm used to the cast, I hope I'll be able to drive."

The rest of the morning passed pleasantly enough with Paul and Caitlin sitting on the porch. He told her about Wolf Crossing, how his family had lived there almost as long as hers had owned the ranch. They compared notes on raising a deaf child in a hearing world. And he told her about his wife's love for making pies and cakes and entering them in the county fair.

"She says she has to practice, but if I eat all she cooks, I'll be too fat to get in the truck to drive her to the county fair."

Caitlin laughed. "I look forward to meeting her."

"Once you are feeling better, we'll plan on a barbecue. Peg's a great cook as well as champion pie maker."

"We'd like that."

"Our place doesn't hold the same appeal as yours, though," he said.

"What does that mean?"

"Horses. Susan is crazy about riding. We've given her lessons, but don't have a place to keep a horse. All she talked about was how Brandon said she could go riding with him and Zack. As long as they're with him, I'm okay. I'm not that good a rider myself."

"Me, either. But Zack knows what he's doing."

"That's one of the reasons I brought her today. That and the chance for her to be with your brother. He made a great impression on both of us."

"He'll love showing off the place." Caitlin didn't voice her fears that he was becoming too attached to the ranch. Time enough for her to deal with that when they left in the fall.

Caitlin, with Paul's help, had lunch prepared when Brandon and Susan came into the house several hours later. Both were pink from the sun. They looked happy.

Susan loves to ride, Brandon signed. *Can she come another day and help out? She learns fast.*

Fine with me, but we need to check with her parents and with Zack, Caitlin returned.

And we need better communications, Paul signed. *Today wasn't a good day to come, Caitlin is hurt.*

I'm so sorry you were hurt, Susan said. *I rode Bonny Boy and Brandon told me about your fall. There is no wind today so it's hard to imagine.*

Caitlin nodded gingerly. *Just be careful riding him. Ready to eat?*

When lunch was finished, Susan and Paul left. Brandon helped clean up the kitchen and then hung around while Caitlin put away all the food and milk.

Any more chores? she asked.

Some. Zack wasn't too happy to have Susan come with us. But she rode fine. I know he's in charge, but you own this ranch. Tell him it's okay for me to have friends over.

Caitlin wasn't sure of Zack's role in this. He wasn't a child-care worker and had probably felt like a baby-sitter or camp counselor today, watching the two novice riders. She'd have to clear things with him in the future. It wasn't fair to him otherwise.

But what if he refused? Then what would she do?

I'll talk to him, was all she promised.

The opportunity didn't come until dinnertime. Caitlin heated soup and toasted some bread with cheese. It was as much as she felt like doing. When Brandon came to eat, Zack was with him.

"I would have cooked dinner," Zack said, looking at the pan on the stove and the toast squares still beneath the broiler.

"I managed this much, no more."

"Sit, we'll take it from here."

Caitlin wasn't going to argue. She was tired and frustrated. She could hardly do anything with her wrist incapacitated. She hadn't realized how much she used it in a day.

"Zack, thanks for watching out for Susan Simmons. I didn't know they were coming or I would have said something."

Zack had put Brandon to work getting the plates and silverware.

"Yeah, Brandon explained he'd e-mailed her after meeting her and asked her out here. Forgot about it when you fell. No harm done."

That surprised her. She'd been prepared for a reminder about that not being part of his job.

He caught her eye. "Expecting a different reaction?"

She nodded. Somehow this man never met her expectations.

"It's Brandon's home. If he wants friends over, so be it."

"He wants her to come again and help out."

"You can use the help," Zack said, setting a bowl of soup in front of her. Brandon followed with the toast.

"How much help would she be?" Caitlin asked.

"She could learn—same as you and the kid. Have Brandon teach her." Zack sat down and began to eat.

Caitlin stared at him, unable to believe what she'd heard. He'd been so against their staying, not wanting anything to do with either of them. What had changed?

He looked up and caught her staring. She dropped her gaze to the soup. It was steaming slightly. Taking her spoon, she began to eat.

"I checked with Jason at the feed store," Zack said. "There were one or two inquiries about your ad."

"Really? I thought he was going to let me know if someone showed interest in the job."

"If it gets that far. I told him to push a bit. One of the men is going to call you, I think. Sooner he's on, the sooner I can leave."

Caitlin didn't want Zack to go. But he'd been up-front all along about wanting to leave. She had hoped working with her and Brandon would have shown him the advantage of staying.

"I wish you would remain until the place sells. The new owners may even want to keep you on," she said. "It's not as if you have another job. What will you do until you find one?"

"Might head back to Texas. The winters are better there."

ZACK CONTINUED TO EAT. Two weeks ago he'd been alone on the ranch missing Clyde and wondering if he should be looking for work. Now he was caring for a woman, teaching teenagers about cattle and still working until he fell asleep from exhaustion. The nightmares hadn't been so prevalent lately. He must be doing something right.

It wasn't that Brandon was much trouble. The kid was so eager to learn everything, Zack could hardly keep up. And he had to admit, Caitlin had pulled her share without complaint.

He'd even handled the crisis of her fall, though the flashbacks and memories of other people injured in a rocky place kept crowding his mind. Still, he felt a quiet sense of accomplishment that he'd been able to do what was needed and get her to help. Clyde had said the memories would fade enough to enable him to live a normal life. Zack hadn't believed it at the time, but maybe. At least for this crisis he had reacted appropriately. Maybe he would again if put to the test.

THE PHONE RANG.

Caitlin rose and went to answer it.

"Miz Jackson, this is Pete Trannor. I saw your ad at the feed store for a cowhand. I'm hunting work."

"Could you come out in the morning? I could interview you then," she said. Turning slightly, she saw both Brandon and Zack watching her. If this cowboy worked out, would Zack really leave? She didn't like that idea at all.

"Sure thing. Be there around nine."

"Do you know how to find the ranch?" she asked.

"Got directions from Jason. Be seeing you."

After hanging up the phone, Caitlin went back to the table. Signing and talking, she informed the two men of the conversation.

"Do you know the man?" she asked Zack.

He shook his head. "Never heard of him. But if he's new to the area, I wouldn't have." He scraped back his chair and rose, carrying his soup bowl to the stove and replenishing it.

"Do you think you'd want to interview him, too?" she asked as he resumed his seat.

"Why?"

"You're much more knowledgeable about the workings of a ranch than I am. You'd know the questions to ask and be able to judge if he's really any good or not."

Zack took another spoonful of soup. "Guess I could."

"He'll be here around nine."

He nodded. "Give me time to look at that mower in the morning. As soon as the ground dries enough, I want to get that hay cut. The forecast is for dry weather the next few days. Sooner we get it cut, sooner we can get it dried, baled and stored."

"Maybe this Pete Trannor will work out and be able to help with the cutting, too."

"Clyde usually hired extra summer help by this time. Haying's hard work. Once we get it cut, then baled, we have to bring it in from the field to store in the back part of the barn to keep it dry. Sell the extra bales."

Caitlin took a moment to sign the conversation to

Brandon. He nodded, his eyes alight with the thought of new challenges. She was happy at the possibility of another influx of cash. The clinic charges hadn't been cheap.

Zack left right after he and Brandon cleaned up. Brandon went into the office to use the computer and Caitlin walked out onto the porch. She still didn't feel good, but it was too early to go to bed.

Hesitating only a moment, she continued walking toward the bunkhouse. She wanted company after being alone all day.

She heard the clang of metal on metal coming from behind the barn. Changing direction, Caitlin followed the sound and soon found Zack deep in the works of an engine that had to be the mower. The large machine showed patches of rust and scraped paint. It was old, but if it worked, so what?

Zack swore and hit the metal again. Caitlin stifled a giggle. This was not a happy man.

"Trouble?" she asked.

He lifted his head to look at her. "You might say. This engine is a piece of junk."

She came closer and peered inside. The only thing she recognized was the grimy dirt clinging to every part.

"No wonder it won't work, it's filthy."

"Gets that way. Can you manage to climb up into the driver's seat and try to start it?"

She eyed the mower dubiously. Stepping gingerly, wishing she had use of her right arm, she soon sat on the hard driver's seat. She was up high. Glancing around, she wondered what it would be like to drive the mower.

"See the button to the right of the draft shaft?" Zack called. "Push it and hold for about three seconds."

She complied. There was a grinding sound.

"Okay, stop!"

Caitlin waited a moment, but when he didn't speak again, she got down and went to stand beside him. Several tools were spread on the ground, and a couple balanced on the edge of the engine. She peered over his arm. He seemed to know what he was doing, but she was totally baffled. How could any one person learn enough to run a ranch? There wasn't a service station nearby, so Zack had to do the work. She couldn't even imagine a tow truck large enough for this piece of equipment.

"What happens if we don't cut the hay?" she asked.

"It'll go to waste. We need hay in the winter to keep the cattle alive."

"Maybe I'll sell the herd, then we wouldn't need it."

"You could sell the hay if you sell the herd," he said, still working on some connection in the engine. Finally he gave another shove to the tool he was using and the bolt moved. In only moments he held the part in his hand.

"Needs cleaning. Let's hope it works when that's done." He turned toward the barn.

Caitlin walked beside him.

"How do you know how to do that?" she asked.

"Learned engines as a kid—on cars, but this is similar."

Going to one of the storage shelves in the barn, he pulled out a glass jug marked Kerosene. Pouring some in an old coffee can, he dropped the part in. "By morning we'll know if that'll work or not," he said.

She watched as he wiped his hands on a grimy towel.

"What made you decide to become a cowboy?" she asked.

"I wanted a change from the city. After I got out of the army, I headed west. No particular destination in mind. Then saw an ad for a cowboy at a ranch in Texas. I applied. The man who hired me thought I'd last a day. I stayed nine months, then found something better. Learned all I could at every job."

"When did you come here?"

"Over two years ago. I was still green. Clyde taught me a lot."

He placed the towel back on the hook and looked at his hands. They weren't much cleaner.

"I need to go wash up."

"I want to hear more," Caitlin said.

"About what?" he asked, turning to look at her.

"About you, learning to be a cowboy, the army. My father was career army. I have to say I'm not so gung ho as he was."

Zack nodded. "I'm not gung ho army."

"Why did you join?"

"To get out."

"Out of what?"

"Brooklyn. The neighborhood I grew up in wasn't the best in the world. We saw the army as our ticket to better things."

"We?"

His expression closed. "A friend."

"Where is he now?"

"Dead." Zack turned and walked away.

Caitlin stared after him. She hadn't known. Apparently they'd been close. Had it been a woman? Most likely a buddy.

She didn't think she imagined the bleak look in his eyes. Sighing softly, she wandered back to the corral and leaned against the fence, gazing at the horses. One ambled over and put its head on the top rail. She rubbed its nose gently.

"I was looking for company," she said to the horse. "Were you as well?" After a moment, curiosity satisfied, the big animal moved away.

"Guess not. Or at least not with me." She watched them a bit longer. The sun had set; twilight grew darker.

She turned and went back to the house.

Getting some water in preparation to go up to her room, Caitlin was still by the sink when Brandon came in. He immediately saw her and began signing.

Wayne's summer plans changed. His mother is pregnant and sick all the time, so they are not going to Hawaii. Can he come here? He wants to come. I told him how much I'm doing and he wants to help out. Zack said we'd have lots of work with cutting hay. Wayne could help. If Susan comes out, that's one more who can help. And you won't be able to, so they could do your work.

Caitlin's initial reaction was to refuse. But she asked

him about Wayne before turning him down. And the more Brandon told her about his friend, the more she began to wonder if he could come to visit—and actually be of help. She was going to be almost useless for the next few weeks while her wrist healed. If they hired Pete Trannor, that would ease some of the burden for Zack. But having teenagers around—would that help or hinder?

Yet kids had been working ranches over the summer for years. It would be good for the boys and they could help move the bales of hay. Zack had said that Clyde had hired college kids. Wayne and Brandon were only a few years short of college.

Let me think about it. And talk to his parents. They might be horrified at the thought of their son going to Wyoming and working on a ranch. She wasn't sure she'd let Brandon go off with people she didn't know.

Would Zack see the visitor as more work, or a help? Or would he even be around if Pete hired on?

CAITLIN WAS ON the front porch the next morning when the ubiquitous pickup came down the drive. She watched as an older man climbed out and glanced around. In a moment he headed for the house. Zack appeared in the large opening to the barn, then also headed for the house.

Caitlin rose to greet Pete when he reached the porch. Once introductions were made, she invited both men into the office of the house. She knew nothing about hiring a ranch employee, but the man looked the role, the hat well worn, yet clean. Boots, of course, but polished to a shine. The jeans and shirt looked new.

"I asked Zack to help me," she explained when they all sat in the office. "I know very little about ranching. And I'll be up-front with you. This place is for sale. I can't guarantee any length of employment."

Pete nodded, looked square at Zack.

"Been working for a lot of years. Know most of what needs to be known."

Zack nodded. "Tell us where you worked."

The interview had started. It was almost two hours later by the time Zack glanced at Caitlin and gave a small nod.

She smiled. She liked everything Pete had said, but left the final decision to Zack. She was glad he approved.

"Want to look around the place?" Caitlin asked. She'd love for him to join them, but was cautious enough to be sure to call and verify all references before making an offer.

"I would," the man said.

Zack rose. "I'll show him around."

"Thank you. It was nice meeting you, Pete. I'll call these references while you two look over the ranch."

As she had hoped, all references were sincere and glowing. One rancher said he kept hoping Pete would come back. When asked why he left to begin with, the man said he had only a limited number of year-round positions and those were filled with family men who had been with him for years. But if one of them left, he'd want Pete to take over.

She then called Harry to let him know what she was doing and to get a range of salary to offer.

"If Zack will stay, I'm making him manager," she said.

"Hmmm," the lawyer said. "He knows the place. Doesn't have that much experience, however."

"He knows more than I do."

"Your choice, Caitlin. There's money enough for the time being."

"We're cutting hay soon. If there's extra, maybe we can sell some of that."

"Every bit helps. Come fall you'll have a lot of cattle to sell, that's your primary source of income."

Caitlin went outside to offer Pete the job. She didn't see the men. When she entered the barn, it was empty. Checking the corral, she noted all the horses were gone. Obviously when he said he'd show Pete the ranch, Zack had meant the entire spread. Brandon must have gone with them.

It was late afternoon when the three men returned. Brandon was becoming very proficient at riding, Caitlin thought, spying them from the window.

She wrapped up the work she was doing on the computer and checked on the roast she had in the oven before going outside. Waiting on the porch, she watched as they all came from the barn. It was like seeing three generations of a family. Pete was older, yet carried himself like a fit younger man. Zack was in his prime, walking with that special cowboy gait. Brandon was the youngest, but he was already beginning to resemble the others in the way he wore his hat and carried himself.

"Nice place you have here," Pete said when they drew closer.

"Thank you." Caitlin smiled at him. "Want to work with us?"

"Be pleased to."

"Then you're hired. When can you start?" she told him how much she could afford and that the job came with room and board.

"Need to pick up my horse where I've been boarding it. Could get back late tomorrow."

"He can bring his own mount, which helps you out," Zack said. "You'll need to buy another one or two before fall if you're still working cattle."

She looked at him. "I'd like to speak to you about that if you have a moment."

He nodded warily.

"Pete, can you stay for dinner? It'll be ready at six and it's a long drive back to Wolf Crossing."

"Be pleased to. Maybe Brandon can show me the bunkhouse while you and Zack talk."

A moment later Caitlin faced Zack. He didn't look precisely welcoming, but she was determined to get this over with.

"What?" he growled.

"I want to offer you the position of manager of the Triple M Ranch," she said formally.

ZACK STARED AT HER. He was leaving. He'd told her that enough times. What part of it didn't she get?

"Before you say no, think about it. From all the people I talked to today, Pete is a good worker. Brandon is learning fast, you said so yourself. We'll be here through the summer, unless the ranch sells first. You don't have to leave. I know you don't like being around me, and I'll try to stay out of your way. But the ranch really needs you."

"I don't dislike you," he said. What was he doing, discussing the situation? He needed to get packing, figure out where to head to next. Get away from Caitlin, her brother and the memories of Clyde. He wasn't considering her offer.

"Please, just think about it for a few days. You'd be totally in charge. You could make changes if you think they are warranted. Hire as much help as the money allows. I'm coming to the realization this place isn't going to sell fast. I need someone I trust to run it properly until it does."

"It's your ranch, you run it," he said.

"I don't know enough."

"Neither do I."

He watched her indecision.

"You know more than I do. And I think you're the type to search for answers to what you don't know. Anyway, that's my offer."

"I'm not your man, Caitlin. Until four years ago, the only time I'd been on a horse was when I was sent to inner-city camp programs."

"I expect my uncle was teaching you every single day."

Zack lifted his gaze to the land. The rolling hills touched his soul. Taking a breath, he could smell the grasses and the cattle. He was a city transplant who had thrust down deep roots. No matter where he worked, he'd want it to be outside. He liked this part of the country. And she was right. He had picked up a great deal of knowledge from Clyde. They'd never ridden out without the older man regaling him with stories that imparted wisdom and knowledge.

But to even consider staying would mean he was getting involved. How much more would the place come to mean to him if he actually managed it?

He didn't want ties.

He started to refuse. But something kept him quiet. It wouldn't hurt to think about it for at least a day.

"I'll let you know," he said.

CAITLIN WENT INSIDE to check on her roast. The meal was ready to dish up when the men filed into the kitchen.

"Need some help?" Pete asked, as he watched Caitlin try to serve the plates one handed.

"I guess I do," she said.

Everyone served himself and Brandon heaped food on a plate for his sister.

I can't eat all that, she signed.

You have to get your strength back, that's what Zack says.

She glanced at the man already standing by the table. Was Brandon going to start spouting words of wisdom from Zack? He couldn't choose a much better man, she mused, thinking of their father and Timothy. Brandon hadn't had stellar role models in his life.

Once seated, Caitlin asked Pete about the last place he'd worked. He proved to be entertaining as he described the other men on the ranch, and some of the cantankerous horses.

Caitlin signed as Pete talked.

After a few moments, Zack reached over and caught her uninjured hand. "Eat, before your food gets cold. We won't talk until you can translate again."

"Oh, sorry, I didn't even think," Pete said.

Caitlin could hardly think herself. She wanted to wrap her fingers around Zack's hand and hold on. His touch was warm. His hand, rough from the work he did, offered security. He squeezed hers slightly and let go.

Brandon watched intently. *What did he say?* he signed.

To stop talking and eat.

He grinned and nodded.

The next few moments were silent as they continued the meal.

Caitlin was touched that Zack had thought enough about both her and her brother to stop talking so she had a chance to eat and Brandon wouldn't be left out. Their own father had never done that.

How hard had life been for her brother? she wondered. She'd left home only a couple of years after her mother had died. She'd never really considered how difficult it must have been for Brandon.

Pete left right after dinner with a promise to return the next day as soon as he got his horse.

Zack headed off—probably to work on the numerous chores that never seemed to end, Caitlin thought. Brandon did the dishes. She was left with little to do.

She wanted to wash her hair. The scrape on her head was starting to itch, a good sign of healing, but it was driving her crazy. There had to be something she could do to get relief.

She went up to the bathroom, eyeing the old-fashioned tub. No handheld shower device. So unless she wanted to risk soaking everything, she couldn't really use it. And how would she wash her hair one-handed?

She'd ask Brandon. Maybe they could use the kitchen sink.

When she returned to the kitchen, it was empty. She checked in the office, but he wasn't there. Had he gone out to the barn? Feeling grumpy, Caitlin headed outside.

Brandon had already saddled his horse. Zack was nearby.

"Where is he going?" she asked. "I don't want him riding off alone. He could fall or something like I did."

"Relax, he's just going in the field behind the barn with Hank to practice. We brought a couple of steers down with us this afternoon. He'll be fine. We'll be right here."

Caitlin watched as Brandon checked the cinch, then swung up on the horse's back as if he'd been doing it for years. She smiled. He really was having the best summer of his life, she thought.

"You want something?" Zack asked.

"I was going to ask him to help me wash my hair. I don't want to get the stitches wet, but I really want clean hair."

The minutes ticked by. Then Zack said, "I could help."

She looked at him, feeling an unexpected warmth

wash through her. For an instant she pictured this large cowboy with his hands in her hair, lathering it up, running his fingers through when rinsing to get the shampoo out. She'd never had anyone wash her hair but the salon workers. Could he really do that?

But she was desperate. "You're on," she said. Zack could wash her hair right now. She'd have to wait another few hours for Brandon.

Caitlin led the way inside, going upstairs to get towels and her shampoo. When she returned to the kitchen, Zack had run the water and gotten it warm. He'd also taken off his hat. He must have run his fingers through his hair a few times because it stuck up in a couple of places. She squelched the urge to smooth it down. They were here to wash her hair, not his.

"I can't get the stitches wet," she said.

"I know."

Nervous, she set the shampoo on the counter and looked at him. "So how do we do this?"

"I thought you could kneel on one of the chairs and hold a towel against the stitches to block any water. Then I'll use the sprayer device in the sink to wet your hair, lather it up and rinse."

"Sounds like a plan."

He brought over one of the chairs and soon Caitlin was leaning over the sink, a towel pressed against her forehead to keep it dry.

The warm water felt heavenly. In only seconds she could feel his fingers massaging her scalp as he worked in the shampoo. She closed her eyes, resting her arms on the edge of the sink, and gave herself up to the blissful experience.

Surprisingly, Zack seemed to know exactly what to do to keep the water from her scrape. He carefully rinsed her hair, and lathered again. This time he seemed to thread the strands through his fingers as if giving each one special attention. She could become addicted to having her hair washed this way, she thought.

The warm water of the final rinse had hardly stopped when he wrapped her head in one of the towels she'd brought.

"Face still dry?" he asked.

She nodded, sitting up on her knees and then wrapping the towel more securely.

"Thank you. With only having the use of one hand, I couldn't do it myself."

"I'll brush it out for you," he offered. "Where's your brush?"

She hadn't thought that far ahead.

"Upstairs, I'll go get it."

"I'll wait on the porch. The warm air will dry it fast."

A few minutes later, Caitlin sat on a bench while Zack stood behind her, gently working through her tangled hair with a light touch.

"You've had experience," she murmured. It was pleasant on the porch. She couldn't see Brandon but heard the thumping of the horse as it ran, stopped and resumed. Hank barked once or twice. What she could see were the vibrant colors in the sky as sunset approached. The mountains in the distance were mere smudges.

"I used to brush my grandmother's hair," he explained. "She has arthritis and it's difficult for her."

"Where does she live?"

"Back in Bed-Stuy, our neighborhood in Brooklyn."

Caitlin couldn't picture this tough cowboy as the kind of boy to patiently brush his grandmother's hair.

"She must have enjoyed that. Who brushes her hair now?"

The silence was momentary, but Caitlin suspected she'd hit a sore spot.

"No one, I guess. She must do it herself."

"Maybe your family rallies around," she said.

"There's only the two of us left."

"Are you close?"

"I haven't seen her in more than six years," Zack said.

The steady movements of the brush were hypnotic. Caitlin closed her eyes, enjoying the sensuous moment. And fascinated by the bits Zack had revealed of his life.

"Invite her to visit," she suggested.

"I have. She thinks anything beyond New Jersey is the wilds of the old west. She won't come."

"And you don't want to go there to visit her?" she asked.

"Not yet," he said. "Maybe one day." He reached over her shoulder and handed her the brush. "Your hair is tangle free."

Caitlin knew he was going to leave. She didn't want him to.

"Stay a little longer," she said. "I could get us some iced tea or coffee."

"I don't need anything," he said. He pulled one of the chairs from against the wall and sat in it. Rocking back on the rear legs, he adjusted his hat low on his face and gazed out over the ranch.

"It's so peaceful here," she said, almost afraid to say anything that would break the shared intimacy.

He nodded.

"Did you and your friend Billy want to be cowboys?"

He slanted her a glance. For a moment Caitlin didn't think he would answer her.

"Never came up. We thought we'd do our stint in the army, go to college and become millionaires."

"Only he didn't make it out," she said softly. "Were you there when he died?"

Zack nodded. She could see the muscles in his cheeks tighten.

"That must have been devastating."

Zack rose. "All war is hell. Billy was just one in a long list of dead. He never had a chance." He crossed the porch and stepped off.

Caitlin surged to her feet. "Don't go. I won't ask any more questions if you don't want."

He turned slightly. "I don't talk about the war."

"Maybe you should—get it out…lose some of its horror."

"That'll never happen. War is all about horror."

"My father used to talk to my mother about the places he'd been. She was a good listener. I remember him saying once that he didn't know what he'd do if he had to keep everything bottled up inside."

"So are you some pop psychologist?"

"No, just someone who could listen."

"I'll remember that if I ever want to talk."

"You do that. I'm going to have some ice cream. Do you want some, or would you rather walk off in a snit?"

"I'm not in a snit. I choose not to discuss the past with anyone."

"Ice cream or not?"

Zack turned and walked back until he stood right in front of her. "What kind?"

He was deliberately crowding her space. She took a step back. He took a step forward. When she bumped against the door, she couldn't retreat any farther. He was hardly a hand's width away. If he was trying to intimidate her, he was not succeeding. The feelings he was causing had nothing to do with fear.

"Chocolate, Rocky Road or Butter Pecan?"

"Rocky Road is my favorite, Butter Pecan was Clyde's. He kept a supply all summer long."

"So some of this could be months old. Does ice cream ever go bad?" She didn't dare take a deep breath, afraid she'd brush up against Zack. From the dancing lights in his eyes, he knew he was making her uncomfortable, and was amused by her reaction. Maybe she should turn the tables.

She put her good hand on his chest and pushed. The

resistance beneath her palm surprised her. He stepped
back easily enough, then caught her hand. For a
moment they stared at each other. As his head lowered,
Caitlin drew a breath, taking in the scent of the man,
feeling the warmth of his skin as he brushed his lips
over hers.

CHAPTER EIGHT

ZACK DIDN'T WANT TO LET GO. Caitlin was warm and sweet. Her mouth moved against his and long-dormant desire spiked. He tightened his embrace, imprinting the feel of her against his body, soft where he was hard. When her tongue touched his, he wanted more. He'd been too long without female companionship. But it hadn't bothered him before.

Now, with this sweet woman in his arms, it did. He wanted more than some chaste kisses. Much more.

Her brother was in the field. It was still broad daylight. But none of that mattered. He wanted more. Just a few more moments of pleasure, her arms tightly around him, her mouth driving him wild. Her scent imprinted on his soul forever.

A sound from the barn penetrated and Zack slowly ended the kiss. He didn't want Brandon coming out and seeing them. Who knew what conclusion the teenager would jump to.

He eased back, his arms still around her. Caitlin withdrew almost as carefully. When he let his arms drop, he felt empty.

She stared at him, her eyes wide with questions. He wished he had some answers.

"Probably a dumb idea," he mumbled. He needed to get away. Return to the bunkhouse and make plans to leave. With Pete starting, Caitlin wouldn't be left in the lurch. She'd be able to get another capable hand before long.

"Probably." Her hand rested on his chest, her fingers moving slightly, sparking excitement in every cell of his body. He caught her hand, brought the palm to his mouth. Kissing her, he watched the emotions flare in her eyes. She wanted him as much as he wanted her.

"I'm heading off now," he said. It was safer. Staying around Caitlin would prove too hard to resist.

For a moment he saw disappointment in her gaze. "Stay for ice cream. That's all. Brandon will be in soon. He'll want some, too."

He kissed her hand again. "Just ice cream, then."

She nodded. Pulling her hand free, she turned and scooped up her brush, which had fallen. "Want me to bring it out here?"

"That might be best." He couldn't believe how much farther he'd been willing to take things if the teenager hadn't been nearby.

He needed to back off. Caitlin was not the kind of woman to want a casual affair. And he wasn't going to get involved.

When she went inside, he turned and almost laughed. How involved did he need to become to want to go to bed with her? Pretty damned involved.

He leaned against the railing. Things were changing too fast. The reason he was here hadn't altered. He'd let Billy down. He'd fled the memories he hated.

Becoming attached to the Jacksons was as stupid as trying to hold on to Billy.

"Rocky Road," she said, coming out with two bowls of ice cream. She'd chosen Butter Pecan.

"Thanks." He sat on one of the chairs and began to eat. Glancing at Caitlin, he saw she was watching him.

"I really want you to consider the manager's job," she said.

He took another bite of ice cream.

"Told you I'd think about it."

She took a deep breath. He could still feel the imprint of her breasts against his chest. He looked away. For the first time in a long time, however, he didn't relish the thought of the privacy of his room. He wanted to stay—a little longer anyway.

What was the proper protocol? Did he apologize for kissing her? Make some comment about how fantastic it had been? Or ignore it as if nothing had happened?

It didn't make a lot of sense. His life the last four years had been solitary. He liked it that way. No ties, no complications, no risking any connections because he knew firsthand how fast a friend could die.

As soon as he was finished, he'd check on the boy and then turn in.

She ate tiny scoops of ice cream, making a sound of pure bliss as she slowly savored each spoonful.

Zack wondered if she made similar sounds when she made love.

Scowling, he looked away and concentrated on mentally listing the tasks ahead.

"I'm not getting involved with anyone," Zack said. Might as well make that perfectly clear. Even though she'd said she was going back to San Francisco, and he talked about moving on, he wanted no misunderstandings. No clinging, no crying goodbyes.

Caitlin looked at him. "A kiss isn't a lifelong commitment. Even a marriage isn't a lifelong commitment these days. I'm not too high on men right now. I learned that lesson the hard way. I'm happily single again, as the saying goes, and plan to stay that way."

That surprised him. "You don't want to get married again?"

She shook her head.

"What happened?"

"He fled the country about two steps ahead of the law and a boatload of angry clients. Seems he felt he could enjoy life better in the islands somewhere— using other people's money." She laughed. "Oh, the irony just struck. If he'd stayed honest a couple of years longer, we'd still be married. And could expect six million dollars from the sale of the ranch. Oh, how I wish I knew how to contact him to tell him!"

"You don't know where he is?"

"I do not. But even if I did, the law gets first dibs. One day we were visiting with friends, the next he was gone. Two days later the cops descended."

Zack wasn't sure what to say. "He hasn't been caught?"

"There are some places in the Caribbean where they don't honor U.S. extradition. Guess he found one of them. All I know is he left me holding the bag. It took months to get squared with the law, for them to believe I had no idea of what he'd been doing or planning. If I ever get my hands on the man, he'll rue the day he left me with his mess."

"Tough break."

"Shows me I can't trust my judgment in people. I tried going into business for myself—doing events planning. I can throw a mean party."

Zack asked, "What happened?"

She shook her head. "I didn't have any money after Timothy took off. And not a lot of experience in anything but throwing parties. I might have done all right if my second client hadn't bilked me and then bad-mouthed the services I provided."

"Bilked you how?" He was growing fascinated by her story.

"I threw this lovely poolside party for fifty at the woman's estate in Woodside. Elegant hors d'oeuvres, wonderful wine, all the trimmings. Everyone said it was a great success. When I tried to collect, however, she said it wasn't up to her standards and she refused to pay for anything. She even began spreading the word that my services were poor and not worth the time or money. Who knew if I might steal something from clients like my husband had? Just thinking about that makes me want to scream."

"But there must have been a contract or something binding that protected you," Zack said.

Caitlin shook her head slowly. "I wasn't smart enough then to have a contract. I couldn't pay all the vendors as promised. It took me most of six months to get them paid off. In the meantime, no one would extend me more credit when I couldn't pay on past orders. Pft, so goes a budding career."

"So what did you do?"

"Waited tables."

"A waitress?"

"I'm pretty good at it and the tips are fantastic. I'm not qualified to do much else, and jobs are at a premium in the Bay Area. I want to stay there because of Brandon."

"What about your parents?"

She took a deep breath. "My father died just after Timothy took off. His will had been made after my marriage and he thought I was set for life. He left almost everything to his wife."

"Not your mother."

"My mother died when I was sixteen."

Zack thought over what she'd said. "What about Brandon?"

"What about him?"

"Didn't your father leave him provided for?"

"A small stipend only—to supplement his schooling at the California School for the Deaf. It's a state-run school that costs nothing for Brandon to attend."

"Why not an equal share with his wife?"

She shrugged.

"There had to be a reason."

"I guess."

"And it is?"

"Stop pushing. It's none of your business."

"Most of what you told me wasn't my business.

You wanted to let me know. So what's the hang-up with Brandon?"

"My father wasn't Brandon's real father," she blurted out.

That did startle Zack. "Who was?"

"I don't know. I found out when my mother died. I don't think Brandon knows. He just thinks our father was a cold, unfeeling military man. Being at the school for the deaf helped, since he was away from home most of the year."

"But your father took care of him on vacations?"

"Mostly. I don't think he wanted his fellow officers knowing. That's why it's so important I sell the ranch and get some money. I'll be the only one responsible for him until he's old enough to earn his own living. And you know that won't be as easy as for some kids."

"I don't know about that. He's a good worker. Learns fast. Once he settles on something, he'll excel."

"He thinks he wants to be a cowboy," she murmured.

"And that would be a problem because why?" Zack asked.

She looked at him. "I always thought of him working with computers or something, making lots of money."

"Maybe money isn't as important to him as it is to you," Zack suggested.

She flared up at that. "Money is important to everyone. Do you know how hard it is to earn a living if you're not skilled or have some kind of special education? I want him to have choices."

"He has choices. Just because he's only sixteen doesn't mean he isn't starting to become a man. He'll have to try things to know what he wants. So far he takes to this work like he was born to it. He's always asking questions. But never the same one twice. Give him some slack, Caitlin. He could make a good rancher."

"What did you want to do when you were sixteen, become a cowboy?" she asked.

"No, at sixteen, I was car crazy. There was a man at a garage who gave me a job—taught me all about engines. I thought I'd open a service garage myself maybe, or work for him all my life."

"Now you work cattle, a far cry from cars."

"Life has a way of changing plans. I'm not saying ranching is the right thing for your brother. But I do think it is his decision, not yours."

"I guess. I just—I don't know, I thought we'd both get jobs in some city and see each other more often than we do when he's at school. I know he's ten years younger, but he's all the family I have. He'll feel differently when we sell this place. Then he'll be able to do anything he wants."

Zack didn't argue the point. If in fact Brandon wanted to be a cowboy, having several million dollars behind him wouldn't hurt.

He rose. "I'll take the bowls inside," he offered. Time enough to move on. Hearing Caitlin's past made him yearn for things that couldn't be. They were scarcely friends. Would never be more. He had too much baggage to get involved with someone. And she had different dreams than he did. A few more weeks together—if he stayed around—and they'd go their separate ways.

CAITLIN WATCHED ZACK HEAD for the barn a few minutes later. She wished he'd stayed longer. That he'd told her more about his past than the fact he'd liked cars at sixteen. Still, it was the longest conversation they'd had, so maybe it was a good sign.

"For what?" she asked herself. His kiss had been wonderful. For the first time in a long time she'd felt desired and cherished. Not that she was interested in any kind of long-term relationship. Her trust in others was shaky. She and Timothy had been married nearly six years. And he'd totally fooled her.

Zack was not interested in her in that way either. It was just chemistry or something.

Explosive, she'd say. But if he'd asked, she'd have gone anywhere with him earlier.

Feeling deflated, she stood up. She was tired, her head ached and her wrist throbbed. Time for bed.

She had enough on her plate without worrying about a cowboy she'd only met a couple of weeks before. Knowing she was being impatient didn't stop her from wanting faster action on the sale of the ranch. She was worried Brandon would totally learn to love the lifestyle he saw here and not want to return to California. Where would that leave her?

AT BREAKFAST, BRANDON ASKED again if his friend Wayne could come for a few weeks.

I'm not up to it, Caitlin said, holding up the cast.

We'd be a help—we can cook. And there's lots more to do around here with haying starting, he countered. *I bet Zack would like the extra help.*

Wayne ever done any haying?

No, but he could learn as fast as I will. And Susan said she'd come out and help. She could even stay a few days, save her parents bringing her out and back.

I'll ask Zack. He might not want teenagers around. This is your place. Just tell him.

I asked him to be manager. It could take years to sell the ranch. I need someone who knows how to run a ranch to be in charge. If he is in charge, he gets veto vote to visitors.

Brandon frowned at that, but didn't argue. *Ask today, okay?*

Caitlin didn't respond immediately. She didn't know if Zack would accept the position. Asking him to put up with a couple of other teenagers didn't seem like a good way to tip the scales in her favor. Yet, if Brandon wanted his friends here, what would it hurt? She liked Susan. She was sure she'd like Wayne.

I'll ask. Get me Wayne's parents' phone number. I'll need to discuss things with them as well.

He jumped up and ran from the room, not wasting a second.

Caitlin hoped Zack would say yes—both to staying and to having visitors.

When Caitlin went out to the barn in the early afternoon, it was deserted. Two of the horses were gone. Zack and Brandon had left her behind. Not that she felt up to riding. Bonny Boy came to the corral fence and put his head over.

She rubbed his nose. "I know you didn't mean to toss me, but I'm not up to riding again for a while. One day, I promise."

He blew on her hand and then ambled away.

When she walked into the cool barn, she saw a piece of paper near the door. Zack had written a note to Brandon, telling him of the chores that needed to be done, and then asking Brandon to bring his horse to the hay field. Zack had taken the mower out to see if it'd work.

Caitlin smiled, knowing Brandon would have followed every instruction to the letter. A couple of weeks ago he'd never been on a horse. Now he could ride, was working with a cattle dog and was helpful enough to go out to meet up with Zack. She could see a growing confidence in her brother since he'd been on the ranch.

Maybe being a cowboy wouldn't be the worst thing Brandon could do. It sure suited Zack. She wondered what he'd been like as a boy. Car crazy at one point. Weren't most teenage boys? What would he have done if he hadn't been sent to a war zone?

Hearing a truck, she went outside to see Pete arriving. She wished she'd had Zack's answer before the man arrived. She'd like to start off with Pete reporting to Zack. Oh well, for sure life didn't always go the way she wanted.

Pete quickly unloaded his own horse, put away his things and spoke briefly with Caitlin. He got general

directions from her, saddled up and rode out to find
Zack and get started.

Caitlin went to the office. The last couple of days
had given her time to figure out the programs her uncle
had used. Now if she only knew what things meant.
Was it good to have the number of head of cattle she
had, or should she decrease the herd? Or increase it?
Was she going to be able to sell some of the hay for a
quick source of income, or have to find some other way
to stretch money until the fall sales?

She called Wayne's parents and reached his
mother. Explaining who she was and why she was
calling, she was surprised at the easy compliance in
Mrs. Bronson's attitude.

"Wayne is so disappointed we're not going to
Hawaii. When his friend invited him to a working
ranch, we thought that was wonderful. He and Brandon
have been friends for several years, you know."

Caitlin murmured an appropriate response. She
didn't know Brandon's friends. First she'd been too
tied up with Timothy to visit his school often. Then too
tired from working long hours making a living.

"Would he be able to fly there? I know Brandon said
you drove out, but that would be really difficult for us,"
Wayne's mother continued.

Caitlin hadn't even thought about that. Where was
the nearest airport?

"We'd have to check, but I think he could fly into
Casper. We could pick him up there and bring him to the
ranch." Good grief, it would take a day to get to Casper
and back. And she thought Wolf Crossing was far.

"He doesn't know much about horses or cattle, but Brandon said he could learn. We've all read Brandon's e-mails, he sounds like he's having a wonderful experience. What a special summer it would be for Wayne. He needs something like that about now. I'm pregnant, and it's changing everything."

"I still need to make sure my manager is okay with the idea. He'd be the primary teacher for the boys," Caitlin cautioned. She knew both boys would be thrilled. She didn't think Zack would be, however. But somehow she had to make him see it was a good thing.

After promising to call later to confirm dates and all, Caitlin hung up.

No sooner had she replaced the phone than it rang again.

"Hello?"

"Caitlin? Charlie Johnstone here. Calling to see how Hank's doing."

"Just fine. Brandon is working with him and the two of them seem well suited. He responds to hand signals now."

"Didn't know at first the boy was deaf. He's working out well, according to Zack. A good worker. Looks a lot like your mother."

"He does. More than I do."

"She was a wonderful woman."

"I miss her a lot."

"The thing is, I have some pictures from that summer you two stayed with Clyde. Thought maybe someday you'd want to see them."

"I'd love to. Why not come to dinner here one

evening. Even though it was before Brandon was born, I'm sure he'd love to see pictures of our mother."

Caitlin had a startling thought. Brandon had been born the spring after their visit to Uncle Clyde. If Charlie had photos, he must have seen her mother often. Maybe he knew if she'd been partial to someone that summer. Maybe her mother had fallen for some cowboy. Or even Charlie himself! She swallowed. Was she actually talking to Brandon's father?

They arranged for an evening a couple of weeks later and Charlie hung up. Caitlin stared at the phone. If Charlie was Brandon's father, would he storm in and demand custody?

Maybe she should call back and cancel.

Or maybe, a small voice said, you could see what he has to say.

AS SOON AS DINNER WAS OVER that evening, Caitlin asked Zack if she could talk to him in the office. Brandon smiled, his excitement obvious. She hoped Zack would agree to working with Wayne if he came to stay for a few weeks.

Once in the office, Caitlin shut the door. Nervous, she went to sit behind the desk, then wondered if that had been the best tactic.

He stood near the window, watching her.

"I know you may not have thought fully about my offer," she began.

"I thought about it. I'll stay."

She blinked. She felt certain she'd have to argue the point, offer more money, or accept defeat.

"Oh, good. Thank you."

"I probably won't be doing things much different from your uncle Clyde," he added.

"Sounds fine to me. I'll rely on you." She cleared her throat. "There is one other little thing."

Zack said nothing. She could have used an encouraging nod or something.

"Brandon would like to invite a friend over."

"Susan?" he asked.

"Well, yes, Susan, too. She's dying to come ride some more."

"Susan, too? Who else?"

"There's this friend of Brandon's from school, Wayne Bronson. Actually, Brandon thought he could come and help out around the ranch. You'll need men to load the hay on the wagon and bring it to the barn. They'll need some training, but they're both young and strong and anxious to help."

Zack narrowed his eyes. "You're asking me to take on another deaf kid? Teach him and Brandon about ranching? Make that three if you're including Paul Simmons's daughter."

It did sound a bit daunting put like that.

"The only difference between those kids and any other kids is the way in which they communicate—visually rather than aurally. They are young, intelligent, and excited about the chance to spend the summer working on an actual ranch. Brandon has been a help, hasn't he?"

"Sure, but he learns fast. Plus this is his family's ranch. He wants it to succeed. But it's a dangerous business. What if one of those kids falls from a horse like you did, only with more severe results. Then what?"

"What if they don't? What if they do exactly as they are instructed and blossom from a summer of work in the sunshine and fresh air. They'll learn new things, like riding and cattle and…and hay!"

Zack's lips twitched. "Yeah, hay is important to learn. I can't do that, Caitlin."

"Please, Zack. I promise they won't be trouble. I'll get a release signed by their parents. You won't lead them into any deliberate danger. Everyone understands there are some inherent risks in life. Think what a wonderful summer these kids would have."

ZACK STARED AT HER. She was serious. For a moment he flashed back to the kids on the dusty road in Afghanistan. They didn't have a wonderful summer. Hell, they wouldn't have any more summers. Dead by roadside bombs. From their own people. Limbs blown off, eyes staring at nothing.

He swallowed and looked around, grounding himself in the mundane aspects of Clyde's office.

He'd tried to save the children, but too much trauma, too much blood loss had made it impossible. Now she was asking him to be with kids, take them out where danger lurked. Risk their lives when they were safe and whole. He couldn't do it.

"Please," she said softly.

He shook his head. "I can't. They wouldn't be safe."

"Yes, they will be. If you don't want to, can I ask

Pete? Please let these kids do this. It will be good for them, really."

He didn't want this. If they came, he'd leave.

Wait. He turned and gazed out the window. He'd just told her he'd stay as manager. Now he was ready to run. Clyde had told him the pain would ease. It hadn't. Zack could still see those women and children. Still hear the wails of the mourners. He could feel the warm sticky blood on his hands, as he tried so hard to save just one.

"Zack?"

He looked at Caitlin. "All right, if Pete says he'll work with them, then fine. Keep them away from me." With that he left. He needed to get out into the sunshine, see that he was back in Wyoming, not some dusty roadside where death and destruction was only a mortar shot away.

He walked out to the barn. Pete and Brandon were working in the yard with Hank. The dog glanced his way, but his training held and he stayed with Brandon.

Zack kept walking.

CAITLIN SCARCELY SAW the men during the next few days. They rose early to feed the stock and do minor chores, then headed for the hay fields. By the second day she felt well enough to try to ride. Brandon saddled Bonny Boy for her. If she brought the horse to the stairs leading to the porch, she could use the steps to give her height, swing up with minimum effort and no undue strain on her healing wrist.

Her heart was in her throat when she perched on the

horse's back. But a couple of turns around the yard and her confidence returned.

The next morning she had Brandon saddle her horse before he took off. She packed lunch for all the men, then headed toward the sound of the mower. The faint hum grew louder as she approached until she wondered how the men could stand it without going deaf!

Brandon was unconcerned, but both Pete and Zack wore bright red ear coverings.

Pete stood beside Brandon as they watched Zack in the distance make the turn with the mower and rumble back toward them. Zack saw her first. Slowly he brought the machine to a halt near the other two and turned it off.

"Giving trouble again?" Pete called.

Zack shook his head and nodded toward Caitlin, who urged Bonny Boy closer now that the loud racket had ceased.

They were appreciative of the lunch, and especially the beverages.

Next time, bring a barrel of cold water, Brandon signed. *This is the hottest it's been. Zack says it's one of the worst job a cowboy has to do but it needs to get done.*

She flashed a look of gratitude toward the cowboy, now walking around the mower, studying different sections. If nothing else, the man was a strong role model for hard work.

She'd never seen him relax, much less goof off. He was nothing like—

Stop! she admonished herself. She could not compare all men to Timothy. She knew he wasn't the norm. But it was hard after living with the man for so long.

That day set the pace for the ones that followed. Caitlin could see the difference to the field each noontime. More and more hay was cut. Once that was done, they would rake it into rows, turning it a bit and letting it air dry. Then the old baler would follow the windrows and pack it into bales for transportation.

TEN DAYS AFTER HER ACCIDENT, Caitlin drove to town to have the stitches removed and to have the doctor check her out. She didn't tell Brandon or Zack she was going. They were at a critical stage with the hay and she was capable of driving herself.

The doctor's visit went smoothly. The stitches were removed and he pronounced her wrist to be healing nicely.

Planning to stop for lunch before returning home, Caitlin headed for the diner they'd eaten at before.

Upon entering, she looked for a seat. It was crowded.

"Caitlin?" Charlie Johnstone beckoned from one of the booths where he sat alone.

She smiled uncertainly and wound her way through the tables. He was coming for dinner in a couple of more days. She hadn't expected to see him before.

"Join me?" he invited, standing as she approached.

"Thank you. I should have realized lunchtime would bring a crowd, but I didn't expect this." She slipped into the booth opposite Charlie.

"I've just ordered. Let me get the waitress back here. Then you can tell me what happened." He gestured to the cast.

Once Caitlin had placed her selection, she looked over at him and explained about the accident.

"I came in to see the doctor today to get the stitches out. I drove myself because the men are working on the hay. And in three days I have to drive to Casper to pick up a friend of Brandon's who is coming to stay for a few weeks—to learn all about ranching."

"Another deaf boy?" the rancher asked.

"Yes, they attend school together."

"You know Paul Simmons's girl? Susan, I think her name is?"

"Sure do. She's been out to visit and is coming again when Wayne does."

Charlie looked at her for a long moment. "Quite a group you'll have," he said.

She nodded.

"Need any help?" he asked.

She glanced up. "Doing what?"

"Might need some more horses. I have a couple of old ones that work well, but aren't up to the strain of a full-time ranch hand. Think they'd be perfect for kids still learning. Tack'd go with 'em. Might come over and lend a hand. That Zack seems a loner. Never much participates in things in town. He okay with this?"

"He's been helpful to me and Brandon. Still, I'm sure he'd appreciate some additional resources. The kids each need a horse and I'd like to be able to ride out and watch as well."

Had Zack thought of that aspect? She bet he had. What were his plans to make sure everyone had a horse to ride? Maybe she should double-check with him. But ever since he'd reluctantly agreed to have the kids for the summer, he'd kept away from her.

Or was it the kisses? She still thought about them each night before falling asleep.

Charlie was looking at her oddly. She dragged her thoughts away from Zack and his kisses. "Did I miss something?"

"I said I'd bring two horses over when I come to dinner day after tomorrow, if that suits you?"

"Yes." She smiled as she studied Charlie's features to see if she saw anything to suggest that Brandon might be related to this man. His gray hair had once been dark, like Brandon's. But dark hair was the rule rather than the exception in hair color.

"Want me to go with you to Casper?" Charlie offered. "Long way for a girl to go alone."

Caitlin almost smiled. She was more than capable of making the trek and she'd long ago stopped being a girl. But she didn't take offense. "Brandon's going with me. We'll be fine, but thank you for the thought."

Their meal arrived, and when they began to eat, Charlie asked how they were settling in at the ranch. She told him and turned the conversation to memories she had as a child. He spoke warmly about her mother, but gave her no clue to indicate the two of them had had a closer relationship than casual acquaintances.

Caitlin wished she had just one conclusive piece of evidence. Would Charlie's pictures offer anything?

CHAPTER NINE

CAITLIN DID SOME QUICK shopping at the local super-market, picking up a cake mix and frosting to bake a welcome cake for Wayne and Susan when they arrived. She chose several baskets of fresh strawberries, some fresh vegetables and then on to bread. She tried to get an assortment of things to appeal to everyone. She was picking Susan up on the way back from the airport. She hoped the adventure would work out.

As long as Zack was in charge, she didn't worry.

She had not taken lunch out to the men, telling them earlier they were on their own that day. When she unloaded the groceries, she noted the kitchen was not as pristine as she'd left it. They must have returned home to eat lunch.

Caitlin was getting quite proficient with her cast, and soon had a huge pot of spaghetti sauce simmer-ing. She began boiling the water, knowing it would take a long time.

When the tired men trekked into the kitchen shortly after six, she took satisfaction from the look of delight on their faces with the aroma filling the air.

My favorite! Brandon signed.

"What he said," Pete added. They had all washed up in the bunkhouse, so were ready to eat.

"What was it?" Zack asked.

"Don't know, but he looked happy as a clam, so I figured it was something about how great the grub smells. Do thank you for including us in with your meals," Pete added to Caitlin.

"Brandon said spaghetti is his favorite," Caitlin explained. "And I'm happy to have you and Zack with us each night." She began to pass out the plates so they could serve themselves at the stove. Her arm wasn't up to heavy lifting, and it made things easier this way.

Zack let the other two heap their plates, then gestured for Caitlin to go. "You next, you fixed it all. Where were you when we came in at lunch?"

"Went to have the stitches out. Saw Charlie Johnstone at lunch. He's coming to dinner the night before we go for Wayne. Said he'd bring a couple of horses for the kids to use."

Zack nodded. "Maybe I'll call him tonight and see what he's bringing."

"I told him you were in charge." She handed her plate to him. "Would you mind? I want lots of sauce on my noodles. I'll put the garlic bread on the table. The salad is already there."

"What did the doctor say?" Zack asked.

"That I could wash my hair myself now," she said, smiling brightly at him. She would miss Zack doing it. He'd washed her hair a half-dozen times now. But there had been no more kisses like the first time.

"Maybe I should wash it once more—just to make sure."

The look in his eyes made her knees go weak. The intensity surprised her, and the flash of desire. For a moment she wished her brother and Pete were out with the dog, that she and Zack were alone. Their gazes held for a long moment. Finally he broke contact and scooped up some dinner for her. Taking it to the table, he placed the plate down and held her chair for her. Then he got his own food.

Caitlin was aware of every move Zack made. She tried to keep the conversation going, but as at other meals, he suggested she eat first and then interpret for Brandon.

"Brandon's teaching me to sign," Pete said. He glanced at Zack. "Think the boss man's learning, too."

Zack scowled. "None of that, Pete."

The old cowboy laughed. "Doesn't want to be boss, missy," he said to Caitlin.

"He agreed," she replied calmly, her heart jumping. Surely he wasn't going to change his mind.

"And as boss, if you don't do what I say, I'll assign you stall clean-out forever," Zack growled.

Pete laughed, mimicking the action so Brandon could catch on. The teen laughed as well.

"In a couple of days, we'll have three signing kids around. Watch the conversation, then," Caitlin said.

WHEN DINNER FINISHED, Pete said he was going to the bunkhouse to watch a show he wanted to see on TV. Brandon was off to use the Internet to talk to Susan and

Wayne and finalize plans. They'd both be on the ranch in two days.

Zack didn't get up from the table right away. Caitlin looked at him quizzically. "Not anxious to be somewhere else?" she asked.

"Does seem as if everyone deserted," he said.

"Want some more tea?" she asked.

"Sure."

She brought some fresh ice from the freezer and filled his glass. She added some iced tea to her own glass and sat back down.

"That was a good dinner," he said, twirling his glass around and around with his fingers.

Caitlin thanked him. "How's the hay coming?"

"Ready to bale starting tomorrow. Pete and I drove the machine to the field. Brought back the mower and rake. When I have some time, I want to tear down those engines and really work on them. Might get another year or two out of them."

She didn't state the obvious, that in two years she hoped this ranch belonged to someone else. Thinking about that seemed surreal. She had the day-to-day activities to take care of.

"You want to talk to Charlie while I do the dishes?" she asked.

He nodded. She brought him the cordless phone. Taking the last of the items from the table, she quickly ran hot water over the dishes. Using her left hand, she washed them with a soapy rag and then put them in the drainer in the side sink. Once finished, she sprayed everything with hot water. Best she could do and so far no one had gotten sick.

She listened as Zack discussed horses with Charlie. The other man must have offered help because Zack made some suggestions on where he needed backup.

He finished the conversation before she finished the dishes, but didn't leave. Caitlin wiped down the counters, rinsed out the rag the best she could and draped it across the edge of the sink.

"All done?" he asked.

She turned and nodded. He was still at the table. Rising, he grabbed his hat and headed toward the front of the house. "Let's sit on the porch and talk," he said.

Her heart jumped again. She hated it when people said, *Let's talk*. It was never good.

Once she was seated on the porch, she smiled brightly, as if that would ward off bad news.

"What's up?" she asked.

"Do you know what you're doing having these kids out? Look at you, second or third day riding and you conked yourself on the head, needed stitches and broke your wrist. How much better do you think these kids are going to do?"

"Probably lots better. Brandon has been working with you or Pete almost every day, and he hasn't had a mishap. Don't assign them anything dangerous. They'll love working and helping. That's all most people want—to be needed. You said normally by this time of year Uncle Clyde had hired on a bunch of extra hands—including a college kid. We can use the help, right?"

"How much help are green kids going to be?" he argued.

"More than no help at all. Or even me with my broken wrist. I can't do much until it heals, but I can keep the meals coming. The kids can help with the haying. Or is that too dangerous, because of the machinery?"

"Being around horses and cattle isn't a walk in the park," he said.

"I know, but I have to believe they'll be fine. They really want this, so they aren't going to ignore rules. Just make sure you train them the right way. I can't think of a better role model for teenagers than you."

Zack stared at her for a long moment. "You're crazy. I'm no role model. I can hardly make it through the day on my own."

"Now you sound crazy. You're the most together man I know."

Zack took off his hat, ran his fingers through his hair and replaced the Stetson. He shook his head. "I'm not. If you think I'm going to have much to do with these kids, you don't know me at all. I want to stay away from people, not become a role model, or work with others. I'm a loner."

"Keep telling yourself that and maybe one day you'll believe it," she said.

"It's the way things are."

"There must be a reason. You said you and your friend Billy—oh, because he died? Is that it? Don't get close to someone because if they die, you'll be hurt?"

ZACK ROSE AND WENT to the railing, then leaned against a post. He stared out over the land. "Don't try that psychology on me. I have my reasons."

"I'm not asking you to be friends with Brandon and Wayne and Susan. Just teach them some skills for riding and working cattle. They'll give you their very best in exchange. And if they get hurt or something, you'll know what to do."

"Knowing what to do isn't always enough. Sometimes nothing is enough."

Caitlin was silent for so long, Zack turned to look at her. She was studying him with a speculative expression.

"Tell me what happened to Billy. Let me understand, please."

"He died, I told you."

"Were you there?"

He turned his back. It was still daylight. He could get a horse and ride until he was too tired not to sleep. He could check on fencing, make sure the water pumps were working, make sure—

"Zack, were you there?"

"Yeah, I was there. I had my hands on two of the bleeding wounds, but there were more than I could staunch. He bled to death. I couldn't stop the blood. I couldn't save my best friend. All the medical training I had was worth spit. I couldn't save him. Or the children. God, the children, shattered by car bombs, shot by their own side because they waved at us or took our candy. They never had a chance. They should be running in some playground, attending school, dreaming of what they could be when they grew up."

He closed his eyes, but snapped them open again. The scenes engraved in his mind made him feel sick. Would he ever forget the faces, the futility of trying so desperately to save those kids, even when his CO had ordered him to step away? He had to save them.

Clenching his hands into fists, he willed away the images. Yearned for peace.

He felt her hand against his arm, gripping for comfort. Only there was no comfort from the nightmares and memories he had. Nothing to ease the pain of not saving Billy.

"I never even went home to see his mother," Zack said. Why was he telling Caitlin this? He hadn't told anyone else, not even Clyde. Maybe because he needed to make her see that he wasn't the man to run the ranch, to teach children.

"I mustered out at Langley and headed west, as far from the old neighborhood as I could get. Never even saw my grandmother or Ellie, Billy's mother. She was like a second mom to me as I grew up, and I never even went back."

"It would have been too hard," Caitlin said softly, rubbing her fingers against his arm.

Zack turned and looked at her. She was soft and sweet and looked as innocent as a newborn. Except her life hadn't been the perfect storybook tale as it should have been.

He pulled her into his arms, clinging to her, feeling the contact, knowing for once he wasn't alone. It was a gift bigger than he deserved.

"I'm sure she understood. She would have been

weepy and clingy and that was the last thing you needed," Caitlin murmured, rubbing his back, leaning against him.

"Maybe some day you can visit, or call her. Just to talk. You both loved her son. She'd understand."

"I should have gone home. Should have told her I tried my best to save him."

"She knows that. Both Ellie and your grandmother know you tried your best. If anyone could have saved him, you would have. You know that, too, Zack."

"There wasn't anything I could do. Two other corps men helped. Nothing. He was dead in minutes. Gone forever."

"I know. Death is so final."

He heard the sympathy in her voice. One part of him wanted to thrust her away and go off alone. Another part wanted to continue holding her, breathing in the scent of her, feeling her warmth thaw some of the ice around his heart and soul. Could the words she was saying be true?

Did Ellie know he'd done his best? Billy had been his closest friend all his life. There was a gaping hole where he should have been. There was no one to talk to late at night. No one to share the satisfaction he derived from working on the land, mastering a horse. No one to reminisce with. Hell, no one to go out and get rip-roaring drunk with.

"I can't imagine the horrors of war," Caitlin said. "I do rest easier knowing you have a medic background. You were so cool when you found me, and knew exactly what to do. Not every ranch has that, and they still hire on workers."

"Not kids."

"These kids are two years away from being old enough to live out on their own. How will they get the experience they need if someone doesn't give them a chance? It's only a few weeks, Zack. It'll work, it has to."

"And if not?"

"We'll cross that bridge when we get to it, I guess."

She shifted slightly and Zack was instantly aware he was holding a beautiful woman in his arms. The need for comfort fled as a new need took its place. He buried his face in her silky hair. It smelled like flowers and Caitlin.

She had her own baggage. Her husband had left her with a mess and probably a strong distrust of men. Yet she trusted him. At least on the ranch. Would she trust him with more?

What more was he willing to risk?

She pulled back a little and looked up into his eyes. "Don't you truly think we can make this work?"

He stared into her blue eyes, wishing they were alone on the ranch, that he had put clean sheets on his bed. That she'd smile at him the way she often smiled at her brother. No, not quite like her brother, but with desire and want in her eyes.

"What, the kids or us?"

She blinked. "Us?" she almost squeaked.

He didn't respond except to kiss her.

He felt the hesitation before Caitlin kissed him back. Her mouth was sweet. Her tongue met his when he traced her lips. He could feel the strength in her arms as she held on tightly. The unforgiving feel of the plaster cast dug into his back. He didn't mind; he was holding heaven in his arms.

When she pulled back, Zack half expected her to ask him to leave. Instead, she glanced at the house, and then took his hand in hers.

Moments later they were in her room.

"Brandon is used to my going to sleep early ever since the accident," she said, closing the door gently. "He won't hear us." She turned, but before she could take a step, he tossed aside his hat and drew her into his arms, his mouth finding hers instantly.

Twilight was beginning to fall. Soon it would be dark. For now the light allowed him to see the shine in her eyes, the rosy-pink of her cheeks, the dampness of her mouth. He kissed her again. And again. Until kisses alone weren't enough. Touching, tasting, exploring, nothing was enough.

He slowly unbuttoned her shirt, while her one hand fumbled with his buttons. He finished first and gazed at the lacy encased breasts, his heart catching. She was so incredibly beautiful.

"I want you," he breathed, absorbing her fragrance, feeling the softness of her skin against his fingertips.

"I want you, too," she said, trailing kisses across his chest, his shirt finally open.

In only moments he lifted her and placed her on the bed. It was so much better this time than the last time he'd put her to bed. This time he joined her. There was no concussion to worry about, no injuries, only the silky feel of her skin and the fire that threatened to consume him from the inside out.

He kissed her again and let his fingers learn all her secrets until he swept them both away to a private place.

ZACK WOKE WITH A START when a door closed.

Caitlin moved, rubbing her bare leg against his. "Brandon going to bed. What time is it?"

"Don't know, after ten, I think."

"Ummm." Her hand brushed against his chest, moving to his neck. She threaded her fingers up through his hair. "Sometimes you run your fingers through your hair and leave it in spikes. I always want to smooth it down."

He drew her hand to his mouth and kissed the palm, then wrapped his fingers around it and held it against his chest. "So do it."

She giggled softly. "Right in front of Pete and Brandon? Like that sure wouldn't cause comment."

"Where do you plan to put these teenagers you have arriving?" he asked.

"What do you mean?"

"I thought the boys might like to stay in the bunkhouse with me and Pete. Give them the real flavor of being a cowboy. You're still doing meals, right?"

"Of course. Then Susan could have the room Brandon's been using. There is another bedroom I started cleaning before my accident. And the one Uncle Clyde had. But I know they'd prefer the bunkhouse."

"Two more rooms in the bunkhouse can be cleaned

tomorrow. I'll hold off another day or two before baling the hay, give it more time to dry."

"Charlie Johnstone's coming to dinner on Friday," she reminded him.

Zack nodded. "He and I spoke about the horses he's bringing. He offered to help in other ways, too. Odd, that. Never knew he offered to help Clyde. Of course Clyde probably forgot more than Charlie knows. Not the case with me."

"He probably feels ranching is too much for me. I'm not Clyde."

"I noticed," Zack said, squeezing her hand slightly. For a little while he was just a guy with a girl. He took a breath. It was nothing like New York. But also nothing like Afghanistan.

He tugged her closer. "I'll have to get back to the bunkhouse."

"Right away?" she asked, then kissed him.

"Not right away," he said, drawing her even closer.

WHEN CAITLIN AWOKE, she was alone in the bed. She stretched her arm over to the place where Zack had been, but the sheets were cool. He'd been gone awhile. Glancing out the window, she saw dawn on the horizon. Time to get up.

Uncertain, she continued to snuggle beneath the covers. How was she going to face him? She wasn't a person who did one-night stands. Except for a boyfriend she'd met at college, Timothy had been her only lover. Now Zack.

And to compare the two would be difficult. Timothy

was polished and sophisticated. Zack made her think she was the only woman in the world for him ever.

Should she act cool, as if last night was just like any other night? Or should she expect their relationship to change, to become more intimate?

Suddenly she worried he'd think one night together gave him rights he hadn't pushed for—like kissing her in front of Pete and Brandon. Or even more?

They needed to discuss things.

She wished she could call Beth and ask her opinion. But her friend was still on her cruise—with a husband who never caused a bit of trouble.

Caitlin wasn't sure she could tell her friend everything—certainly not about the special kisses, the licks and strokes that Zack had shared with her late into the night. She wasn't even sure she wanted to admit she had practically dragged him to bed and now felt as shy as a teenager on a first date.

She threw back the covers and got out of bed, grabbed a robe and some clothes, then headed for the bathroom. When he came in for breakfast, she'd tell him they needed to talk. Establish some kind of ground rules.

He'd turned her topsy-turvy and she wanted to know what to expect next.

WHEN SHE ARRIVED in the kitchen, someone had started coffee and there were toast crumbs on the counter. But Brandon wasn't there. He'd already gone out to see the horses, she had no doubt.

She prepared her own breakfast, and waited for the men to come in.

Pete showed up at six, Brandon on his heels.

"Where's Zack?" she asked, starting on the next pan of eggs.

"Don't know," Pete said, sitting at the table and pouring a cup of coffee. "He wasn't around when I got up and his truck is gone."

Her heart sank. "Gone?" He'd left, just as he'd said he would. She stirred the eggs, not seeing them, seeing only the dark eyes that had witnessed too much, the reserved man who didn't want to get involved. The ardent lover who had taken her to heights last night that she'd never reached before.

He couldn't be gone.

"Seems unlikely he'd take off without telling someone," she said, trying to think. Last night had changed things, they could still work together. He could still give Brandon tips on riding and handling cattle.

"Maybe. He's a hard man to get to know. Keeps himself apart, you know what I mean?"

Caitlin nodded. She had thought they'd breached that barrier, but apparently not. Where could Zack be?

She went through the motions of serving breakfast to Brandon and Pete and even poured another cup of coffee for herself, but she couldn't drink it. She felt her world tilting off center. Would her taste in men always gravitate to those who had no true feelings for her?

A spurt of anger flared. She was not the trusting wife she'd been with Timothy. Wiser now, Caitlin knew she didn't need anyone else to make it. If Zack had proved too much a coward to see things through, so be it. She was made of sterner stuff.

"If he's gone, we'll have to look after things ourselves," she said.

Pete glanced up. "Gone as in for good?"

"You said his truck was missing."

"I thought he went to get a part or something. Why would he leave?" The old cowboy looked puzzled.

What? Brandon signed.

Caitlin thought of the times Zack had told her he wanted out. No one else knew that. Could it be he just went on an errand? Without telling anyone? Unlikely.

I'm wondering where Zack went, she signed.

Probably to get the part for the engine that keeps cutting out, he said, finishing the last of his meal.

Caitlin stared at him. *I thought maybe he left, moved on.*

Brandon frowned. *Why? This is his home. He works here.*

We'll see, won't we?

If he returned, good. If not, she would deal with it. She began to clear the dishes.

If he hadn't left, she might just fire him for giving her such worry.

Once the dishes were stacked in the sink, and Brandon and Pete back in the barn, Caitlin left the house and crossed quickly to the bunkhouse. She had to know.

She peeked into each bedroom—there were six in all. Most were dusty with a blanket thrown over the beds. Two were occupied, one obviously Pete's. The next one had a neatly made bed and not a single item of personal belonging showing. But looking into the drawers, she saw jeans and shirts. There was another pair of boots in the closet and a new hat. She drew a deep breath of relief, and smelled Zack. This was his room, and his clothes were still here. He was coming back.

Leaving quietly, she slipped by the barn and hoped no one had seen her. At least she could get through the day knowing he hadn't gone for good.

It was late by the time the truck drove past the house. Caitlin was in the office and almost dashed outside to confront the cowboy who had given her hours of worry. But she remained at the desk, listening, hoping he would come and see her.

BY DINNERTIME, she was ready to throw in the towel and go find him. When the men came in to eat, Zack was right behind Pete. But he didn't even look at her. She served her plate and left the rest for the men to serve themselves. Sitting down, she waited until the others were ready before beginning to eat. She glanced at Zack.

"I didn't know you were going off today," she said. Proud her tone sounded casual, she clenched her good hand in her lap and waited.

"Needed a part for the baler. Thought they might have it in Wolf Crossing, but no luck. I had to go to Casper."

She nodded and began to eat. Today had not gone as she'd anticipated, but he was back on the ranch. Time enough later to discuss their night together.

CHARLIE ARRIVED LATE the following afternoon, towing a four-horse trailer. Brandon and Pete were on hand to unload the horses—all four of them. Caitlin heard the commotion and came from the house to see what was going on.

"Hello," she called as she hurried to join them.

"Howdy. Brought a couple of extras. Know those kids will be running these horses ragged. All are good steady mounts. I talked to Zack about them."

Sure, Zack was talking to Charlie. He had hardly said two words to her since he'd returned. And when she'd said she wanted to talk with him, he'd pleaded extra work and disappeared so fast she almost hadn't seen him go.

She watched as Pete and Charlie backed the horses down the ramp, handing the halter lines to Brandon, who then led them into the corral. They ambled away once released, checking out their new abode.

Once all were in the corral, Charlie closed up the trailer.

"Come in, I have iced tea. Dinner won't be for a little while," Caitlin said.

"Let me get the pictures from the truck." He pulled out two fat photo albums and turned to walk with her back to the house. Brandon was already in the corral, patting one of the new horses. Hank sniffed around the hooves.

"They won't kick the dog, will they?" Caitlin asked.

"They're used to cattle dogs. And Hank's used to staying out of their way. They'll be fine."

"If you don't mind the kitchen, come on back so I can finish dinner and visit," Caitlin said.

"Smells mighty good," he said when they entered the house.

"Pot roast. I've learned to fix hearty meals here. Zack turned his nose up at one meal that was all salads, eating rabbit food as he called it, and ended up fixing a huge sandwich with half the ingredients in the refrigerator."

"We work hard, like to fill up," Charlie said.

He put the albums down on the counter out of the way. "We'll look at those after dinner."

"Have a seat," Caitlin said, pulling out a chair for him to use. She quickly poured iced tea for the guest and went back to the biscuits she was making. It had been hard to roll out the dough with her cast on, but she'd managed. Every time she accomplished a task, she felt better. She was beginning to hope the place wouldn't sell fast. Brandon wasn't the only one having a wonderful summer—despite the broken wrist.

"You sure look like your mother," Charlie said with a sad smile.

"Thank you," Caitlin said. "I always thought she was beautiful."

"Me, too." He took a sip of tea. "I remember her that summer you two spent here. She loved riding, swimming in the river, cooking over a campfire. Guess traveling around the world with your father made her adventuresome."

"I remember riding horses that summer, going out with Uncle Clyde and watching cattle walk around. I'm sure we were doing more, but that's most of my memories. And the swing on the tree near the barn."

"I put that up for you," Charlie said. "Clyde suggested it, but I was a much younger man than he was back then."

Caitlin hadn't remembered Charlie from that summer. "Did you come to visit a lot? I don't remember."

"No reason you should. I came a lot the last few weeks you were here." He turned his glass on the table. "Do you know why your mother brought you here?"

Caitlin shrugged. "To visit. We were between moves, I think. Seemed like we moved every two or three years in those days. After Mom died, we didn't move as much. I guess my father put in for transfers in earlier years and then stopped."

She hesitated. "Was there another reason?"

He looked at her. "If there were, I'm sure you would have known. Your uncle sure was happy to have you stay for so long. I suspect your mother was always his favorite relative. He would have left the ranch to her had she still been alive."

Caitlin nodded, knowing Charlie probably didn't realize the place had been left solely to her. She planned to share it with Brandon, so there was no problem there. But it was odd that Clyde had left it to her alone.

Dinner was delicious. Each of the men complimented her on the savory pot roast and fresh vegetables that were steamed to perfection. When she brought out strawberry shortcake for dessert, there were groans of delight.

Zack did not say much during the meal, but Caitlin caught him studying Charlie several times. The rancher seemed to fit in perfectly. He and Pete swapped stories, trying to top each other with more outlandish tales.

Caitlin was kept busy translating for Brandon so he wouldn't miss out. He laughed at many of the antics.

She even caught Zack laughing at one point. It changed his entire appearance. She stared until he caught her eye, his smile fading as he turned away. She almost stormed over to demand he talk to her then and there. Charlie said something else that was funny and she turned back to translate for Brandon.

When the meal ended and they were ready to push back from the table, Charlie offered to bring over the albums. Pete and Zack decided to stay to see the photos as well, so dishes were cleared and the large books brought to the table.

The first picture showed Tricia Jackson up close. She was laughing at something and her eyes sparkled in the light. Caitlin felt a pang. Her mother seemed so young in the photo. She'd only been a few years older than Caitlin was now.

Involuntarily, she reached out and touched her cheek. "Mama," she said softly.

Brandon signed, *She was pretty, wasn't she? You look a lot like her.*

Caitlin nodded, glancing up to catch Zack's gaze. He said nothing, just looked at her, then back at the picture.

"Look how happy she was—I don't remember her that way," she said, studying the photograph again.

Charlie cleared his throat, as if covering for a display of emotion, then flipped the page. There was Tricia with Caitlin. The little girl sat on a horse that looked way too big for her. Tricia was smiling up at the young Caitlin, who beamed from ear to ear.

"You started riding early," Pete said.

Zack glanced at Brandon, then Charlie. "Nice pictures. You take them?"

"No, some Clyde took, gave me copies. He probably has a box of pictures somewhere around."

Caitlin flipped slowly through the album. She remembered her mother as a rather sad woman who put up with the military manner in which her husband ran their home. Caitlin thought back, remembering her mother's laughter—rarely heard after Brandon was born. Had she mourned the fact her baby was deaf? She'd never indicated that to Caitlin. But why would she? Tricia had been the adult, Caitlin the child. Or had she been mourning the loss of Brandon's father? Caitlin had never considered that angle before.

There was a picture of Charlie and Tricia. For a moment, Caitlin didn't recognize Charlie. He didn't look much older than her mother in the photograph. With his cowboy hat and snug jeans, he looked hot. Had her mother thought so?

"Did you spend a lot of time with them?" Caitlin asked, hoping her voice sounded casual.

"Clyde and I had been friends for years. My wife had recently died when you two came for the summer. I guess I spent a fair amount of time over here. Sometimes you and your mother came to my place for dinner. Once I took her into town to see a movie."

It didn't sound like a passionate affair to Caitlin, but he would hardly admit to such a thing after all these years.

When she turned the page again, she saw her mother

and another cowboy, this one younger, and even from the photograph, Caitlin could almost feel the sex appeal.

"Who is that?"

Charlie frowned. "Stan Elliot. He worked for your uncle that summer. Left right before your mother did. Just worked in this area that one summer."

Caitlin stared, mesmerized. She couldn't tell the cowboy's hair color, but he was tall, like Brandon, and lanky. Another photo showed Stan with Tricia. And another. They were clowning around, and once again Tricia was laughing. More of Caitlin and her mother, and Uncle Clyde. Good grief, he'd looked ancient in those days. He'd been in his seventies back then.

The photographs finished too soon for Caitlin. For a little while she could wrap happier memories around herself and relive that summer.

"You had a mighty pretty mother, Caitlin. You favor her," Pete said, rising. "Charlie, want to come see how Brandon does with Hank? They're working real well together."

"Don't mind seeing that," Charlie said. He smiled at Caitlin. "Keep the books for a while. I want them back, mind, but can lend them for a while."

"Thank you."

Zack hung back when the others left. Caitlin got up from the table to start the dishes. She ran water in the sink. "We need to talk," she said.

"About?" he asked.

"The other night."

"What about it?"

She turned and looked at him. "That's what I wanted to ask you. Was it just a one-night stand? Do you think we have something going or what? I wake up and you're gone—as in, no one knew where you were. I thought you'd left. You've said you want to go often enough."

"I would have told you if I was pulling out."

She waved her hand in dismissal. "What about us?"

He sighed and looked across the room at her. "There is no *us*. You own a ranch, I work here. We had a night together. That's all it was. There's too much baggage in my life to do anything but get through each day. You'll sell this place and return to California. Let's leave it the way it is."

"And how is that?" She held on. She would not give way to the sudden sadness that swept through her. Their night together hadn't meant as much to him as it had to her. She swallowed. Could she live with that?

"The way it's been."

Turning back to the sink, she turned off the water. She'd wanted to talk, she just didn't like the way the conversation was going.

"Is Charlie Brandon's father?" he asked.

She almost dropped the pan she'd picked up. "Why would you ask that?"

"The way he kept looking at Brandon during dinner. And there's something around the eyes, the way they both smile. They favor each other."

She bit her lip and began washing the pan. "I don't know," she said at last.

"But he's not your father's son?"

She shook her head. "I learned that right when my mother died. Brandon was in the car crash, too, and needed blood. He and my father weren't compatible. My father was never the same toward Brandon after that. But Brandon was so little, I don't think he noticed. At least I've always hoped he didn't. Dad supported him. His name is on Brandon's birth certificate. I think it was a face-saving tactic—don't let anyone know the son wasn't his. But he left him next to nothing in his will. Dad couldn't bring himself to leave another man's son a legacy."

"Sounds like he didn't leave you anything either," Zack said.

"I was newly married to Timothy when he wrote his will. Guess he figured I was taken care of." She didn't need to voice the hurt she'd felt when the will had been read.

"So what did he think would happen to Brandon if he died before the boy was earning a living?" Zack asked.

"Schooling is pretty much taken care of, so I guess he thought I'd take him during vacations. He was right. He's my brother no matter who his father is. Do you think it could be Charlie?"

"Maybe. I'm thinking Charlie is wondering, too. Is it possible?"

Caitlin draped the drying cloth over the edge of the counter. "Brandon's birthday is in early May. I suppose it's possible. I never really thought about it until after I found out. Mostly, I couldn't believe my mother had been unfaithful. It was a shock. I was sixteen and she was my idol. I loved her so much. Much more than my father. Is that horrible?"

"Not especially. You must have had your reasons."

"My mother was a loving, warm, wonderful person. My father thought he was in the ranks of the military at home and at the front. It wasn't a harmonious household. In retrospect, I think getting away from my father was a big factor in rushing into marriage with Timothy. He was the exact opposite of my father—a charmer from the word go. That's why he was so successful in scamming so many people."

"Does Brandon know?" Zack asked, leaning against the counter, arms folded across his chest.

"Not that I'm aware. He hasn't asked any questions and Mom died about ten years ago when he was six. A drunk driver smashed her car and killed her instantly. He walked away unscathed."

"Tough break," Zack said.

Caitlin nodded. "Do you think his father could be Charlie?"

"That cowboy in the later pictures sure seemed to have a thing for your mother."

"Charlie asked if I knew why Mom had come visiting that summer. Could that have anything to do with it?"

"Ask Charlie."

"I can't just come out and ask if the man had an affair with my mother—oh, and could he possibly be the father of my brother?"

"I guess that is a bit awkward. I'm betting a man who's kept a secret for this long isn't going to let anything slip."

CHAPTER TEN

THE NEXT MORNING CAITLIN WAS up early. She and
Brandon were going to pick Wayne up at the airport in
Casper, then swing by the Simmons's home in Wolf
Crossing to pick up Susan. By dinner tonight, there'd
be a full table in the kitchen.

Zack had left for the hay field before Caitlin was
even up. He had gone to the bunkhouse as soon as
Charlie had left last evening. So much still had to be
said, but he was avoiding her. He told Pete he wanted
to analyze the hay, then get back to put the part in the
baler and start it up.

Caitlin wished Zack had stayed to say goodbye.
Their relationship was anything but normal. She liked
being with him, yet was cautious about letting herself
trust anyone. He couldn't get past his experiences from
the war and made sure she knew there was no future
for them. Sleeping together had not miraculously
forged a stronger bond. In fact, she knew it had driven
a wedge between them that might always be there.

She'd tried to tell him she was only in Wyoming
for another couple of months, then would return to
California.

To what she wasn't sure. Especially if the ranch hadn't sold by then. If she could just find an inexpensive place near Brandon, find work and earn enough to go back to school, at least she'd have a plan for the future. She liked working with people, and might pursue something in the travel industry. If, as Jeff had said, it took years to sell the ranch, she would be foolish not to make plans for the fall.

As they drove east toward Casper, she gazed at the land. There was so much of it that showed no signs of man. So different from the crowded Bay Area with homes and businesses lining every square inch. The traffic was hardly noticeable compared to bumper-to-bumper back home. She knew Montana had the nickname big sky country, but it could equally be applied to Wyoming. She loved the huge blue dome overhead.

She suddenly had no desire to return to California's congestion.

At the airport, Brandon and Wayne were glad to see each other and their hands flew as they caught up on news. They were in the same class at California School for the Deaf and had been friends for years. Wayne was excited about working on the ranch and Brandon quickly brought him up to speed on what he'd learned so far.

They sat in the back seat together so it was easier to communicate. Several hours later, Caitlin stopped for Susan. The three teenagers quickly fell into conversation. Susan sat in front, but turned around to sign with the boys. It was after seven by the time Caitlin reached home. She was tired from driving all day. There was still supper to prepare.

Boys in the bunkhouse, Susan upstairs in the main house with me, Caitlin signed. *Segregation—boys with the cowboys, girls together. Brandon, you and Wayne take one of Susan's bags, she'll get the third and then you go find out from Zack where you'll be sleeping. Dinner as soon as I can fix it.*

The three teens scrambled around to follow Caitlin's orders. In no time, Susan's things were in the room Brandon had used and the boys were lugging Wayne's suitcases to the bunkhouse, Susan following to see where they were staying.

Caitlin washed her face and brushed her hair before heading for the kitchen. A large sheet of paper was taped to the cabinets.

"Dinner on us," a bold hand had written.

"Thank you!" she said softly and turned to head out toward the bunkhouse.

The aroma of cooking meat met her as she rounded the corner of the barn and approached the bunkhouse. A large grill stood near the stoop, and she could hear the sizzling as she walked closer. Pete and Zack stood over the grill. They looked up when she came into view.

"Glad you're back, we were getting worried," Pete said. "Thought we'd save you fixing dinner."

"And we wanted to fire up this old grill," Zack added. "If we're having a barbecue with neighbors soon, I wanted to make sure it worked." He glanced at her, then back at the meat cooking. She tried to ignore the prick of hurt. The closer she got, the more aware she felt of him. She wished he'd lean over and kiss her. Urge her to run back to the house for another night of passion. Even a friendly smile would be welcome.

When the teenagers came out, they gravitated immediately to Zack. Brandon introduced Wayne. Caitlin translated softly in the background. Zack shook hands with the visitor. Caitlin was glad to see he didn't try to dodge them. She knew he felt they didn't belong, but she was happy for her brother to have some friends to hang out with. If things worked out, Wayne could stay the rest of the summer.

Caitlin was ready for bed long before anyone else was. She told Susan the main door would be unlocked and to come in when she wished. Bidding the others good-night, she headed for the house. Glancing back, she felt wistful. She'd hoped Zack might have walked with her, but he was describing the next day's work to the kids, drawing pictures in the dirt with a stick.

She should be glad he was dealing with them so well. But she wanted some attention from the cowboy herself.

THE NEXT DAY SET the routine for the following ones. Everyone was up early—Wayne and Susan excited beyond belief. Caitlin made sure they ate a hearty breakfast, gave everyone two water bottles, and watched as Pete and Zack led the cavalcade out.

She could have gone, but wanted to get the meals planned. Feeding two more teenagers, in addition to Pete, called for portions she wasn't used to cooking.

Her wrist didn't ache as much as it had. The scar on her forehead wasn't as noticeable as earlier. She was getting better. Maybe she'd ride with them later, once she felt caught up with the household duties.

Mid-morning, Caitlin began working on the books again. She was learning more and more about the operation of the ranch by seeing what time of year her uncle incurred expenses or deposited large sums of money. The place was profitable, no doubt about it. The extraordinary medical expenses prior to his death had run it perilously close to the red, but if Zack could keep the business going this year, it should resume its healthy profitability. She and Brandon could earn a comfortable living from the ranch.

Maybe instead of planning to return to California when Brandon did, she should think about staying. She had a home. She could wait for the sale here as easily as in some apartment in the Bay Area. It would mean Brandon wouldn't have any family close by, but as long as they owned the ranch, he could come for vacations.

She'd have to give that some thought. It was so far from what she'd envisioned and she wanted to make sure it wasn't tied directly to her wish to stay near Zack. Not a very wise reason to change her future plans.

Yet, she had no one close in the Bay Area except Beth, and they'd proved this summer that e-mail worked well. She could invite Beth to visit, catch up with all the news and show her the new Caitlin.

Could she make it work?

Hearing a loud noise, Caitlin went to the window. Zack had obviously gotten the baler working. She watched as he maneuvered the awkward machine away from the storage area and out toward the fields.

Pete was working with Wayne in the corral, having him mount and dismount. Earlier he'd been learning the different gaits and how to cue a horse. Susan and Brandon had also been on horseback. Now both of them sat on the top rail and watched Wayne. Their horses stood outside the arena, tied to the fence, half dozing.

Caitlin hoped the teenagers would prove to be of help once they'd learned the basics. And she crossed her fingers there would be no more accidents. She didn't know what that would do to Zack.

She returned to her computer and logged onto the Internet, then looked up reports from the war zone. She wanted to better understand the horrors he'd faced. And find out if there was anything people at home could do to help those returning.

At noon everyone but Zack trooped in for lunch.

"Where's Zack?" Caitlin asked.

"Still out in the hay field," Pete told her. "He wants one of us to bring him a horse around four."

"He needs lunch," she said.

"Figure the man knows what he's doing. You want to ride out and give him lunch? I planned to take these young'uns out this afternoon. Wayne'll be ready for the open range by then. Boy's learning fast."

Caitlin asked the teenagers how they were doing, and was flooded with a rush of enthusiastic signs.

They would be dog-tired at the end of the day, Caitlin knew. But the kind of tiredness that came from solid accomplishment.

Wayne complained he didn't have a proper hat. He was wearing a ball cap.

When Caitlin interpreted, Pete said he'd seen one in the barn that Wayne could use until he got his own.

We'll have to go to Fallworth, Wayne can get a hat there, Brandon said. *He could use some boots, too.*

He'll have to make do for a day or two. Then we'll go, she returned.

Wayne grinned in delight.

As soon as they finished eating, the three teens dashed from the house.

"I wish I had some of that energy," Pete said. "Nice lunch, Caitlin. Appreciate it. I landed on my feet with this job."

"I think I got the better end of the deal," she said. "You didn't know you'd be teaching a bunch of kids how to ranch, did you?"

"No, but it makes a man feel good, passing on things he's learned. They are so eager. Guess I better get back out there before they lose some of that enthusiasm."

"I doubt that'll happen any time soon. It's a special opportunity for them. You aren't having any trouble communicating?"

"Naw. That Brandon knows right much what to do and he's telling them. I usually just point to a trouble spot, he can recognize what's wrong. Makes those hands fly and the problem's corrected. A couple of times I took a page from Zack's book and drew a diagram in the dirt. Works perfectly."

"Don't let them do more than they are ready for— no matter how much they push," she said.

"Zack would have my head. He wants to vet them before moving to the next step. They'll be working on cleaning tack this afternoon—and the stalls. Not that there's much to do with the horses in the corral, but they can learn. We'll have a ride later when we take Zack his horse."

"Let me know when you go, I'd like a ride myself."

Pete touched the brim of his hat and headed out. Caitlin quickly cleaned the kitchen and started dinner. If she got it all cooked, she could warm it up when they returned from the ride and not leave the stove on when gone.

It was a beautiful afternoon. A few clouds hovered over the distant peaks, but nothing that looked like rain. She was pleased to have her horse saddled when she went to join the others. Pete had had Wayne and Susan saddle it up for the practice. Pete held the reins of Zack's horse as they rode out. The three teenagers led the way, Brandon proudly displaying his knowledge of the ranch.

Caitlin fell in beside Pete. She kept alert, not fully trusting the twelve-hundred-pound animal she was riding. She'd let down her guard before with dire consequences. She didn't want to do that again.

She heard the engine long before she saw the machine. Cresting a slight rise, they all stopped and looked at the field stretching out before them. The baler was about a third of the way down the field. Every few moments a rectangular bale of hay fell out of the back. There were rows of bales ready to get onto a wagon and back to the barn.

"That'll be our task for the next few days," Pete said. "Hauling all that hay back to the barn. Plenty of feed for the winter months. Good thing these kids have energy, they'll need it. Bucking hay is hard work."

"Especially in this heat."

"Won't work midday. Too hot then. Early morning and late afternoon are the best times. We can stack them in the barn during the midday hours—cooler there. Once it gets too hot, we'll all be glad to rest."

The machine slowed and stopped, the engine idling. Zack climbed down from the cab and motioned for them to come closer.

The horses plodded down the slight incline and over to the baler. The horse Susan rode eyed the machine warily. The others didn't seem bothered by the noise. Caitlin was on alert.

When they reached Zack, he came to Caitlin. "Ask if Brandon wants to learn how to drive this thing," he said. "We can do a couple of sweeps before heading back."

"He doesn't drive," she said automatically, eyeing the large farm equipment with some trepidation.

"He's old enough to learn," Zack said, looking at Brandon.

"It's too dangerous."

"Caitlin, what's he going to run into? Some unmowed hay? The thing's too wide to ever tip over, even if we had hilly terrain. He just has to point it where he wants to go and run the gears to engage the baling mechanism. If he's going to be a cowhand, he needs to expand his skills."

"He's not," she said.

"For the summer he is. Tonight you can get permission from Paul Simmons and Wayne's family. The others can take turns tomorrow. Ask if they want to."

She gave him an exasperated look. "Of course they'd want to. Are you kidding?"

"Then what's the problem? I'm not going to let them get hurt. You want a turn first?"

"I have no desire to learn to drive that thing." She knew Zack wouldn't deliberately let them get hurt. It was just the machine looked so lethal and her brother was still a kid. Only, he was growing up this summer. And she could not hold him back.

"Okay, I'll tell Brandon." She signed to her brother. His face lit up and he slid off his horse almost before she'd finished. Handing Susan the reins, he hurried to the cab, glancing over his shoulder to look at Zack as if to say *let's go.*

I want a turn, Wayne signed.

Me, too, Susan said.

I'll check with your parents tonight. If it is okay with both of them, then tomorrow you can have turns, Caitlin signed. She trusted Zack knew what he was doing.

For a moment, she went still. She did trust Zack. He was nothing like Timothy. His word was rock solid. And he knew how to manage the teenagers—letting them learn and push limits, but keeping them safe.

Pete signaled and they turned the horses and rode away from the machine. In only moments the sound of the engine changed and it began to crawl forward. A few moments later, a bale of hay tumbled out the back and plopped on the ground.

"They'll be a while. Let's get the others riding. I want Wayne to get practice. Susan is pretty good," Pete said, nudging his horse. He continued to lead Zack's horse; Susan had Brandon's. Caitlin almost suggested he tie them to one of the bales of hay, then realized exactly how much the horses would love that.

Wayne had been awestruck by the cattle they'd seen and was anxious to look at the main herd. Susan had fallen in with Caitlin and talked a little, studying everything Pete did with close attention. Another hero in the making, Caitlin thought, smiling.

An hour later they returned to the hay field. The machine had been turned off, and Zack and Brandon were standing around a bale of hay, Zack pantomiming. Caitlin was relieved to find everything as it should be. If she had been able to afford the insurance, Brandon could have started learning to drive a car after his birthday. But that was one expense she couldn't swing.

Oh, dear, what about insurance on the ranch? She'd have to check on that before she let those kids drive.

Zack nodded and clapped Brandon on the shoulder. The teenager smiled broadly.

When everyone had mounted and started for the house, Zack fell in beside Caitlin, slowing down until they dropped behind the others.

"Brandon did fine with the machine. I won't let him drive it without supervision, but next year, he'll be ready to do it on his own."

"I hope it doesn't take until next year to sell this place," she murmured.

"What are you going to do if he wants to work the ranch?" Zack asked.

"He's sixteen. This is a novelty for him. He loves computers. Once the adventure wears off, he'll be glad to go back to his city life."

"He will, or you will?"

"What do you mean?" Caitlin asked.

"He loves this. He's eager to learn everything. He's glad his friends have come to spend time here, but even if they weren't here, he'd want to learn everything. It may be a passing fancy. But what if it's his niche in life?"

"It's not."

"What if it is?" he persisted.

"I don't know. He has to finish high school and then go to college before he starts a career. It's too early to tell."

"Maybe. But he's asked me to get him some information from the University of Wyoming on ag courses. He questions me all the time about things, beyond what a casual curiosity warrants."

Caitlin didn't want to hear that her brother wanted to be a rancher.

"Don't encourage him," she said.

"I'm not encouraging him. But I will answer a direct question when asked."

"And how do you do that? You don't sign."

"He talks. And usually forms the questions as yes or no so I only have to nod." Zack was thoughtful a moment, then said, "He could come by it honestly, the desire to work the land."

"We don't know if Charlie or that other cowboy is his father."

"I didn't mean that, I meant Clyde. Your mother is descended from a long line of people who owned this ranch. Only one family's owned it since the country was settled. Might be Brandon's heritage."

She thought about the journal she was reading, a few pages each night. The life her great grandmother Elizabeth described was hard. Of course they hadn't started out with the amenities Caitlin took for granted like electricity and plumbing. Despite the hardships, Elizabeth had loved the ranch. She had grown up on another ranch and moved to the Triple M when she'd married. That was the life she'd known. Brandon had known army bases and urban living. This was just a phase he was going through. Didn't all boys want to grow up to be cowboys at some point in their lives?

Yet she had not been happy in the Bay Area once Timothy's perfidy had been uncovered. This last year especially had been hard and lonely. Here she was learning new skills, discovering things about herself, like the fact she could be alone and not necessarily lonely.

And she had the chance to be with her brother. That would end when they returned to California. He had to board at the school, since she couldn't afford to have him commute back and forth.

As they rode behind the others, Caitlin studied the teenagers. This was a great environment for them. No drugs. No gangs. No traffic accidents. The list of advantages grew as she considered life in California.

If, and it was a big *if,* Brandon really wanted to ranch, why not? She couldn't impose her goals on him. He soon would be old enough to decide for himself. The fact he'd asked Zack to get him information about the university showed he was thinking about college. Just not the way she'd expected.

It hurt a bit that he'd asked Zack. Did Brandon believe she wouldn't help him find out about the programs at the University of Wyoming?

She thought to herself that having Zack as a hero wasn't a bad thing for her brother. So what was the problem? Didn't she feel being a cowboy was worthy of Brandon?

It wasn't that, she suddenly realized. It was a fear of being left out.

THE NEXT MORNING ZACK HITCHED up the wagon to an old tractor and made preparations to get to the field to start baling. Pete would drive the tractor while two of the teenagers loaded the wagon with the bales already made. They'd rotate, one driving the baler, the other two loading. He was pushing to have everything finished by the end of the week.

"I can come help—maybe drive the baler myself," Caitlin said as she watched Zack work.

"You stay away from anything that will set back your wrist healing," he said.

"But you need help," she said.

He looked at her over the back of one of the horses. "We'll manage fine with the kids loading the bales on the wagon." He looked at the western sky. "Weather's supposed to be good for the next week. We should get everything undercover by then."

"I wish I could help," she said.

"Bring out lunch around noon," he said. "Can you find us?"

She nodded. If she could have changed any one thing this summer, it would have been to be more vigilant when riding Bonny Boy so she wouldn't have fallen. Now she just had to wait out her recovery.

"That so feels like woman's work."

"You are a woman."

The way he said it had her looking at him again. For a moment the others seemed to fade away and it was only Zack and her, separated by a tractor. These last few days had been hard. She couldn't help remember their night together, and wish for more. What had scared him away?

Or hadn't he enjoyed it as much as she had?

No, he had not faked anything. She yearned for the closeness she'd felt for a few hours. For the feeling of being joined to another.

But Zack was all business.

He sent the others ahead and stayed back to saddle her horse. He instructed that no one was to touch the machine until he got there.

"Normally I wouldn't have Bonny Boy standing so long with the saddle on, but there's no way you can cinch it up tight enough. You can mount using the block over there, right?"

"Yes. I'll bring lunch, not to worry."

"I will worry. What if he shies again and you fall? Or if you get lost and wander around all afternoon in the hot sun? Dammit, Caitlin, this is not the place for you."

"Give me a little credit. I'll manage. Women have for eons. And I can find you by listening for the baler. It makes such a racket I would hear it from forever. I just head for the noise."

He nodded, double checking the horse.

"Go on," she urged him. "I bet the horses outdistance the tractor anyway, and they got a head start."

"A man can only take so much temptation," he said, leaning down to kiss her.

Caitlin scarcely knew what was happening before the kiss was over. He'd ignored her for days, then kissed her?

"I was not tempting you," she said. She pulled his head down for a longer kiss.

"Just breathing tempts me," he said, gently putting her aside a moment later. "Charlie's coming over tonight for the barbecue. Do you know how to start up the grill?"

She shrugged. "I can figure it out. I'll take care of the homefront, you take care of those kids."

Zack nodded and started out.

Caitlin heard the noise the tractor made. It rivaled the baler. Didn't farm equipment have mufflers? It was a wonder they weren't all deaf.

He pulled the large flatbed behind him, soon moving out of sight.

She watched wistfully, wishing she were going with him, or that he had stayed. Or that she had a clue about what he thought of the two of them.

CAITLIN PREPARED LUNCH early to allow time to ride out to the hay fields. She managed to get on her horse and followed the tracks the tractor had left that morning. The noise of the machine made a perfect guide. It was hot, not a cloud in the sky. She hoped everyone was taking care not to get overheated or sunburned.

When Zack spotted her, he stopped the baler. The quiet alerted Pete, who glanced over and saw her as well. With a big grin, he cut the motor on the tractor. Brandon looked up. He was on the wagon, stacking bales of hay. Wayne was on the ground, lifting them to the wagon.

Zack waited for Susan to climb down from the baler before hopping down himself. He'd been watching for Caitlin. He was getting too involved with these kids, but couldn't seem to stop things from spinning out of control. The way they had the other night when he'd slept with Caitlin. It had been the first time in a long while he'd made love to a woman. And he couldn't forget a single minute. He wanted to be with her. She filled most of his waking thoughts, and a few sleeping ones as well.

He'd tried pulling back, treating her like a business professional, nothing more. But it didn't stop the longing. He watched her as she drew closer. She rode competently, and was trying to do her share even with an injured wrist. For a fleeting second, he wondered if they could make something work.

But her fall proved how dangerous life could be. There were no land mines or assault weapons on a ranch, but cantankerous cattle, heavy machinery and unpredictable horses could wreak almost as much havoc. He turned away. He couldn't bear the thought of Caitlin ending up bleeding to death on some rocky outcrop.

She rode over to the tractor and let Brandon help her dismount. Once Caitlin spread out the blanket she'd brought, Brandon and Wayne flopped flat out, pulled their hats over their faces and closed their eyes. Zack waited for Susan to sit, then sank down near the edge.

"Tough morning?" Caitlin asked Pete. She flicked a glance toward Zack. He didn't blame her for being peeved. But he wasn't going to lead her on. They had no future together.

"Don't think these young bucks knew how much work haying can be. But they're doing fine. Might quit a bit early today and go swimming."

"Where?" Caitlin's tone brightened.

Zack thought it was a great idea. The kids deserved a treat after working steadily all morning. The river would be perfect. And he'd love to see Caitlin in a swimsuit. "The river," he said.

"Can we swim in it? I thought it was for cattle to drink."

Pete chuckled. Zack looked away to smile. Sometimes she said the darnedest things. "Yeah, but we can still swim in it. They aren't that picky. The water's shallow enough to warm up so it's enjoyable. Doesn't move fast this time of year. So we'll put in another hour or so after lunch, then head for the stretch that cuts across your property."

"Sounds wonderful. You all must be hot as blazes working out in this sun. I didn't realize until I was riding how hot is it."

Zack nudged Brandon's foot with his own. "Caitlin, ask them if they're ready to stop?"

She quickly signed the question. Brandon sat up like a shot, shaking his head. *This is fun. Tiring, but look how much we've done.* He shook Wayne, who opened his eyes.

Want to quit?

No way, I want to eat and drink a gallon of water and then get going. I bet we fill that wagon today.

I don't want to, either, Susan added. *I'm just getting the hang of the baler.*

Zack watched as Caitlin took in their reactions. She shrugged and nodded. These kids weren't afraid of hard work. And their sense of accomplishment grew with each task they mastered. He wouldn't let them work too hard. Pete's idea of a swim was a good one. They'd have to quit early enough to get back to the house by the time Charlie arrived.

When Caitlin handed out the sandwiches, her fingers brushed his. Deliberately? Her eyes held his for a couple of seconds when he met her gaze. Dammit, a man could only take so much. He moved into the shade of the wagon and began to eat. Putting distance between them didn't lessen his desire, but it was prudent.

He glanced around at the contingency on the blanket. Cutting hay this year was different from previous years. It felt like a family operation more than a business. Last summer Clyde had hired a half dozen men to bring in the hay, some with little or no ranching experience. Since he'd primarily wanted labor to store the hay, experience hadn't been required.

This year, however, the process felt different. These kids were soaking up every new experience like a sponge. And even though Brandon and Wayne had known each other for years, Susan fit right in. The three of them worked well together and seemed to enjoy each other's company.

They reminded him of Billy and himself when they were kids. Different setting, but the same kind of camaraderie.

He looked away. He hadn't thought about Billy in a couple of days. No nightmares recently, either. Clyde said he'd get over the worst of it one day. He never wanted to forget his friend, but he wouldn't mind the crushing sense of loss to fade. Sometimes he wondered what Billy would have thought of the changes Zack made in his life. He wasn't going to be some hotshot businessman living in a penthouse near Central Park. Wasn't going to be a doctor or mechanic. Of all the things they'd discussed growing up, cowboying had never been one of them.

Now he was working a spread as a manager. Only because he knew a bit more than the new owners. What would Clyde think of this arrangement? He missed the old man. One day, he'd miss Billy like that, a poignant ache of what might have been if a land mine hadn't ended his life too soon.

As lunch progressed, Zack began to grow uneasy. He was fitting in too well. He had made a pact with himself, not to let emotions enter into day-to-day life. He didn't want to become attached.

But it was already too late. He cared what happened to Caitlin and her brother. He enjoyed teaching Susan how to run the baler and instructing Wayne in riding. This was a summer like no other. It would end soon. He'd do best to remember that.

Rising, he tossed his napkin in the bag Caitlin had brought for trash and started for the baler.

"Time to work already?" Pete asked, surprised.

"I'm getting back to work. Lots to do." Zack refused to look at anyone. He had let down his guard, but that didn't mean he would let himself get in too deep.

CHAPTER ELEVEN

TWICE CAITLIN CALLED Charlie Johnstone and postponed their planned barbecue. The first time was after everyone had voted to swim instead of entertain. Even Caitlin had had fun, though she'd only gone wading, not wanting to get the cast wet.

They were all caught up in getting the hay in before the weather turned. The next day was a repeat of the first. The cowboys headed out while Caitlin worked around the house until it was time to take lunch. Then she returned home, gathered bathing suits and towels and rode back out for fun at the river.

No one wanted to stop playing in the cool water early enough to have a barbecue with their neighbor.

Caitlin was having as much fun as the teenagers—and Pete. The only one who didn't join in was Zack. He'd reverted to the same taciturn man he'd been when they'd first arrived. He claimed there was too much to do to go swimming, but if Pete could spare some time, surely he could.

Caitlin also saw the light on in the barn late that night. Pete said Zack was keeping up with everything but pushing too hard. Something had to give soon or he'd burn out.

A few days later when Caitlin called Charlie a third time to cancel, he asked what was going on.

"We're trying to get our hay in before the next rain, which is forecast in another couple of days, so Zack is running flat out."

"Need some help?" he asked.

"I don't know. Zack's working with the kids and Pete. They're bringing in hay every day. It looks as if most of it has been baled, but loading it goes slowly."

"I have two men I could spare for a couple of days. Nothing around here is critical right now."

"I'd have to ask Zack. He's the manager of the ranch."

"Tell you what, I'll call him tonight, make the offer. I'll tell him I'm getting antsy being put off so much. I'm looking forward to seeing Tricia's kids again."

Once again Caitlin wondered if Charlie was Brandon's father. How would she ever find out?

"That'd be great. I'd love to count on Saturday, but according to Zack, ranching doesn't stop for the weekend. So I'm not too sure about that."

"I'll find out when I offer the men's help. How are you doing otherwise?"

"Fine."

"And that brother of yours? How are he and his friends doing?"

"Great. They love it. Who would have thought teen-agers would take to hard, hot work so much?"

They chatted for a little longer. When Caitlin hung up, she sat back in the office chair and gazed out the window. She knew her great grandmother Elizabeth had favored the view from the kitchen—of the trees near the spring. Caitlin liked this one, however. In the distance, the smudgy horizon of the mountains against the blue sky still gave her a thrill. The green grass was high, offering lush forage for the cattle.

She thought about Zack. They had managed to stay out of each other's way without causing comments from the others. However, tonight she had business to discuss. She'd received all the statements from the bank, and even with watching every dime and getting virtually free help from Wayne and Susan, they would run out of funds before long. Zack had to advise her on how to get an influx of cash.

CAITLIN WAITED UNTIL after dinner to seek Zack out. The boys were in the bunkhouse with Pete. Susan had asked for computer time to e-mail her parents. She was excited about all that was going on and wanted to share her experiences with them. They'd taken some digital photographs earlier and she wanted to send them as well so her parents would see her actually working on the ranch.

Caitlin went to the barn. From what Pete had said, she was pretty sure she'd find Zack there.

As she walked inside, she looked with satisfaction at the hay that rose high against the back wall. More than half had been brought in. When finished, the stacked bales would occupy a major portion of the barn. The stalls were on the side by the corral. In winter, Zack had said, the horses spent time outside, but he usually brought them in at night. The temperatures dropped in winter months and the barn afforded shelter.

He was sitting on a bench, working on something leather with a tool.

She knew he'd heard her. He kept working.

"Hi," she said.

He looked up. "Need something?"

She shrugged and straddled the bench, looking at the leather strap he was working on.

"I need to talk to you about money."

That caught his attention. With six million and change coming in, what did she need? She hadn't gone through Clyde's money yet. He'd seen what she'd bought.

"What about it?"

"There's not a lot of it."

"There has to be. This is a profitable ranch."

"Clyde didn't have any insurance. That last illness cost a bundle. We're cash poor, according to the lawyer. If we can hold off until the fall, and the price of beef remains where it is now, then we should be okay. But I need something between now and then—that is, if you and Pete want to get paid and we all want to eat."

It should not have surprised him, but it did. Clyde had never said a word.

"How much are we talking about?"

"I'm not sure. I've been going over his books for the last few years, trying to see what is seasonal so I know what to expect. Taxes are taken care of until later in the year. The monthly expenses seem to be fairly steady, but there are a couple of expenses I'm not sure about. The biggest infusion of cash each year is in the fall."

"When he sold the steers."

"So if we sell some now, will that tide us over?" she asked.

"Could. It'll mean less in the fall. You'd have to look into it."

"You have to. I don't know even what questions to ask."

He was silent for a moment.

"Charlie called earlier," Zack said at last. "He's sending some men over to help tomorrow. We should finish getting the hay in sooner than expected. Once we see how much we have, you could sell off what you don't anticipate needing." He could talk to Charlie about the best plan. The older man knew better than he the ins and outs of keeping a ranch afloat.

"Will that be enough?"

"Heck, Caitlin, I don't know. This is one reason I didn't want the job. I'm not experienced enough in ranching to have a ready answer."

"Then ask Charlie. You two talk the same language."

He nodded, resuming the work on the strap. He was making a new one for one of the saddles. This kind of work he liked.

After a minute he looked up. She hadn't left.

"Clyde had some investments that paid quarterly. The attorney is looking to see if he can sell some shares for ready cash. It would be better for a prospective buyer to think this is a profitable ranch."

"It is a profitable ranch. Something else?" he asked.

"No. I'll just visit for a little while. The boys are watching TV in the bunkhouse. Susan's on the computer. I don't know where Pete is."

"He likes to listen to country music. Works out fine with the TV muted for closed-captioning and his music blaring. Everyone's happy. Unless I want it quiet. This is the best place for that."

"Or the house. Come up there if you want quiet."

"I don't think that's a good idea."

"Why not?"

How did he tell her he wanted things to go back to the way they'd been before she'd arrived? She'd be hurt and he didn't want that.

"It just isn't," he said.

She didn't respond. A few minutes later she got up and left without saying another word.

Zack waited until he could hear her steps in the yard before looking up.

He could still smell the lingering trace of her scent, the strawberry shampoo she used, the sweetness that was Caitlin herself. Damn, he wished she'd never come to the ranch to disturb his peace. He'd had everything the way he wanted. Now he was yearning for things that could never be.

His world was crashing in on him. Those teenagers looked up to him as if he were the only cowboy on the planet. Even Pete deferred to him in most matters, and the man had decades more experience.

But it was Caitlin who bothered him. He wanted her. And the more he saw her, the more she came to mean to him. Then one day she'd leave. And he'd be alone again. Better to build walls now to hold off any future heartache.

Still, he wished he'd handled things better. He hadn't wanted to hurt her and he was afraid he had.

BY SATURDAY AFTERNOON all the bales had been stacked in the barn. The equipment had been parked in the large shed behind the barn and the haying was finished for the year. Brandon and his friends had acquitted themselves well. Wayne improved in his riding daily. Susan was getting as proficient as Brandon.

Charlie arrived around four. Pete had the grill going and Caitlin had the steaks thawed. She and Susan had made a huge chocolate cake for dessert and she'd asked Charlie to bring some ice cream from Fallworth. The men who had helped with the haying had also been invited to stay.

Caitlin watched the preparations, thinking about the parties she had put on for Timothy. They'd been lavish, with a caterer supplying the food and drinks, florists decorating their home. She'd often had a new gown to wear.

Now she was in jeans, boots and still had a cast on her arm. The food was home cooked, though plentiful. And somehow, it seemed as if everyone was having a great time. Never mind that there weren't couples—she and Susan were the only females in the group. But the respect the men had for each other shone through.

Caitlin enjoyed the stories they told. Each man was, of course, the hero of his own tall tale. Some were hilarious. Her hands were flying as she interpreted each one for the kids.

Once or twice, she caught sight of Zack on the perimeter. He had a beer and seemed to join in, but she could tell he had to make an effort. If he had his way, he'd be back in the barn working. Or riding off into the distance.

Charlie came to sit beside her after the meal was finished. The cake had been a big hit.

"Nice of you to include my men," he said, sitting on the bench she'd pushed away from the picnic table.

"They were super helpful. Did Zack talk to you?"

"About finances?"

She nodded, looking across the yard to where Zack was talking with a couple of Charlie's cowboys.

"Yes, he did. We discussed options. You'll have to make the final call. I think you can get some quick cash now and more in the early fall. It's a good ranch. Your family chose well when they picked this spot."

"I found a journal from an ancestor. Elizabeth Martin. She loved it here. I'm beginning to see the appeal. It's far from what I'm used to, but it's growing on me. I better get back to San Francisco before I turn into a cowgirl." She spoke the words lightly, but in the back of her mind the prospect of staying was beginning to take root.

"Would that be so bad?" Charlie asked.

"Brandon keeps talking like he wants to continue ranching. Do you think he'll change his mind when the novelty wears off?"

"Might. Might not. From what I see, he's not afraid of hard work. And if he's still talking about ranching after cutting hay, he's seen some of the worst of it. Of course, he might change his mind after a winter here. Nothing like San Francisco—or what your mother told me about that place. She liked it best of all the locations your father was stationed."

"Did you and she talk a lot?" Caitlin asked carefully. She kept her gaze on the far horizon, wondering more about her mother that summer than she ever had before.

"Your mother came to visit because your father wanted a divorce. She was anxious to talk about what she'd done wrong or what she might do to change his mind. By the end of the summer she had about accepted things. Then he called up and asked her to come back, said he'd changed his mind."

Caitlin swung her gaze back, staring at him in disbelief. "They separated?"

"You were too young to know what was going on. She was a wonderful woman, didn't deserve the heartache your father put her through. He thought he'd found another woman and wanted out of his marriage. Never did learn what happened, but when he called, your mother went back. I never heard from her again. She never wrote Clyde again after that Christmas."

Caitlin was shocked by the revelation. She searched her memory for any indication that it was true. What had happened? Who would know at this late date? Her father was dead. As far as she knew, her father had met Marjorie after her mother had died. The woman probably knew less about his background than Caitlin.

"Was she close to anyone while she was here?" Caitlin asked.

"Your uncle—he was crazy about your mother. Never had any kids of his own. He thought she was special."

"And the cowboy in the pictures?"

"They went dancing a few times." Charlie glanced at Brandon. "Your father was a fool to want to leave your mother. Guess he recognized it before it was too late."

"I don't think she was happy. Maybe she could never get beyond that betrayal."

Charlie looked at her. "I'm sorry to hear that. She was a special woman. You favor her. Guess Brandon favors your father."

"Not so much." Caitlin was dying to ask this man if he'd had an affair with her mother, but she couldn't. What if he had? It wasn't any of her business—unless he was the father of her brother. If he was, would he acknowledge Brandon? Want to establish any kind of family tie? Or would he repudiate him?

She would do nothing to hurt her brother.

Rising, she began to gather the plates and utensils from the table. "I better get this all cleared off before it's too dark to see." Was there another way to find out the truth? Someone had to know.

"Let me help," Charlie said, joining her. Caitlin smiled and nodded, her mind churning with ideas to find out the truth.

"I appreciate your sending the cowboys to help out. Zack said we wouldn't have gotten all the hay under cover this quickly without them. Another storm is coming in, I hear."

"This hot weather has to break sometime. Glad they could help. That's what neighbors are for."

She could think of several former neighbors who had not rallied to help when Timothy's crime had been uncovered, and at least one who had gone out of her way to hurt Caitlin.

"I think you made a wise decision in giving Zack the manager's position," Charlie said a little later when all the dishes had been cleared. He leaned against the counter, watching as Caitlin squirted liquid soap into the rising water in the sink.

"Here, let me do that," he said when he saw how awkwardly she was managing. "You fed us, least I can do."

"I don't mind."

He gently moved her aside and rolled up his sleeves. Caitlin grinned at the sight. Charlie was a special kind of man.

"Zack said he had all the kids take turns operating the machinery, under supervision, of course," Charlie commented. "They are having the time of their life."

"Brandon just turned sixteen, so he could have a driver's license, but living at the school he doesn't really need one. And auto insurance is so expensive." Caitlin stacked the rinsed dishes on the rack. She'd let them air dry and put them away later.

Charlie paused a moment in his dishwashing. "Just turned sixteen?" he repeated.

She nodded. "Early May. He was thrilled Zack let him drive in the field. Maybe if he learns to maneuver that heavy equipment, driving a car will seem like a piece of cake."

Charlie didn't say anything, but continued to wash.

Caitlin glanced at him, but his expression gave no indication of what he was thinking.

"Wondered where you had gone," Zack said a minute later, entering the kitchen through the back door. "Your men are heading back. That storm looks like it's heading this way faster than originally predicted."

"Almost finished here. Got a couple of things to check with you before I go."

"I can finish," Caitlin said. "Thank you for your help."

Charlie nodded, rinsing his hands and drying them. He replaced his hat and headed for the door. "Mighty fine meal, Caitlin. Thanks for inviting my crew as well."

She finished cleaning the kitchen and headed for the office, reining in her curiosity. She booted up the computer to check her e-mail, then hesitated a moment before reaching for the phone. She had to look up the number. It was still early evening in California.

"Hello?" The cool, cultured voice grated on Caitlin's nerves. She remembered the warmth of her mother's.

"Marjorie, it's Caitlin. How are you?"

"I'm in perfect health. Where are you?"

"I'm in Wyoming."

"Still at that ranch?"

"We're staying the summer. It's a nice break for Brandon."

"And you as well, I dare say. Why are you calling?"

No family feelings there, Caitlin thought. "I wanted to ask you something about my father."

"What?"

Caitlin heard the wariness in Marjorie's tone.

"I just learned he and my mother separated for a time before Brandon was born."

"That was before I met him, Caitlin."

"I know. But you were his wife. He must have confided some things to you about his past."

"What goes on between a man and his wife is private."

"Did he ever say anything about my mother being involved with another man?"

"You mean Brandon's father? If he'd had any suspicions before her death, don't you think he would have ended that marriage in an instant?"

"Sounds to me like he tried to end it that summer we spent in Wyoming."

"What is it you want, Caitlin?"

She took a risk. "There's a man here who might be Brandon's father. I want to know if it's possible."

The line hummed in the silence that followed. Caitlin was almost afraid Marjorie had hung up when she finally spoke again.

"Your father said something once and only once. Something about raising some damn cowboy's son. You know your father didn't have to keep supporting Brandon. He wasn't his child."

"He didn't know that for the first six years of his life. Hadn't he bonded with Brandon at all in that time? How could he have raised Brandon for six years and then want nothing to do with him?"

"Your father was a difficult man sometimes, as I'm sure you realize. I can't help you further. Find some cowboy who lives there."

"What?"

Caitlin thanked Marjorie and hung up. That had not been helpful.

She heard the distant rumble of thunder. It had grown dark while she'd been talking. Going to the window, she felt the stirring of fresh air. The storm would bring cooler temperatures. She was glad the hay was safely stored.

Brandon came into the office a few minutes later.

Nice barbecue, he signed. *I like Charlie and his cowboys.*

Me, too, Caitlin replied. *You and Wayne and Susan are working well together. I'm proud of you all.*

Good, I want to talk to you about an idea I have. Let's turn this ranch into a working one, and offer summer vacations to deaf teenagers. Like Wayne and Susan. They learn fast, they love horses. And there aren't a lot of places that offer vacations to deaf kids. Only a couple that offer ranch experience. Don't say no before you think about it.

Caitlin looked at him in surprise. Her immediate reaction was to say no. She knew next to nothing about running a ranch, period, much less taking on the responsibilities of deaf teenagers.

Brandon continued with ideas for camping out and fishing expeditions. He suggested having different sessions for early summer, midsummer and late summer, to coincide with school vacations. Caitlin knew how to sign. He bet Zack could learn quickly. And Pete.

She didn't want to squelch his enthusiasm right away, but the undertaking would be huge.

Let me think about it, she signed.

Truly, or are you just stalling? he asked.

She wouldn't admit to stalling. *I'll think about it. Talk to some people, like Paul Simmons. Maybe Zack.* It would sure impact his job. She had a mental picture of how he'd react. It had been hard enough talking him into having Wayne and Susan—and he'd already known Susan.

They are sure to go for it! Maybe we would end up hiring some deaf cowboys, too.

We couldn't get it going this summer, no matter what, she cautioned. *And by next summer, the place might sell.*

That's just it. Don't sell the ranch. I want to live here. I don't want to go back to California.

School is in California.

You could homeschool me. Maybe Susan could stay and be homeschooled with me.

Caitlin shook her head. *You are getting too far ahead of yourself. We are not ranchers.*

We come from ranchers. We could learn. Please, think about it. Please.

CAITLIN REMAINED IN THE office after Brandon left. She was stunned at his idea to stay and run a camp for deaf kids. What about school? She wasn't a teacher. And the prospect of all the money the ranch would bring when it sold was hard to give up. They'd never have to worry about anything.

Except what to do for the rest of their lives.

But to establish a camp for deaf kids based on a few

weeks of living here? Maybe she should offer to let him stay for a year, see how he liked being homeschooled and isolated from other kids his age, then discuss a camp.

She went up to her room to get ready for bed, arguments against his plan forming. Hoping to become sleepy, she took the journal and began reading. Because of the small writing, she took a long time to make her way through each page. Usually she managed two or three each night before falling asleep. Tonight the words began to blur before she finished the second page. Clicking off her light, she settled down to sleep.

Thunder woke her some time later. She sat up, startled. The curtains at the windows billowed out. She heard the sound of rain on the roof, smelled the scent in the breeze.

The sky lit up and thunder cracked again.

This time she got up to close the window so rain couldn't blow in. There was a light on in the barn. Were the kids still up?

Throwing on a robe, she slipped on her sandals and went to check on Susan. The girl was fast asleep. Thunder wouldn't bother her.

Caitlin went downstairs and peered out again. It was raining. The barn was lit up. Either someone was working late, or the light had been left on. Not a problem either way, she thought. But something prompted her to look again. Maybe she'd dash across the yard and check.

She found an old slicker that had belonged to Clyde.

Flinging it around her shoulders, she went outside. Her feet were muddy and wet within five steps. The wind whipped the coat open and the rain soaked the bottom of her nightgown.

By the time she reached the barn, she regretted her hasty decision.

It was warmer inside. The sweet smell of fresh hay filled the air. Glancing around, Caitlin didn't see anyone. She went to the tack room and peered in. No one.

About to reach for the light switch, she heard a noise. Instantly on the alert, she looked into the back part of the barn.

"Who's there?"

"Get down," Zack called.

She looked around, then walked toward him. He was kneeling behind two stacked bales of hay. Thunder rolled. He cringed and ducked. "Get the hell down before you get your head blown off," he yelled.

She ducked instinctively and looked around again. Was someone else in the barn?

"Zack?" she asked, inching closer.

He looked at her. Suddenly the tension left him and he uttered an expletive, rolling over to sit on the packed ground, leaning against the hay. He rubbed his eyes with the heels of his hands.

"Not again," he said in disgust.

Caitlin dropped the raincoat and went to sit on the edge of the bale, watching him warily.

"What happened?"

He closed his eyes. "Flashback. Thunder sounds

like gunfire and if I'm not ready for it, I think I'm back in Afghanistan with all the damn horrors that place held."

"Does it happen often?"

"Whenever it happens, it's too much. But no, not often. Less frequently since you've been here. The thunder is the trigger." He glanced at her. "What are you doing out in the rain?"

"I came to see why the light was on. Were you working?"

"Yeah. Couldn't sleep."

"Everyone else can sleep through this."

"Pete's probably awake, but he has better sense than to get up and go out in the rain," Zack said.

"As long as I don't get struck by lightning, I like it. It smells fresh and clean and the air is much cooler."

Another bright flash came from outside, followed a couple of seconds later by thunder.

She looked at him.

"I'm not going to freak on you," he said, rising to his feet. "I'm here and grounded. Besides, the storm's moving away."

"I called my stepmother tonight," she said.

"Why?"

"To see if she knew anything about my parents." Caitlin told Zack what she'd learned from Charlie.

"Leave it alone, Caitlin. If your mother had wanted the man to know, she would have sent word. Brandon believes your father is his. What does it hurt to leave it that way?"

"Most of the time I think that. But then I think, what

if he has a great father somewhere who just doesn't know? Brandon would benefit by having a father in his life, don't you think?"

"What if it's that cowboy and he turns out to be a drunken fool who doesn't earn enough to keep himself together?" Zack countered.

"Then it would be better not to know," she agreed. Rising, she picked up the slicker and flung it over her shoulders. Her robe was not warm enough now that the air had cooled.

"Brandon suggested we keep the ranch, operate it as a cattle ranch and offer deaf kids a chance to come and work," she said.

"You told him no, I hope," Zack said. He walked to the tack room and switched off the light. Heading for the door, he turned to look at Caitlin. "You did say no."

She followed more slowly. "I haven't yet. Of course we can't do it. Can we?"

"No."

"Why not?"

ZACK STARED AT HER. "Why not? Because it's a dumb idea, that's why not. Ranching is hard work, not some camp activity for kids."

"We're talking teenagers, not young kids. They could work. Wayne and Susan are working."

"I don't believe what I'm hearing. It's not a good idea."

"I want to hear concrete reasons why not."

"You don't have the proper staff or training. You don't have room. You don't have the skill. You don't have the insurance. You don't know anything about teenagers."

"I was one once," she said mildly.

Zack was getting annoyed. Was she truly considering the idea?

"You need people who can communicate with the kids."

"You manage."

"Only because we're not doing that much and I can write down most of what I have to say."

"You could learn ASL," she said.

Zack stared at her. Then he frowned. "If you have any other deaf kids come out, I'm leaving. I'm not going to take the risk."

"Zack, we'd make sure we're as safe as we can get. There are no guarantees in life. If we wanted to live risk free, we'd never get out of bed in the morning. And we wouldn't have pillows in case we might suffocate or blankets to get tangled in. We'd sleep on the floor, but wait, then we'd all have to live in the sun belt so we wouldn't freeze without covers."

"You're being ridiculous. I'm trying to have a rational conversation."

She reached out and caught his arm, her fingers pressing tightly.

"I am, too. Sort of. Think about the opportunity for kids who are often denied the same experiences as hearing kids. How many kids might learn to love it and want to work in ranching? How many lives could you touch by doing this?"

Zack couldn't believe the woman who had arrived

ready to sell in a second would pass up six million dollars to put in years of damn hard work to give some strangers a few weeks on a ranch.

"I'm not buying it, Caitlin. What about the money?"

"What money?"

"The money you stand to get once the ranch sells."

"What if it doesn't sell? Or not for ten years? Maybe this is an alternative."

One he couldn't condone. He flicked off the overhead light, plunging them into darkness. He wanted to get to his room and shut the door—on her and her wild ideas. Every time he began to get comfortable, Caitlin changed the rules. Why couldn't she understand he didn't want to be involved?

"You really want this?" he asked.

Caitlin's grip on his arm eased. He wished he could see her in the darkness. Dumb move turning off the light.

"Brandon wants it," she said. "I told him I'd look into it."

"Tell him it's not feasible."

She was quiet for a moment, as if gathering her thoughts. He was not going to be talked into staying if this was the new plan.

"There are nine years between Brandon and me, almost ten. We weren't close as kids because of that age difference. Now we have a chance to build something together. Something he feels strongly about. Maybe we can't make it work, maybe he'll change his mind in another month. But I think I owe it to both of us to look into it. My initial reaction was like yours—impossible.

But the more I've thought about it, maybe it might work. Not to make a lot of money. I'm hoping the ranch will come back into the black and be self-sustaining. Then we could offer kids a chance to come at little or no cost. We'd teach them teamwork and riding—skills they wouldn't have an opportunity to learn elsewhere. Who knows? As Brandon said, we may make some cowboys out of them. Haven't you ever wanted to be in on the ground floor of something really great?"

"And you think this would be?"

"We'd be doing a good thing for kids each summer. And the rest of the year the ranch would be just us."

"Just us," he repeated. *Us.* There was no *us.* He couldn't take that risk.

"I'd want you to stay, Zack. I really would."

He heard the words, but superimposed on them were the echoes of words he and Billy had shared growing up. *It'll be us against the world. We'll make it so big the neighborhood won't know what hit it. You and me are a team.*

It was to be Zack and Billy all the way. Only a land mine had ended that. Ended Zack's faith in the future.

"Think on it, Zack. Maybe tomorrow you and Pete and I can brainstorm questions we'd need addressed before continuing. It's only a thought right now. But the more I consider the possibilities, the more I see possibilities. We have the ranch anyway, which can provide us a living. If it works out, great, if not, at least we tried."

"In the six weeks you've been here you've gone from wanting to sell the place instantly to wanting to live here and work it?" he asked. She couldn't have changed her mind that fast. What was she up to?

"There's still a lot to decide. And the way everyone talks about the winters, maybe I will reserve a final decision for a few months. But I've been reading a journal from one of my ancestors, telling about the hardships they endured, and how much they loved this land. I've never had a place to call home for more than two or three years. We moved so much with my dad. Then Timothy and I moved three times in the five some years we were married. Brandon doesn't have a home either. This could be it for both of us."

"Or a disaster in the making. Think of all that could go wrong."

"Think of all that could go right. Maybe I want to take a chance. I did what I thought was right all my life. I ended up married to a crook and then got stiffed by a woman who should have been my friend. I'm young, healthy, and have had this ranch given to me. Maybe it was meant for a better purpose than just lining my pockets with a bunch of money."

"You still need money to run it, until you get it in the black again," Zack warned. Why was he fighting so hard against the idea? Could he at least give it some thought? If only to point out the pitfalls.

It was apprehension, plain and simple. He couldn't deal with kids coming to the ranch. His time here would be limited if they turned the place into some camp. He should have left weeks ago. Maybe now was the time to make the break. Pete could run things until she got more help. And Caitlin was smart. She could learn the important business aspects of the ranch quickly. Charlie would help her. Or one of her other neighbors.

"Please, Zack, just think on it overnight," she said.

He could think of other things he'd rather do overnight. Being alone with her for starters.

"I'll think about it." Time enough in the morning to decide when to leave.

"Want to come in for some hot chocolate?" she invited. "I'm too cold to go back to bed right away."

A prudent man would say no. But if he were leaving soon, what could a cup of hot chocolate hurt?

"Sure."

Caitlin put the slicker over her head and ran for the house. Zack ran beside her, his hat keeping the worst of the rain off his face. The rest of him would dry.

Once in the kitchen, Caitlin switched on the light over the stove. It provided plenty of illumination for making hot chocolate, yet gave the room a cozy warmth with shadows that fit the rainy night.

Zack put his hat on one of the chairs.

"Need any help?" he asked.

"No. I have some of that cake left. Want a piece?"

"Yes. That was a hit at dinner."

"Everyone likes chocolate cake, I guess," she said. "You could get that while I fix the drinks."

In a short time they sat at the table eating cake and drinking the hot beverage. Zack didn't talk about her plan for the ranch. He didn't want to talk much at all. The quiet suited him.

She seemed equally content to be silent.

A few moments later, he began to wonder what she was thinking about. Did she dwell in the past, or was she looking toward some nebulous future? Sometimes just being in the present was enough. It was what he did best these days.

Caitlin licked the last of the frosting from her fork and pointed it at him. "Did you ever think how long sweets have been part of our lives?"

"Never thought about it."

"Me either, until right now. In the journal I'm reading, they made popcorn balls, peanut brittle, candy apples, had taffy pulls and made pies and cakes. I've never been to a taffy pull."

Zack frowned. "Did you ever want to go to one?"

"Actually, I don't think I've ever heard of a real one. I've read about them in books. Might be fun. I know Brandon likes caramel apples. I bet he'd like candy ones as well. Anyway, we could do things like that if we had a camp—show what a ranch was like a hundred years ago."

He leaned back in his chair and looked at her. With the soft kitchen lighting, she seemed even younger than she was. Her robe covered her nightgown completely. Was it sheer and lacy or plain cotton? He'd much rather talk about that than apples. He'd like to take the robe off and see that satiny skin again. Taste her, touch her, lose himself in her sweetness and heat.

He finished his chocolate. He knew he had to get going. It was after midnight and he was starting to have thoughts about his boss that had no place in his life. He'd made his choice, now he had to stick to it.

"Zack, please consider it. Whatever we decide, I want you to be a part of the ranch."

"That may not be possible," he said, startled she'd picked up on his thoughts.

"If you could do anything you wanted, what would that be?" she asked.

"Bring Billy back," he said without hesitation.

"Oh, if you could change the course of your life, then I wouldn't have my mother die. Wouldn't have married Timothy. Would have finished college. But I'm talking about right now. What would you do?"

"Kiss you."

CHAPTER TWELVE

CAITLIN FELT HEAT FLOOD through her. She stared at him. "We tried that, and you ignored me for days."

"So I'm stupid. I'm just talking about a kiss."

She swallowed. Her mind went blank. She wouldn't mind being kissed by him again. She'd loved it before. But would he then grow all distant and ignore her again? She enjoyed their time together; she didn't like being ignored.

He rose and reached for his hat. "Forget it, Caitlin. Thanks for the chocolate."

It was decision time. Yes or no?

She surged to her feet and crossed the short distance.

"Okay," she said, looking up at him.

He stared at her for a long moment, then dropped the hat on the floor to reach for her, drawing her into his arms, snug against his chest. He was so slow she grew impatient but at last he lowered his head until his lips touched hers.

For a moment she thought that light touch was going to be all. Then he deepened the kiss. It was magical. She closed her eyes and kissed him back.

Forgotten was Timothy's betrayal, the problems with finances and raising a teenager. Tonight was for her alone. A passionate kiss that reaffirmed her femininity. An embrace that set her body on fire and had her yearning for more.

Zack was not staying. She knew that. But she wasn't asking for forever. She just wanted now. Tonight.

He moved his hands over her back, molding her soft body against his harder one. She wanted more than a kiss, but couldn't give in to her desire with Susan asleep upstairs. Or the boys in the bunkhouse nearby. What if someone awoke and needed her?

Zack slowly ended the kiss, moving to trail his lips across her jaw, down her throat to that soft pulse point. Her good hand touched his hair, his cheek, his neck. She wished she had both hands available to learn every inch of him, to feel what her eyes could see.

He rested his forehead on hers and gazed into her eyes. "I have to go."

She reached up to kiss him again. The soft token flared into another passionate embrace. Endless moments ticked by. Caitlin wished she could shed her clothes and his and feel his skin next to hers. Spend the night together in pleasure and delight.

He ended the kiss, stooped to reach for his hat and turned to leave, all in one fluid motion.

Caitlin was half tempted to step out into the backyard and let the rain cool her heated skin. She felt less like sleeping now than she had when she'd come in for hot chocolate.

THE NEXT MORNING DAWNED CLEAR. The air was cooler but promised to heat up by midday. Caitlin heard the horses whinnying in the corral and Pete calling out something. She dressed quickly and hurried to the kitchen to get breakfast going.

She barely had the bacon cooked and the pancake batter made before they started trooping in. Susan came in first. A minute later Pete came, heading right for the large coffeepot.

"Nice day," he said. "Might get us some swimming in later if we do all the chores first."

Caitlin nodded, signing his comment to Susan. Her face lit up.

Wayne and Brandon clumped in. Caitlin looked beyond them, expecting to see Zack, but he wasn't there.

"Zack not eating?" she asked Pete.

"Haven't seen him today. Truck's missing."

Caitlin felt her breath catch. She was not going to panic. He'd left once before without telling anyone. He probably had run into town to pick something up for— for what? All the machinery was working as far as she knew.

"Tell these kids we want to do saddle checks before getting the horses today," Pete said. "Make sure that leather is getting good care. A saddle is a cowboy's best friend. A good one, that is."

Caitlin conveyed the information. Then Brandon asked her about the camp. Wayne and Susan immediately wanted to know what he was talking about, and before long all three were making suggestions to Caitlin on how to run it and how they could help.

I bet my father would have some good ideas, too, Susan signed. *He'd volunteer to help. I've often heard him say he'd do that at the school if it were closer. Maybe some of the teachers from the school would want to come for a vacation as well.*

Caitlin nodded. That was a thought. Maybe it wouldn't be as hard to staff as she'd thought. Still, there was so much to think about.

Signing as she spoke, she looked at Pete. "I asked Zack to see if you and he could talk with me this morning about the idea Brandon has for a summer camp for deaf teens. Letting them actually work on the ranch. You and Zack would have a better idea of what they could do—based on these kids." She smiled at the three teens.

Where *was* Zack? Caitlin wondered. Why hadn't he told anyone where he was going?

Pete asked Caitlin to sign instructions to the kids on how to clean their saddles using saddle soap. Then he told them to work on all the saddles in the tack room and he'd check on them when he finished talking with Caitlin.

Pete poured another cup of coffee when the teenagers trooped out.

"Want to talk about that camp idea now?" he asked.

"Yes, but let's move to the office," Caitlin suggest. "No dirty dishes there."

Soon they sat facing each other. Caitlin outlined Brandon's idea, adding her own growing conviction it could work. They could try it for a year and see what happened.

"I thought this place was up for sale," Pete said.

"It is, but no one has expressed any interest. The real-estate agent said it could take years to sell. This would be something we could do immediately. I'm growing to love it here. This house, old as it is, beats a tiny apartment with a washing machine down the block. I don't know if I can homeschool Brandon, but it's something else I can look into. And if so, all the better. He'll have time to see if he really loves ranching, or if it's a passing fad."

"Can't have kids run your ranch," Pete said. "They don't know enough. By the time they learn, they'll leave."

"I would have regular cowboys as well. But I'd really want the campers to have tasks to do, so they *are* learning, not just playing."

It was late morning by the time they finished discussing all the pros and cons they could think of. Caitlin was going to get in touch with other camps for the deaf and see what aspects she hadn't thought about. Then she wanted to talk to Wayne's parents and Susan's, to get their initial reaction. There was a lot to do before finally deciding to give it a try, but at least she was exploring the possibility.

She wished Zack had been part of the discussion. Even knowing he didn't approve, he would have solid insight into the plan. Where was he?

The sound of a truck in the driveway came through the open window.

Caitlin went to look out. Disappointment flooded her when she saw it wasn't Zack's. "Somebody's stopping here. I don't know who. I wasn't expecting anyone."

She went to the front door and out on the porch. A cowboy got out of his truck.

"Zack Carson around?"

"Not at the moment," she said.

"Someone sent him a package. I said I'd bring it by and brought the mail, too," the cowboy said, going around to open the passenger door and taking out a large rectangular box with envelopes and newspapers balanced on top. "Told Margaret at the post office I was coming this way. She said to save you a trip."

Caitlin took the box and thanked the man.

Pete ambled down and touched the edge of his hat to Caitlin. "Guess it's back to work for us. I'll be thinking about that idea of Brandon's."

Who had sent Zack a package? The return address was New York. Was it something from his grandmother?

By late afternoon, Caitlin was pleased with the accomplishments of the day. Dinner was baking. She'd made a pineapple upside-down cake for dessert and had scheduled an appointment with the doctor to remove her cast next week. And she had written a draft proposal for operating the ranch as a deaf camp during the summer months. Paul Simmons had been very helpful with insurance information and enthusiastic about the idea. He'd said he'd contact some of the people he knew at the school Susan attended to get more information.

Caitlin had also checked with the lawyer. He had

been cautious about the undertaking, but agreed to look into it. He'd even made a sensible suggestion that she wanted to take up with Zack when she saw him.

When she'd tested the waters with Charlie Johnstone, the man had quickly offered any help she needed. He'd suggested she consider getting some chickens for eggs and maybe a hog or two to slaughter each fall for pork. There was beef aplenty.

Mid afternoon she heard Zack's truck. She went out to the porch, but he entered the bunkhouse without a glance her way. Later she heard him leave on horseback.

She could hardly contain her enthusiasm when the others arrived from the range later in the afternoon. She took a glass of tea and sat out on the porch while they brushed the horses and fed them. Sipping from the frosted glass, she watched Zack. He had an air of authority the others lacked. Wayne and Brandon imitated him in their mannerisms. She smiled. They'd do well to emulate him.

Finally the men headed for the bunkhouse to clean up and Susan walked briskly toward the house. She smiled when she saw Caitlin and began telling her about their afternoon.

When Susan went inside to wash up, Caitlin wanted to run across to the bunkhouse and see Zack. Ask him where he'd been. Tell him about the various conversations she'd had during the day about a camp. But she had dinner preparations to finish. She'd catch him later.

It was almost eight by the time she finished cleaning the kitchen. She'd be glad to get rid of the cast to speed washing-up time.

When she went outside, she wasn't surprised to see the three teenagers near the corral. It was as if they couldn't bear to be far from the horses no matter what. They looked as if they were swinging ropes, trying to lasso a barrel.

Pete sat in the shade of the barn watching them. She didn't see Zack.

"What are they doing?" she asked when she got closer.

"Zack wants them to learn roping. They've been practicing." He laughed when Susan threw the rope and let go. The entire thing sailed over the barrel, missing it completely. The others laughed at her. She frowned and went to retrieve the rope.

"They're no good, but if they practice, they'll get it," he said.

"Where's Zack?"

"In the bunkhouse, I believe."

She turned and headed for the building.

"Zack?" She no longer knocked, but entered the common room without fanfare.

The package that had arrived earlier was sitting on the table against the wall—still unopened. She'd given it to him at dinner, but he'd merely glanced at the return address and tucked it beneath his chair.

"Zack?" she called louder.

She heard footsteps coming from the back and quickly moved away from the box.

He entered from the hall.

"I was hoping to talk to you," she said.

"About?"

Honestly, the man drove her crazy. Last night he'd kissed her as if she were the last woman on earth. Today he looked at her as if she were a stranger.

"About the ranch, what else?"

She sat on the leather sofa and Zack went to one of the large chairs flanking it. "What about the ranch?" he said, stretching his legs out in front of him.

She glanced at the box. "Is it your birthday?"

"No."

So much for satisfying her curiosity. "I spoke with a lot of people today about our idea of a camp. And the local school board about homeschooling. It really might be possible." She knew it was possible, but after all the setbacks of recent years, she was almost afraid to believe it would work. "I still have lots more to do before giving a definite yes or no. We'd need to fix up this bunkhouse to be able to house more men to work the ranch. And then we'd have to build another building or two to house the students and counselors. Or maybe we only offer camp for boys initially. See how it works. The thing is, I think it could. With a lot of work on my part. Some on Brandon's. Most of it depends on you."

"I don't—"

"Wait and hear me out, please." She leaned forward in her determination to make him share her vision.

"I'll need the money the ranch earns. We would charge the teens a nominal fee. So I'd need money for more horses, for food, transportation to and from town— There are a list of things I came up with and I'm sure as we go, even more will be identified. I've studied the records of the last five years—all my uncle had on his computer. This is normally a very profitable ranch. With proper care, it can be again."

"You may want to hire a more knowledgeable manager," he said.

"I may want to offer you a partnership of sorts."

"What?"

"That's what the lawyer suggested, that I offer you a portion of the ranch for you to stay. How about two hundred acres with another two hundred every five years until you have fifteen hundred acres total? And a percentage of any profit we show. You could start your own herd, run the cattle with mine, and get any proceeds from that. We'd be partners. What do you think?"

ZACK STARED AT HER, dumbfounded. She was willing to offer a piece of the land that had been in her family for generations, just for him to stay and run the ranch while she tried some dumb-fool idea of a camp for deaf kids?

"You could get an expert manager for a small proceeds of the profits," he said. "You don't have to give up your land."

"I was planning to sell it until today. I think Brandon and I can make a nice living on four thousand acres. And I want you as manager."

"Why?"

"Because I don't want you to leave."

He looked at the pretty brunette watching him so earnestly. He wanted to pull her into his arms and kiss her like crazy. Then maybe take her back to his bedroom and make love to her until dawn.

But he couldn't stay and become partners. The thought made him feel sick.

"Can't do it," he said.

"Why?" She looked deflated. Slowly she leaned back on the sofa, the bright sparkle of excitement extinguished.

"We've been through this before, Caitlin. I'm not one for putting down roots, for becoming involved with others. There's a lot of country to see."

"Baloney. You're just blowing smoke. I think you're feeling guilty."

"About what?" That caught his attention. Of course he was guilty. He had not been able to save his friend. What kind of man moved on and became a partner in a ranch when the partner he was supposed to have had lay in a grave in Brooklyn?

"I know what it's like. Truly, I do, because of Timothy. I was so angry at him for being a crook. Then I thought everyone was judging me like I was Timothy. I felt guilty for just being in San Francisco, for trying to make a living for myself. I almost felt as if I should somehow make restitution for what he did. You feel guilty because Billy died and you didn't."

"He died because I couldn't save him."

"You're not God."

"I'm a trained medic. I should have been able to save all of them!" He almost shouted the words. The anguish wouldn't let up.

"All of them?" she said softly.

He closed his eyes, rubbing the heels of his hands against them. Wishing he could erase the images that would never fade.

"That's right—the little girls who will never grow up. The old woman who died with such a stunned expression on her face. The other men in my platoon that I couldn't save. They're all gone. Why was I left?"

"Maybe to make something special of your life as a tribute to them," she suggested.

He dropped his hands and looked at her.

"That's what I feel when I think of this project for Brandon. Timothy stole money from a lot of people— most of whom couldn't afford to lose that money. I can't pay them back. But I can pass on some kindness, something no one else will offer these kids. Maybe that's what I'm supposed to do."

"I'm not a rancher."

"You look like one to me. You weren't a medic before you were trained. You know, even doctors lose patients—in fancy hospitals with a billion dollar's worth of equipment around them. Could such a setting have saved Billy?"

Slowly Zack shook his head. "Nothing on earth could have saved my friend."

"Then why do you think you should have?"

"It was my job."

"Your job was to do your best to patch up wounded soldiers and ship them back to medical facilities. You did your best. I can't imagine you doing anything but. Just as you do on this ranch. I don't want you to leave. Please, Zack, stay and help me and Brandon make this work."

Pete came in, then stopped in the doorway and stared at them. "Is this a private conversation?" he asked.

"Maybe you can convince Zack to stay. I've offered him a partnership. I want him to run the ranch while Brandon and I focus on a camp. He says he can't."

"Now why in the world would you even think that, son?" Pete asked, stomping over to sit in the chair opposite Zack. "This is a good setup. I'm thankful I found work here. Not a lot of places take an old cowboy."

Caitlin smiled. "I don't think of you as old, Pete."

"Nice words, missy." He looked at Zack. "I've been working ranches since I was sixteen. Never heard of a cowboy being offered a partnership before."

"It's a bribe so I'll stay," Zack said, getting up and pacing toward the package. He glared at it and turned to walk back.

"Could be," Caitlin admitted. "But I want you to stay. Whatever it takes."

"I'll screw up," he said.

She shrugged. "You still know more than I do. We can probably rebound from any problems."

"Sounds like a plan to me," Pete said.

Zack paced back toward the wall, turned and walked to the center of the room again. He stopped in front of Caitlin.

"And if there are thunderstorms, what then?"

"We'll deal with it."

"What's with thunderstorms?" Pete asked.

Zack stared at her, suddenly longing to agree. To

know where he'd be in another year or two or ten. To know he was accepted just as he was, failures and all. Wayne and Susan would be leaving soon, but Brandon and Caitlin would stay. And Pete. Could he stay here and keep apart emotionally? Not risk making friends to lose them if the camp didn't work out, or if Caitlin got an offer for the ranch one day?

The camp could fail, the ranch sell, and Caitlin and her brother would take off for California in a New York minute. Better if he left now. Cut the ties before they bound too tightly. Leave before he was left.

"No." He turned, went down the hall to his room and closed the door.

CAITLIN STARED AFTER HIM in dismay. She'd offered the most she had, and he'd turned her down. She couldn't believe it. Had he not understood?

Or was it she who didn't understand? He'd told her over and over that he wasn't comfortable becoming involved. Just because they'd shared a few kisses, made love, just because she had begun to think of them as a couple didn't mean he did.

She'd guessed wrong about Timothy. Looked as if she'd guessed wrong again. This time the hurt went even deeper. How could she be so misguided about men?

"Well, I tried," she said, wishing for more than she was going to get.

She bid Pete good-night and went back to the house.

Her excitement about the camp faded with Zack's unswerving refusal to participate. She was walking a fine line and knew she needed a lot of luck to make the project work. She and Brandon could end up hating Wyoming by the end of the winter. Or they could plant deep roots like Clyde and those who had gone before, and never want to leave.

She went inside feeling drained. Walking up to her room, she grabbed the journal, then lay on her bed to read. But the words blurred and all she could hear was Zack's refusal.

CAITLIN HAD A PILE of scrambled eggs on the platter with sausage links surrounding the mound and hot toast ready for buttering when Wayne and Brandon showed up the next morning. Susan had been up for a while, helping her with breakfast.

Tomorrow, you two can come in and help fix breakfast, Caitlin signed. *I'm not the cook.*

You do it so well, Brandon returned, grinning. He ducked when she threw a pot holder at him.

Pete came to the door. "Caitlin, I need to see you a minute."

"Sure, what's up?" she asked, going to the back door and stepping outside.

The sun was already climbing. It would be another hot day.

"Zack's not around. Truck's missing. I checked his room. He packed up everything. I think he's gone for good."

CHAPTER THIRTEEN

IT TOOK A MOMENT for the statement to sink in. "As in *gone?*" she asked, stunned. Had he really carried through and taken off for parts unknown?

"Lock, stock and barrel," Pete said.

"I'll kill him. Cut him up and feed him to the fish in the river. How dare he do this to me just because I offered him a partnership." Anger flared. She'd been on an emotional roller coaster with the man, but this was the last straw. She was furious.

"Damnedest thing I ever heard of," Pete said.

"He claims he has too much baggage, but so do I. So does everyone. We could have made it work. I thought the land would swing the deal. What an idiot."

"Zack?"

"Me, to think a few kisses meant a relationship. Why can't I learn? Men are the most fathomless creatures in the world. I can't believe I fell for another one who had no intention of sticking around. I should become a nun!" She turned and stomped inside. She was angry. But she was also incredibly hurt. She had wanted Zack to stay. Not only because she needed him to run the ranch, but because she'd truly believed they had something special between them.

She had fallen in love with the man, irritating attitude and all.

He'd left. Just as if she meant nothing.

Damn, she probably didn't.

Three pairs of eyes looked at her. Brandon asked what was wrong. So much for trying to hide her feelings. Before she could control herself, she burst into tears. Her brother jumped up and came to wrap her in his arms. A moment later she felt Susan hug her, then Wayne. They didn't know what was wrong, but they were there for her.

Which Zack should have been.

Finally she drew a shaky breath and nodded against her brother's shoulder. He slowly released her. All three watched with concern.

Zack's gone, she signed. She still couldn't believe it. Caitlin had thought things were finally going right for a change. There'd been special kisses. Special nights. And she liked working together to keep the ranch afloat while she and Brandon learned what was needed.

She'd offered Zack a part of all she had. And he'd not only said no, he'd left.

Brandon asked why. Wayne and Susan asked a dozen questions. Caitlin had no answers. She would never tell them Zack hadn't wanted them there in the first place. They thought highly of the man. She would not destroy that image.

Time to eat—Pete will be in charge for now, she signed. The eggs were cool, so she dumped them back in the pan for a quick reheating. The sausages went into the oven. Silence reigned behind her. She blinked back tears. Time for crying was later, when she was alone. Now she had to rally for the kids and find some way to get beyond the fear that threatened to choke her. How could she manage without him?

When breakfast was finished, Pete sent the kids out to get the horses ready for the day.

"You okay?" he asked Caitlin when they were alone.

"I will be," she said, gathering the plates.

"That man has rocks in his head," Pete muttered on his way out.

"I agree." She bit her lip to stem the flow of more tears. What did it take to get through to her that men could not be trusted? Why not just rip out her heart and stomp on it and have done with it.

At least she hadn't married the guy.

Tears threatened again. She had refused to dream about such a thing, but secretly, deep inside, she had thought they might build a life together. It was that possibility that had got her past the notion that she had to live in California. Even beyond the idea that six million dollars would buy happiness. People brought happiness, not money.

But apparently not all people.

She washed the dishes quickly and then headed for the office. She would not be stopped just because Zack had cut and run. She would explore the camp idea, find a dozen cowboys to work the ranch, and spend her life doing exactly what she wanted!

First thing, she called Charlie.

"I need a favor," she began. "If you can spare a man, can I borrow a cowboy for a few weeks, until I can find one to hire?"

"What brought that on?" Charlie asked.

"Zack left."

"What? When?"

"He was gone this morning." She would not break down again. But the ache in her chest wouldn't go away.

"Why?"

"Because I offered him a partnership," she said carefully.

"What am I missing?" Charlie asked.

"He never wanted to stay. He told me that a hundred times. I just never took him seriously."

"I'll come over and you can tell me the whole story," he said.

"Fine, but think about lending me a cowboy."

It was after eleven when Caitlin heard the truck in the drive. She got up from the desk. Her enthusiasm for the camp had waned as the morning progressed. It wasn't looking as easy as it had yesterday. There were so many things to consider. And her heart just wasn't in it.

She went out onto the porch and stopped dead. It was Zack's truck. He halted near the stairs and just sat there, looking at her through the windshield. She debated going back inside the house, but her feet seemed rooted to the porch.

Impasse. Neither moved. Time ticked by. Caitlin grew angrier the longer she stared at him. Finally she'd had enough and turned, entered the house and slammed the door behind her.

A moment later she heard him on the porch, crossing to open the door.

"What do you want?" she asked when he came in.

"To apologize. I should have told you I was leaving."

"I believe you did tell me many times," she said. Every fiber of her being wanted to launch herself into his arms, hold him so tightly he'd never leave again. But she didn't move a muscle.

"I talked about it but didn't know how serious I was after that first day. Last night was just too much. Billy's dead. I don't deserve to be part owner of a ranch."

"Billy has nothing to do with us. Why did you return?"

"Charlie told me something that made me come back."

"Good grief, you came here because a neighbor told you to?"

"No. Come in here and sit a minute." He walked into the living room and sat on the sofa. She watched warily for a moment, then went to perch on the edge of a chair.

"I'm pretty sure, and Charlie's pretty sure, he's Brandon's father. He fell in love with your mother, and she fell in love with him. Yet, apparently no one around here knew about Brandon until you showed up. If your mother ever told Clyde, he never said anything to Charlie. I never heard your uncle mention Brandon either, though he did talk about you once in a while.

Charlie said they fell in love that summer. They became lovers, then your father called and wanted her back. She felt the ties she had with Robert Jackson were important—more important than breaking up her family and putting her little girl through such turmoil. She left and never returned."

"Charlie told you this when?" she asked. Had her mother really sacrificed her own happiness for her daughter's sake?

"When he found me in Fallworth. I didn't know where to go. I didn't want to stay here, but there's no other place I want to be."

Caitlin frowned. "That makes no sense."

"I stopped for gas, filled up the truck and then sat there wondering where I was heading. Charlie found me there and told me I was a damn fool. He had let the woman he loved go without a fight and still misses her to this day. If he's Brandon's father, then he's missed knowing his son all these years. Do you know what he said—I would never forget you. I would never get over you. I would regret leaving to my dying day."

Caitlin stared at him.

"So he told me I was an idiot," Zack said. "If he could do one thing differently in his life, it would be to go after your mother."

"I can't take your coming on to me, then growing cold, then coming back," she said. "I've done a really stupid thing and fallen for you. You tear my heart up each time you turn from me." Caitlin couldn't believe she was listening to him. When would he begin ignoring her again?

"Then it's about equal. I love you, Caitlin. God, I can't even tell you how much. And it scares the hell out of me. What if something happens to you like it did to Billy? I don't think I could live through something like that again. I think of you when I'm working, when I'm trying to sleep, when you're in the room with me, and when we're apart. You have changed my life. And I'm scared shitless."

Caitlin tried to understand what he was saying. "I'm not in a war zone," she said slowly.

"Ranching is dangerous. Look what happened earlier this summer. What if you'd hit your head on a jagged rock and been killed?"

"Uncle Clyde was in his nineties when he died. If he'd been a stockbroker, would he have lived that long?" she asked.

He stared at her.

She began to smile, her heart thumping so hard she could hardly hear over the blood rushing in her veins.

"Tell me again," she said.

"I love you." He spoke slowly, deliberately. "I'm a mess, have flashbacks, am wary of getting too close to anyone, haven't even seen my own grandmother in longer than I want to think about. But as God is my witness, I love you. I always will."

Caitlin did launch herself off the chair then and straight into Zack's arms. "I love you, too, cowboy. Let's live dangerously and take a chance together."

"Marriage, babies and the whole nine yards?" he asked.

"Yes. You can teach me everything you know about

ranching, and we can pass on the land to our kids when we're old and gray."

His mouth covered hers in an explosive kiss. Hungry for her, he deepened the kiss until Caitlin's head spun.

"Brandon may have something to say about that," Zack said some time later when they lay half sprawled across the sofa.

"He'll want you to learn sign so you two can talk more. Do you think Charlie really is his father?"

"Charlie thinks so. We could ask for DNA testing. The question is, how do you think Brandon will react?"

"I think he'll be okay—eventually. It will be a shock, though. Maybe that's the reason he took to ranching so fast—like father like son." A thought struck her. "Oh no, what are we going to tell them all? They think you left."

"I did. We'll tell the truth. I was a fool to leave, but fortunately came to my senses before I got too far." He nuzzled her jaw. "Maybe my grandmother just might come out for the wedding."

"Was she the one who sent the package?" she asked.

He shook his head. Slowly he sat up, pulling her with him. "The box was from Billy's mother. I haven't opened it."

"Why not?"

"What could she send me?"

"Get it and find out."

He went out to the truck and returned in a moment with the box in hand.

After sitting back beside Caitlin, he used his pocketknife to slit the tape and then took the top from the box, revealing a photo album.

There was a letter. Zack opened it and slanted it so Caitlin could read along.

Dear Zack,

When you get this, I'll be gone. Cancer. Billy always said those cigarettes would get me. I'm sorry I didn't get to see you again, Zack. You and Billy were both special boys to me. You were my second son. I never got to thank you for being with Billy in Afghanistan. It meant a lot to me to know he didn't die alone. I know it was hard on you, son, it was hard on us all. Impossible to believe some days. You may never be able to come back, but we in the neighborhood remember you, Zack. And miss you.

But think back to the happy days you two spent. Remember playing in the spray from the fire hydrants? How about stick hockey? You two were always running in the middle of the street. It was a miracle you didn't get hit by some truck.

I'm sending you my album. No one else will want it when I'm gone. I've spent the last few weeks going over it, writing down what I remember by the pictures. See what memories it brings back for you, Zack. Happy ones, I hope.

I loved you as if you were my own.
Ellie

"Oh, Zack, I'm so sorry," Caitlin said gently.

"I should have gone back," he said, staring at the letter.

"She understood," Caitlin said, squeezing his hand. "It's a wonderful letter." He didn't need another layer of guilt. It sounded as if Ellie understood why he couldn't go home. She opened the album and gazed at a picture of two little boys. One she clearly recognized as Zack. The other had to be Billy.

Zack would come to terms with his past. And now, because of his return, together they had the future.

EPILOGUE

Four years later

CAITLIN CHECKED ON the roast once more. It was about done. As soon as Zack finished his shower, she'd pop the biscuits in the oven and dinner would be ready.

"Dada," little Billy chanted, sitting at his small table in the corner of the kitchen. He was beating on it with a wooden spoon.

"Daddy will be here soon," she told him. Their son had rushed to greet Zack as soon as he had heard his daddy's footsteps on the porch. Now he had to be content to wait. He was used to the routine.

A few minutes later the shower went off. She put in the biscuits to bake. Lifting her son, she placed him in his high chair and scooted it up to the table, which had been set with the fine china and silverware that had belonged to her grandmother. Candles, safely out of reach of toddler hands, sat near the center. Fresh flowers she'd picked up in Wolf Crossing were the centerpiece.

She heard her husband's step and she turned, watching as he entered the kitchen. After more than three years of marriage, she still felt that special thrill every time she saw him.

Zack kissed her. "Dinner smells delicious."

"Thanks. It'll be ready in a sec. Can you get the iced tea?"

He noticed the table.

"Something special?"

"Our last family dinner for a while. Charlie went down to Laramie to pick up Brandon at the university. They'll be here for dinner tomorrow night. Then Brandon will move into the bunkhouse on Sunday. The campers arrive then and we'll be eating with the entire group again."

Her brother had been shocked when he'd learned the truth about his parentage. But he and Charlie had forged a strong bond. When not at the university, Brandon now split his time between the Triple M and his father's ranch.

"Flowers are nice," Zack commented as he went to the refrigerator.

"I got them in town. I mailed the pictures to your grandmother and invited her to come again at Christmas."

He laughed. "She did not like last Christmas here."

"The weather was a bit cold. But she loved being here with you and little Billy."

Zack got the pitcher of tea and filled their glasses. "What else did you do in town?"

"I stopped by the Simmonses'. Susan's home from Gallaudet. She'll be here on Sunday as well. She said she has some wonderful new ideas for our Web site.

And she's excited to be a counselor for the first group of girls we have coming."

She transferred the roast to a platter and handed it to Zack, then dished up the potatoes and vegetables. She had everything on the table by the time the biscuits were golden brown. Before long, each plate had been served, and Billy's bowl had enough bite-size pieces to keep him occupied.

"And we got an e-mail today from Wayne. He's on the way from California. He'll be here this weekend sometime. I worry about him driving all that way."

"They grow up, Caitlin. All three of those kids are twenty now."

"Amazing, isn't it? But the biggest surprise was when I ran into Jeff. Someone wants to buy the ranch!"

Zack put down his fork and stared at her. "You're kidding."

She smiled and shook her head. "Well, not the entire ranch. Vernon Myles's younger son is getting married and Vern wants to buy four hundred acres adjacent to his land to give his son a place to build and run a small operation. What do you think?"

"It's your decision," Zack said. "What do you think?"

"It's the amount of land you'd own if you'd accepted my offer," she said.

"I never wanted your land, Caitlin, I only wanted you."

"Hmm," she said, smiling. "Now you have us both. Anyway, I think it's that section where you used to keep that old bull. I say we sell it and use the cash to pay off the loans we took to build the dining hall and new cottages. That would leave enough left over to expand in the future if we want to. Or a cushion for a rainy day."

Zack resumed eating. "Sounds like a plan. So this is our last meal together for a while."

When camp was in session, they ate with the cowboys and teenage guests in the dining hall built three years ago. Attached to the bunkhouse, it was the perfect place for group meetings, as well as meals.

One of the new cottages would be used by the four girls they had accepted this summer.

So far the camp for deaf teens was a great success. There was a waiting list for each session, and last summer several guests had signed up for this summer before leaving.

She looked at him. "I made one more stop when in town, Zack," she said quietly. "There'll be a new Carson with us this Christmas. Either Ellie or little Clyde."

"You got it confirmed? You're pregnant?"

She nodded, smiling happily as he came around and almost lifted her out of her chair to kiss her. "You constantly delight me, my love," he said.

"You delight me, Zack." she replied softly, feeling her heart overflow. She had it all. Family, friends and a purpose in life. But most of all, a loving husband who supported her in every way.

"I love you, Zack."

HARLEQUIN®
Super Romance®

Bundles of Joy—
coming next month
to Superromance

Experience the romance, excitement and joy with 6 heartwarming titles.

BABY, I'M YOURS #1476 by *Carrie Weaver*

ANOTHER MAN'S BABY
(The Tulanes of Tennessee)
#1477 by *Kay Stockham*

THE MARINE'S BABY (9 Months Later)
#1478 by *Rogenna Brewer*

BE MY BABIES (Twins)
#1479 by *Kathryn Shay*

THE DIAPER DIARIES (Suddenly a Parent)
#1480 by *Abby Gaines*

HAVING JUSTIN'S BABY (A Little Secret)
#1481 by *Pamela Bauer*

Exciting, Emotional and Unexpected!

Look for these Superromance titles in March 2008.
Available wherever books are sold.

"Jeanne proves that one woman can change the world, with vision, compassion and hard work."

—**Linda Lael Miller,** author

*Linda wrote "Queen of the Rodeo," inspired by Jeanne Greenberg, founder of **SARI Therapeutic Riding.** Since 1978 Jeanne has devoted her life to enriching the lives of disabled children and their families through innovative and exciting therapies on horseback.*

Look for "*Queen of the Rodeo*" in
More Than Words, Vol. 4,
available in April 2008 at eHarlequin.com
or wherever books are sold.

REQUEST YOUR FREE BOOKS!
2 FREE NOVELS PLUS 2 FREE GIFTS!

HARLEQUIN®

Super Romance®

Exciting, emotional, unexpected!

YES! Please send me 2 FREE Harlequin Superromance® novels and my 2 FREE gifts. After receiving them, if I don't wish to receive any more books, I can return the shipping statement marked "cancel." If I don't cancel, I will receive 6 brand-new novels every month and be billed just $4.69 per book in the U.S., or $5.24 per book in Canada, plus 25¢ shipping and handling per book and applicable taxes, if any*. That's a savings of close to 15% off the cover price! I understand that accepting the 2 free books and gifts places me under no obligation to buy anything. I can always return a shipment and cancel at any time. Even if I never buy another book from Harlequin, the two free books and gifts are mine to keep forever.

135 HDN EEX7   336 HDN EEYK

Name	(PLEASE PRINT)

Address	Apt.

City	State/Prov.	Zip/Postal Code

Signature (if under 18, a parent or guardian must sign)

Mail to the **Harlequin Reader Service®:**
IN U.S.A.: P.O. Box 1867, Buffalo, NY 14240-1867
IN CANADA: P.O. Box 609, Fort Erie, Ontario L2A 5X3

Not valid to current Harlequin Superromance subscribers.

Want to try two free books from another line?
Call 1-800-873-8635 or visit www.morefreebooks.com.

* Terms and prices subject to change without notice. NY residents add applicable sales tax. Canadian residents will be charged applicable provincial taxes and GST. This offer is limited to one order per household. All orders subject to approval. Credit or debit balances in a customer's account(s) may be offset by any other outstanding balance owed by or to the customer. Please allow 4 to 6 weeks for delivery.

Your Privacy: Harlequin is committed to protecting your privacy. Our Privacy Policy is available online at www.eHarlequin.com or upon request from the Reader Service. From time to time we make our lists of customers available to reputable firms who may have a product or service of interest to you. If you would prefer we not share your name and address, please check here. ☐

HARLEQUIN® *Romance*®

MEDITERRANEAN DADS

In the first of this emotional Mediterranean Dads duet, nanny Julie is whisked away to a palatial Italian villa, but she feels completely out of place in Massimo's glamorous world. Her biggest challenge, though, is ignoring her attraction to the brooding tycoon.

Look for

The Italian Tycoon and the Nanny

by **Rebecca Winters**

in March wherever you buy books.

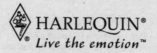

HARLEQUIN®
Live the emotion™

www.eHarlequin.com

HRI7500